Enthusiastic reviews for Lior Samson's novels –

Bashert (The Homeland Connection)

" Perfect! . . . a page turner that spins a good story."

— *Peter Gordon, publisher*

" Samson writes with a crisp elegance, like John Le Carré, and weaves his plot magically, sustaining suspense throughout the novel. The ending is a satisfying and surprising climax."

— *James A. Anderson, author*

" An ambitious novel, . . . moving with the speed of light between interconnected events, three continents, and a group of unique and memorable characters. I recommend it."

- Avraham Azrieli, author

The Dome (The Homeland Connection)

" Suspenseful and timely, . . . I cannot say enough good things about this novel." — *Alan Caruba, critic, BookViews*

" Crisp, sardonic, sometimes amusing, and highly entertaining. [Samson is] a real story teller." — *James A. Anderson, author*

" An excellent read, and very highly recommended."

— *Midwest Book Review*

Web Games (The Homeland Connection)

" An outstanding tech thriller—better than Tom Clancy. . . . This ranks up there as one of the best [thrillers] I've read in 2011."

— *James A. Anderson, author*

" This extraordinary author has the ability to anticipate events in ways that enhance his novels, and *Web Games*, his latest, is no exception. . . . You will not put it down."

— *Alan Caruba, critic, BookViews*

Chipset (The Homeland Connection)

"[A] multi-dimensional thriller that will satisfy discriminating readers who crave realistic stories populated by flesh-and-blood characters."

- Avraham Azrieli, author

"Lior Samson hits another one out of the park. . . . Few thriller writers can match Samson's ability to deliver a gripping story."

—James A. Anderson, author

Gasline (The Homeland Connection)

"Samson turns up the heat with a high-energy plot and . . . a perfect mix of techno thrill and human conflict. . . . a rip-roaring ride. Excellent!"

—Avraham Azrieli, author

The Four-Color Puzzle

"[A]n authentic thinking person's ideal mystery; an eloquent feast of words and an excellent story. . . . [M]ay be the best [book] I have read this year."

—Jeanie B. Clemmons, author

"[A] fast-paced crime story that had me rooting for the hero while also feeling conflicted by his choices. The story challenges the reader."

— Patricia O'Sullivan, author

The Rosen Singularity

"The plotting is ingenious and the characters come through strongly. It succeeds marvelously on the thriller level, but it also delivers a substantial intellectual and emotional kick."

— Rebecca Goldstein, MacArthur Fellow, author

"Vibrant and distinctive characters and thoughtful, yet engaging narratives and conversations, . . . an exciting, pulse-pounding story."

— Laurie Jenkins, book blogger

FLIGHT TRACK

Also by Lior Samson, from Gesher Press

Bashert
The Dome
Web Games
Chipset
Gasline

The Four-Color Puzzle
The Rosen Singularity
Avalanche Warning

Requisite Variety: Collected Short Fiction

Available from Amazon.com and other booksellers.

FLIGHT TRACK

a novel by Lior Samson

GESHER PRESS

Gesher Press is an imprint of Ampersand Press
Rowley, Massachusetts

Gesher Press | Ampersand Press
Rowley, MA 01969
Author site: www.liorsamson.com

Gesher Press and the bridge logo are trademarks of Ampersand Press.

Printed in the United States of America.

5 4 3 2 1

ISBN 978-0-9885275-6-0

Cover and book design: Larry Constantine
Photo credits: Richard Schlamp, "Boeing 787-9";
Curtis Olson, "Night Ocean" (FlightGear rendering)
Set in Alegreya and Alegreya Sans

To the innocent victims of terrorism, whose many voices are lost

We shall meet the enemy, and not only may he be ours, he may be us.
–Walter Crawford Kelly, Jr. (1913-1973)

That which is hateful to you, do not unto another.
–Hillel the Elder

Prologue: Geography

SERGI STANK. He had now spent nearly a week in the mosh pit of a stadium at the center of hell.

Sweat dribbled down his sides and turned to rivulets of icewater in the blast from the air conditioner. He had dragged the desk across his hotel room so he could sit directly in the rush of cold air. This week he was Sergi Cardona, a Spanish businessman who should not have minded the heat of Qatar, but his assumed identity was in continuous competition with the ample Northern European body that carried it. Over the last five days of field work in the crowded capital city of Doha, the temperatures had dipped below 100° only in the all-too-brief nights.

He sat shirtless, the grizzled hairs on his chest and scruffy beard riffling in the mechanical breeze. He wiped sticky fingers on his shorts before opening his laptop to launch a browser and check for messages. The browser was not Firefox or Chrome or Internet Explorer, but a customized piece of software that gave him access to the Dark Web, the vast hidden empire of sites and sources unreachable with standard software. He typed from memory the thirty-two characters of an Internet address in the new IPv6 hexadecimal format, waited until the screen blanked, then typed an ID, passphrase, and a command. The short list of nonsense words that scrolled onto the screen were a coded message telling him that his linking-pin contact with the rest of the network wanted a live chat. That was rare.

When he typed another command, a pixelated face popped up in a small window. It was not the face of the contact, of course, but only an animated avatar, a blocky cartoon with a silly pirate patch over one eye. Sergi had never seen his linking-pin and only rarely spoken with him by an encrypted Internet connection. This call, like the others, would be brief. Like the others, it would not likely carry good news.

The avatar spoke. "We missed one."

"What?" Sergi's heart was already accelerating as he shifted mental gears.

"There was another, out of Singapore."

"How is that possible?"

"It happened. We need to fix the mistake."

"Yes. And the rest?"

"Not your concern. Move."

Sergi looked at his watch. Singapore would be five hours ahead and nearly eight hours away by Qatar Airways on their next flight in the morning. His mind was already juking its way downfield, looking for a path through to a well-defended goal square. "I got it. Post whatever you have about the target at the dropbox."

"We have no assets there, everyone else is committed. Remember, it's Singapore, not some backwater."

"I know. I'll take care of it."

The pop-up window vanished. Sergi quickly navigated his way to the dropbox. As he scrolled through the details, his cold sweat increased. Five time zones. He launched Firefox and clicked through to an airline schedule.

Part One: Astronomy

Chapter 1

GIANCARLO WAS FLYING his dream: captaining a brand new Boeing DreamLiner on a new route. This part of the flight, though, was not his favorite. The rush of takeoff was past and the routine of extended flight loomed. Always a bit of an introvert, today he felt more like curling into a ball and turning off the world than taking to the podium. As he scratched nervously at his left shoulder where the stitching under his epaulet was chafing, he gave one more slow scan of the array of four cockpit displays in front of him that told him the plane was flying itself just fine without any help. He nodded to his First Officer beside him before keying on the cabin PA.

"This is Flight Captain Giancarlo Modica speaking. On behalf of myself, Co-Captain Dale Cornell, and First Officers Hazlina Osmon and Kamal Singh, as well as your entire Singapore-based cabin crew, let me welcome you on board Pacificano Flight 20 to Chicago." Despite the formulaic greeting, his voice bounced in the conversational rhythm that went with his Italian accent. He was in a role, one he had reluctantly learned but that had become habit. "We have reached our cruising altitude of 37,000 feet. With favorable winds tonight, our flying time to Chicago is expected to be a brief sixteen hours and ten minutes." He paused, allowing for the light laughter he assumed would be rippling through the passenger cabins. "Despite the extended delay in our departure caused by some unscheduled maintenance, loading a last minute cargo consignment, and dealing with a missing passenger, we are anticipating an on-time arrival at Chicago's O'Hare International Airport at 6:55 pm local Chicago time. Current temperature in Chicago is a pleasant 23 degrees Celsius, 73 on the Fahrenheit scale. Our route of flight tonight will first take us north, over Vietnam, then on to China and past the capital, Beijing, over the pole, down across northern Canada and into the United States. We will be crossing the International Dateline. So, after a short night and a long day, it will still be Tuesday when we arrive in Chicago.

"I will update you further as our flight progresses. In the meantime, please sit back, relax, and enjoy the comforts of our brand new extended-range Boeing 787-9 DreamLiner on its maiden flight for Pacificano Transocean. Our wonderful cabin attendants will treat you to Pacificano's award-winning in-flight service, starting with complimentary champagne in all cabins to celebrate our inaugural flight. 'The Very Best of the East and West' as it says in our adverts.

"Oh, yes, and while you are seated, please keep your seatbelts fastened for safety, just like we do here on the flight deck. Enjoy the flight."

Giancarlo clicked off the microphone just as a clipped radio message chirped in from Singapore Air Traffic Control.

"Pacificano two-zero heavy, maintain level three seven zero."

First Officer Hazlina responded. "Pacificano two-zero heavy maintaining flight level three seven zero."

"Pacificano two-zero heavy, contact Ho Chi Minh control on one two zero decimal nine."

"Contact Ho Chi Minh, one two zero decimal nine. Good afternoon. Pacificano two-zero heavy."

Giancarlo clambered awkwardly out of his seat. He smiled down at Hazlina. Nestled in her seat, his diminutive co-pilot looked far too tiny to be flying a plane with a take-off weight of over half a million pounds. Giancarlo had flown with her enough to learn how little her size mattered, how capable and tough she was, how she kept in shape with martial arts and filled spare time with target practice at a pistol range. She was so unlike his wife. A wry, close-mouthed smile spread on his face just as she glanced up.

"What's up?" she asked.

"Bio break. Then I'm going to sneak in a short afternoon nap."

"Wait, what about those fatigue management routines we learned last week? I thought we were supposed to stick to the rest and rotation schedules they tailored for this city-pair. On ultra-long-range service, we—"

"I remember the workshop, every boring minute of it, but the Civil Aviation Authority of Singapore is not flying this plane. We are." Giancarlo turned to the jump seats at the back of the cockpit. "You don't mind taking the left seat for a bit, do you, Dale?"

"No prob. Take a break. Not like there will be a hell of a lot to do."

"If I'm not back before we are handed off to Beijing ATC, have Kamal come get me."

"Yeah, looks like my First Officer also has his own personal fatigue management routine. He's already grabbing some Zs." Kamal Singh, seated in the jump seat closest to the cabin door, had his turbaned head tilted back, mouth open, and was snoring lightly. "I don't know how he does that."

== == ==

With the flight attendants busy pouring champagne refills for first-class passengers, the forward galley was empty. Giancarlo crossed over from the lavatory to a narrow door that could have passed for a closet. He unlatched it and climbed the steep concealed steps to the flight-crew rest area where he slipped past the padded seat wedged in on one side to crawl head-first into the right-hand bunk above. The crew rest area was quiet but cramped. Stretched out, with his balding head pressed against the bulkhead, his toes still poked out over the bottom edge of the berth.

He would have much preferred to get a full night's sleep before such a long flight, but the baby had kept Jasmina awake, which had kept him awake. Then, with the baby screaming in her arms, they had fought at the top of their lungs until their voices were hoarse and Jasmina made her threat again. This time she was serious, she had said, and this time Giancarlo believed her.

Had he not been flying the next day, he would have then poured himself three-fingers of single-malt scotch, chugged it, and chased it with another before snoring through the night on the divan in the parlor. In recent years, he had grown too conscientious to drink before a flight, even this flight, which had now taken on new significance as both a beginning and an ending. His days of depression and nights of partying until dawn before flying were twelve years and two wives behind him. He had learned his lessons, at least about flying, then rebuilt his career after moving to Singapore to fly for Pacificano. He was family, they had told him, so his Italian-American cousins hired him despite his rowdy reputation and record of reprimands.

Giancarlo lay in the rest area thinking about Jasmina. He was at a point where life without her was difficult to imagine. He reached up and snapped off the light in the low compartment. Like a concertina collapsing, he let out a slow noisy breath and within a few minutes had fallen into a trancelike light sleep.

He had been out less than a quarter hour when the slight roll of the plane and a subtle change in the engine noise intruded into his dreams and brought him quickly awake. He snaked out of the bunk, shook his head to clear it, and climbed back down the stairs.

Once on the flight deck, he made a cursory survey of the instrument displays. "Here, Dale, let me back at the controls. What's this about?" Dale got up and Giancarlo folded himself back into the pilot's seat. "Why are we changing course? Did Ho Chi Minh redirect us?"

Dale stood behind the pilot. "No. It's in the programmed flight plan, the last one you entered. Hazlina was still trying to raise Ho Chi Minh when the plane started this sharp right turn."

"Well, that makes no sense. Hazlina, you get Ho Chi Minh while I try to figure out what is with the flight control computers."

Hazlina rechecked the settings on the radio. "Ho Chi Minh control, this is Pacificano two-zero heavy. Ho Chi Minh." Her voice could sometimes take on a rasp that some men found sexy but had always annoyed Giancarlo.

He twisted the yoke in an attempt to cancel the roll, then flipped switches, and swore under his breath. "Damn fly-by-wire. I'm trying to turn off the autopilot and nothing is happening, no response. The computers are just not acknowledging any input. What did you do?"

"Nothing. I did nothing. You reprogrammed it, remember? Now I can't get Ho Chi Minh on any frequency. We're entering Vietnamese airspace, they should be screaming at us."

Kamal finally awakened as the plane finished its turn, flattened, and started a steep climb. He wiped his eyes and craned his neck to get a quick review of the displays. "What in hell is going on here?" Annunciators in the cockpit started flashing.

"We've got power out on—" Hazlina scanned panels as she called out the names of systems to the three men. She stopped suddenly and went rigid, staring into the nothing of the high scattered clouds ahead, a look of utter tranquility painted on her face like pancake makeup.

"What is it?" Giancarlo said. She didn't answer. "We're already climbing through three-nine-five, and I still can't override the autopilot. Wait, I have a visual on another aircraft below us. See if you can raise it on Guard."

She switched to the International Air Distress emergency channel at 121.5 megahertz, commonly referred to as Guard. "Mayday, mayday. This is Pacficano two zero heavy, on Guard. We have an emergency. Anyone?" She waited for a response, then repeated the message There was no response. She shook her head. "Nothing. It's all dead."

Giancarlo gritted his teeth. "Shit. And look at the annunciators, it's all wrong, everything's going crazy." Above them, warning lights blinked yellow and red; beeps and buzzes filled the cockpit. "Communication systems are shutting down. we've lost VHF, HF, satcomm, everything. Only the passenger Wi-Fi seems to be still working. Wait, now something is haywire with the AIMS." They watched as the Aircraft Information Management System started a reboot procedure; the plane was losing its brains. "Hazlina? What the fuck?"

He looked over and found her staring at him, a trace of a quizzical smile beginning to twist her lips.

"What is it, Hazlina?"

"MH370. Remember Malaysia flight 370, KL to Beijing, March 2014? Virtually the same track as we were on. You should remember." Her smile flattened into a grim line as she pivoted away from him, spread her hands palms up, and said, *Allahu akhbar.*"

-- -- --

In the business-class cabin, Dante Calabrese finished typing, closed the browser, and shut his laptop. He stared at the glass of champagne that he had not touched. He was tired and by now feeling decidedly drowsy. He would need to be alert later, but now? He closed his eyes, joining the others around him who had already drifted off.

Chapter 2

THE CLATTER AND SQUEAL of steel-on-steel broke the early morning quiet as an outbound Red Line train left Boston's Charles Street Station. Ben Markham was already in the bike lane pedaling his graphite-black Cannondale across the Longfellow Bridge toward Cambridge, just passing the first of the three pairs of massive masonry towers. He thumbed the shifter twice and stood on the pedals in a pointless race to beat the train to Kendall Square.

Everything was a contest to Ben and had been since he was a boy. All his life he had been competing, out to prove something he could never quite articulate. He had been the short, light-skinned kid with sandy hair among taller, darker Israelis, sprinting to beat them down the soccer pitch or exercising his nimble brain to be first to hack into the school computers. Now, for the first time in his life, he found himself scrambling to keep up with his newfound peers.

The train was just slipping underground as Ben flew down off the bridge and coasted, panting, flying past brick-faced buildings toward the Tech Square offices of the Center for Advanced Adaptive Systems Studies.

Before he had accepted the research fellowship, his stepfather had tried to dissuade him from taking the appointment. "MIT's Media Lab is where they do the sexy research, Bini," Karl had said.

Ben no longer liked being called Bini, but he let it slide when it came to his parents. "Sexy?" he responded. "You mean, like, intelligent conference badges that light up when you approach somebody with similar interests or smartphone apps that create enhanced reality for circles of easily bored teenagers? If I wanted to make robots with expressive faces to interact with toddlers, I could do that in our garage." Karl had reminded him that they didn't have a garage, only a parking space behind their Haifa apartment building, but Ben was undeterred. "Look, I didn't get into military intelligence and work my way through the Technion with honors just to crank out digital fluff. I want to do the real stuff, like you." They had both laughed at that. Karl's days of consulting and writing about military technology and industrial security were already well behind him.

-- -- --

At the new Tech Square office tower, Ben chained his bike to the rack in the underground parking garage, then used his badge to summon the express elevator to the CAASS lab on the top floor. The entrance to the lab was marked by a black-and-gray logo that was as forgettable as the name, itself a tossed salad of buzzwords that said so much and so little. Anyone who had to ask what CAASS did, didn't have the clearance to know. The lab did applied math. They did it on government funding that did not appear on budgets.

Ben unlocked the outer office with his badge and eight numbers tapped on the keypad by the door, then reached around through the barely opened door to flip up the middle light switch. The alarm system chirped to let him know he could open the door fully and would have fifteen seconds to authenticate his entry with his handprint. Ben got a kick out of the cloak-and-dagger rigmarole almost as much as he loved the mathematics and the puzzle solving. A taste for skullduggery was encoded in his DNA and reinforced by his years of adolescent online hacking.

As usual, he was the first in the office, a tactic he had adopted to stay in the race with the other young geniuses at CAASS. He would let in the nominal receptionist when she arrived an hour or more later. In his opinion, Victoria was too smart and too butch to be a receptionist. He had always suspected she was CIA, charged with keeping an eye on the Center's staff of geeky revolutionaries, but he knew enough not to ask, even indirectly. Whatever covert agenda she might have, she kept it well hidden under a veneer of verbal sarcasm and playful gestures. On the corner of her desk a black-and-white-striped plush toy held a hand-lettered sign: "Welcome to the Skunkworx."

The rest of the lights came on automatically while Ben, lost in thought, sauntered down the bland blue-gray hallway toward his north-facing office. In the quiet of the building, the faint buzz of a dying fluorescent fixture near the end of the hall was the loudest sound. Ben delighted in these hours before the lab became crowded, before other researchers would interrupt him with questions or requests for help, before his boss would bug him about progress on some project, as if he were a mere programmer finishing algorithms rather than, as he thought of himself, a genius breaking new ground in the application of Bayesian statistics to situational awareness in intelligent interactive human-machine systems.

That phrase of purest tech-speak echoed in his head as he thought again of Karl. He grinned. "Dad, you would be proud of me. If I could tell you about what I am working on, that is." This was another thing he liked about early mornings at the office: he could talk to himself out loud without getting bent-face looks or smart-ass cracks. It was an idiosyncrasy he had picked up from Karl, whose years living alone before marrying Ben's mother had left more than one bad habit as a residue. "Where do I start?" Ben made clicking sounds with his tongue. "I think I should go back to that last simulation from yesterday. I have this nagging sense that I missed something."

He opened the door to his shared office with his badge. The whir of the cooling fans on the computers almost masked a mechanical squealing suddenly coming from the reception area behind him. Ben tensed at the sound, and his hand jerked reflexively toward a sidearm that wasn't there. He had not carried a handgun since leaving the IDF, but his responses were more than just from his training in the Israeli Defense Forces—they were in his very blood. His compact body was as quick as his mind, and both had been leading him into and out of trouble for years.

He slowed his breathing to concentrate on the sound. It was much too early for Victoria to show up. Ben flattened himself against the wall, then slipped along the corridor back toward reception. As the sound grew louder he tried to place it. Something familiar but forgotten, a muffled, pulsing whine he had not heard for years. It seemed to be coming from the locked credenza behind the reception desk. He reached the reception area and knelt down to listen more closely, but the sound stopped. Some equipment, he thought. It's nothing. But he was curious, as always, a curiosity that had long been both an asset and a persistent problem.

The lock on the beige credenza was nothing special, just a simple key-and-tab cylinder so common to standard office furniture. Ben looked around reflexively before retrieving his pocketknife, a constant companion ever since the Hanukkah after his twelfth birthday. One of its blades had been secretly customized in service of his enduring interest in unlocking locked doors. He opened the knife and worked the modified blade into the key slot, jiggled it, twisted, then slid open the cabinet door.

The offending machine, now silent, stood on the middle shelf, with an embossed tape label across its face: "Secure Fax." A single sheet of bright yellow paper rested in the receiving tray. Ben knew he shouldn't read it, but he was already in breach of a bundle of rules. He grinned, a smile others called boyish. "All in or nothing, Ben."

The fax was headed 'Eyes Only' and addressed to General Charles M. Woolyard. "So, Dr. Woolyard, now I learn my boss is a general. What else have you not told us?" Ben read the short fax, handwritten on letterhead of the National Transportation Safety Board.

> We got another, at least we think. This time we have full cooperation and all the plugs and sockets are in place. No one wants to have to be searching half the South Indian Ocean again, so this time I want you and your real-time whiz kids in on it from the start. I'm counting on you to boot up the team and get your best big brains crunching on all cores. I know you are not in the office, but I already tried your cell. Call me ASAP when you get this!

It was signed T. Samuel Parsons, Director, NTSB Aviation Response Research Group. Ben slipped the fax back into the tray and slid the credenza door closed.

He tensed at the clicking of the entry-door interlock and stood quickly enough to bring the sound of rushing blood to his ears. Turning his back to the door, he started intensely scanning titles on the metal bookcase beside the desk.

"Morning, Ben. I figured I'd find you here already."

"As usual, Dr. Woolyard." Ben twisted his head sideways and bent over to continue studying the lower shelves. "Just looking for a spare copy of the AvStat manual."

"Did you try the library?"

"Was on my way there. Just thought I'd check here first." He turned and grinned at the General. "You're here awfully early. I haven't even had time to start goofing off yet. What's up?"

"Later." Dr. Woolyard, nearly twice the age of the oldest of his charges, could be avuncular when needed but fell back on crisp efficiency when pressured. "You can get on with your project or hunt for missing manuals, at least for now. I have calls to make."

Ben took a few steps toward his office, then caught himself. "Oh, right. Library. Almost forgot I was headed there." He crossed in front of Woolyard and took the turn down the other corridor.

Woolyard twisted his balding head to watch Ben enter the library. As he knelt behind the receptionist's desk, his knees cracked. He reached for his key ring before noticing that the sliding door on the credenza was open a crack. "Oh, Victoria, you are slipping." He slid the credenza open and pulled out the fax, then stared at it, puzzled, before closing and locking the slider.

— — —

Ben was working in his office, scrolling across the squiggles of a waveform plotted on his monitor screen, when the phone on his desk rang. He pawed through piles of technical papers and an open manual to get to the handset. "Yeah?"

"In my office. Now."

Ben replaced the handset and took a deep breath before race-walking down the hall toward the corner office with its view back down Main Street toward the Charles River. Woolyard waved him into the room. "So, Ben, sit down. You already know what this is about."

"I do?"

"Of course you do. You read Sam's fax."

"I what? Sam who?"

Woolyard leaned forward with folded hands on his desk. "Do you know, Ben, that I knew your father? Migdal, not Karl, I mean, although I've also worked with Karl. I was just a kid doing liaison with Israel's Aman and Mossad for our Defense Intelligence. I was learning Hebrew and amused by his unusual first name: Migdal. Tower, indeed. You have his short, stocky build and cocky approach to life. And like him, you are a quick thinker, but you just do not have the mastery of tradecraft that served him so well as a clandestine operative."

"I really don't know what you are talking about, sir. My father did work for Israeli intelligence, but he died when I was very young and—"

"Cut the misdirection and bullshit, Markham. You read the fax, a secure fax addressed to me, my eyes only."

Ben scowled in feigned confusion.

"Look, Ben, the faxes feed into the tray upside down, top-edge first; you put the sheet back in the other way around after you finished reading it. I'm willing to bet your fingerprints are all over it."

"Sir, I ..."

"Please understand what I am saying to you now: Let's just say I didn't notice the fax was backwards, that we are not having this conversation, and"—he waved the yellow paper in Ben's face—"I am not going to have this scanned for fingerprints. We have far bigger problems to deal with, so that piece of your record has just been redacted." He slid the paper into a shredder beside his desk that instantly whined into action. "We can save for later the remedial training about picking locks and technical terms like 'secure fax'. We could throw in some lessons in covering your tracks better. Although, I will say that your 'I was looking for a book' line was good enough to fool me at first.

"For now, however, let me bring you up to speed on Sam Parson's message and Operation Flight Track."

Chapter 3

THE CARD HE HELD up against the badge reader at the NTSB headquarters still bore his full name, but T. Samuel Parsons had stopped using his first name years earlier, right after a run-in with the brass that had prompted him to move over to the aviation side of the Board. He had been named Tankut after his mother's Turkish grandfather and Samuel after his African-American father. His face, a handsome hybrid that reflected his heritage, was a mask of placid confidence that he seldom set aside. Acquaintances often described him as a dark-skinned Omar Sharif. Since the brouhaha over the West Virginia pipeline incident, Sam had substituted an initial for his first name, grown out his beard, and latched onto a new girlfriend. He now insisted that the few people around him who remembered him from the early days stop using his old nickname. He was just Sam, no longer Tank. It was a sweeping rebranding exercise, and he had been reinventing himself ever since, cramming to learn more about aircraft and aviation and taking on assignments that others rejected.

His new office was half the size of his old one and was made even more cramped by the line of old filing cabinets along one wall. The beat-up gray metal desk he worked at carried a utilitarian black plastic placard with white machine-carved letters: Director, Aviation Response Research Group. As with Woolyard's group in Cambridge, the name said nothing, and for good reason. The recently formed ARRG dug into places where others did not want any digging, and its interests were not merely forensic but also forward looking.

One of the two phones on Sam's desk rang. He picked it up as he hung his coat on the wall-hook beside his desk. "Parsons here."

"Woolyard here."

"It's about time, Chuck. How the hell are you? You ready up there in Cambridge?"

"Depends. What have you got?"

"Looks like another Southeast Asia passenger plane's gone off track, and, wouldn't you know, my group is still mired in reanalyzing the disappearance of that Malaysian Airlines flight."

"I thought that was supposed to be finished." Woolyard's chiding was gentle but pointed.

"Supposed to be. Our postmortem of MH370 was tasked to devise better ways to respond to events as they happened, but here we are again and hardly any wiser. Not a lot to show for our first years of operation."

"Oh, I don't know. You did a credible job with re-opening that old TWA incident."

"You're talking about Flight 800, the 747 that exploded and crashed in 1996 just after takeoff from JFK."

"That's the one, killed everybody on board. Fuel tank explosion, right?"

"That was the official explanation—from a spark of quote-unquote, undetermined origin. Of course, the conspiracy theorists never stopped claiming it was sabotage or a terrorist surface-to-air missile. A determined cadre of independent experts and amateur analysts even argued it had been a meteor strike. At least now we know the real cause. We also know why the official record will never be corrected.

"But that's all retrospective—twenty-twenty hindsight—always the easier way to see the true nature of things. This time we have to work while events are still unfolding. Is your crew ready to try a flight track in real-time?"

"Well, some of our staff are still coming in. I think a few of these kids never expected that the on-call provision in their employment contracts might actually mean coming in early someday. Nearly all the key people are here, though: real-time text analysis, satellite communications, signal processing, open-source intel, psychosocial. Oh, yes, and somebody you might know—or know of—heads the tracking team. Does the name Karl Lustig mean anything to you?"

"Uh ... oh yes, an Israeli security consultant. I had a brief exchange with him on a gas pipeline incident before he was pulled off the case for some reason. Never understood that. Why? Is he working with you?"

"No, but his stepson is. Ben Markham is one of our rising stars, a math whiz who specializes in fuzzy logic, Bayesian statistics, dynamic systems simulation, and signal extraction from high-noise data, real-time—"

"Whoa, Chuck. It's too early in the morning for such a string of technobabble. And it sure doesn't sound much like specialization."

"That's the point. This kid is all over the map, thinks the big picture but can drill down to the individual pixels. What all that jargon means to us old-guard engineers is that he works on ways to combine soft data—guesses, speculation, ambiguous information—with hard data, then constructs formal mathematical models that can be continually updated to zero in on answers—even in very complex situations. Cool stuff. Anyway, thought you might find it—him—interesting. Another generation is chomping at our heels."

"Yours, maybe, but my heels still have those little wings on them. Speaking of which"—he glanced at his computer screen—"I already have the first of the feeds winging your way."

"I know. I'm looking at the confirmation on two secondary radar data streams right now, and we're getting fresh thirty-day digital-traffic keyword analyses from NSA. Oh, yes, and a promise from the National Security Coordinating Secretary in Singapore that their Internal Security Department will send us everything they have on the crew."

Sam scribbled on a sticky-note. "I'll follow up to make sure Singapore keeps its promise. That's my job. They certainly don't want to look as inept as Malaysia did after MH370 vanished, and they're smart enough to know they can't go it alone. They need us even more than we need them. You should also be getting the Singapore ATC stream any minute now."

"Even more important, Sam, we need the transponder data from the plane and the Inmarsat feeds right away—real-time and recent data history. Those were crucial to eventually figuring out the possible flight track of MH370."

"Okay, we're working on it. And the passenger manifest. It should be pretty clean; Singapore is a lot more disciplined than Kuala Lumpur when it comes to security. Look, I have more calls to make."

He did not even say goodbye before hanging up. He switched to his secure phone and dialed one of the dozens of numbers he had memorized and would never write down. While he was waiting through the rings, he started an email.

This was what he did. He spent his days talking on the phone, swapping encrypted emails, and texting coded messages, working the invisible and distant crowd that were his constituency and his collaborators. He was a detective who never left his desk, a spy who never ventured into the field. He missed the field work from when he was still investigating pipeline explosions, but he reveled in coordinating a network of people who mostly didn't know each other and did not always know they were his eyes and ears, legs and fingers. His tendrils burrowed deep into civilian and military agencies scattered around the globe, all with their own resources, their own agendas, and a shared interest in not losing planes to terrorists.

Sam would have liked a bigger budget and a larger staff, but he knew there were advantages to being too small to attract attention. The lack of resources had inspired him to build a network of connections into foreign and domestic agencies that multiplied what little he had. Sam Parsons was the nexus, the pivot point of the network. He could mobilize people from the FAA, the FBI, the TSA, and dozens of lesser known groups in any number of countries. Some of these contacts were official, but many were sub rasa relationships that could bypass red tape to deliver resources on short notice.

As he waited for the call to be forwarded to an extension, Sam scanned the array of clocks displayed on his computer monitor above a map showing the known, planned, and possible flight tracks of flight PT20. Time was the enemy. If there were to be any chance of taking action, they would have to find the plane fast. It was now 7:28am on the east coast, some two-and-a-half hours after the flight had departed Singapore's Chengi Airport. The alarm had reached him this early in the flight thanks to a covert contact in Vietnam who passed on information from their military radar after the flight had failed to check in with air traffic control in Ho Chi Minh City. Sam had launched Operation Flight Track even before leaving his girlfriend's apartment in Georgetown.

== == ==

Keating Summers, the current Assistant Director for Special

Projects, tapped on the office door frame and didn't wait for Sam to motion him in. He paused just long enough to get the gist of the phone conversation before seating himself opposite Sam. Keating was even darker than Sam. Two generations of interracial marriage had somehow not diluted the violet-black sheen of his South African ancestors. Parsons held up an index finger to gain a minute, and Summers nodded agreement without stirring from the chair.

As Sam's call continued, Keating checked email with his smartphone, then reviewed his appointments for the day. Eventually, he looked up and mumbled. "Right. Talk to you when you are done with your call. My office." He stood to leave but stopped when Sam gestured for him to sit back down. Sam mouthed the words "I'm done" to Keating, then apologized over the phone before abruptly setting the receiver down.

He swiveled in his chair to face Keating. "It's a cliché, I know, but I have never understood the inscrutable oriental mind," Sam put a large hand over his mouth and nose and sucked stale office air between his fingers as he thought about what to say next. "It does not look good for cooperation from the Chinese. They were a lot more engaged over the Malaysian disappearance—more Chinese citizens among the passengers—but that doesn't appear to be the whole story. They seem to have their own network of informants and data pipeline tappers now in place, so they understand what's going on and the implications. At the same time, something is holding them back from jumping on board with both feet. I learned the hard way not to trust the Chinese. They deny hacking into our computer systems even when we confront them with a digital smoking gun."

"I take it that we're not intending to reciprocate by sharing what we know with China."

Parsons laughed. "Too late. We already told them everything

we know." He made a circle with his left thumb and index finger. "Zip. That's what we know at this hour, but we do have the intellectual artillery zeroing in on the target."

Keating, who was Parsons' boss, three pay grades higher, and twenty points lower in IQ, edged toward the doorway. "You'll keep me in the loop, of course."

"As if my brother were the hangman, sir." Keating gave him a look that said the off-beat allusion was lost on him. Both men smiled as Keating left the office muttering something about "the President."

Chapter 4

MARWA FREDERICKSEN HUNG her oxblood leather jacket over the back of the extra chair, flipped her long hair to one side, and sat down at her desk with her back to Ben and without a word said. Ben had always wondered what force of fate had led to her sharing an office with him. Perhaps someone had thought it fitting to put the group's only two Israelis together.

"I'm so glad you finally made it." He did not look up from his work. "Now everyone is here."

"Not everyone," she said without turning from her screen. "Caswell is caught in traffic. So was I. Not everyone can afford an apartment on Beacon Hill just a ten-minute bike ride from the office."

Ben continued to type. "I told you before, the apartment belongs to my late father's holding company. I live there rent free, which is about what I can afford on my stipend. I'm not a paid full-time employee like you." He finished correcting an equation and closed the MatLab program he had been tweaking. "Do you know why you were called in this early?"

"Yes, I know. I got the update from Woolyard at the all-hands meeting after I arrived. That's where I've been the last ten minutes. You were missed." She paused for effect. "Not! I guess you didn't get the word. Head buried in equations, I suppose."

It had not always been like this. They had started off well enough. That had lasted for more than half a minute as she lounged in the doorway on her first day, standing in her skinny jeans and spike heels, winding her brown-black hair around a finger as her dark eyes gave Ben and the office the once over. Ben had reciprocated with a survey of his own and a look nearly every Israeli male masters at puberty. Then they were introduced, and the ethnic contradiction of her first and last names began to become clear. Not only was she married—to a Lutheran minister in a most unlikely match for a Muslim woman—but she was a Canadian-educated Arab Israeli with a Palestinian father. They had been like the two Koreas ever since, sniping in perpetual cold-war tension across an invisible cease-fire zone running down the middle of their office.

Ben gritted his teeth as he launched his program again. "I've been here since before seven—working. While you were being briefed, I was already busy with Artyem on an upgrade to the routines for real-time image conjugation. Oh, pardon my tech talk. You know, mathematically overlaying satellite photos to enhance resolution of small features." Ben was becoming annoyed, as much at himself for getting caught up in her sarcasm as he was actually pissed at her. "Artyem was here soon after the call went out."

"Bully for him. Bully for you. I don't think we're going to find that plane with satellite images, however enhanced they might be by your number-crunching routines, particularly since it's still nighttime over the Pacific. We'll find it by understanding the people and figuring out what they're thinking, what they're trying to accomplish and why."

Ben swung his feet up onto his desk and tilted his chair back as far as it would go. He put on his best imitation of Arabic-accented English. "Please, please, Doctor Fredericksen, psycho-analyze me, and tell me why I stole this plane. No, truly by the Prophet, I want to understand myself before we crash into the sea and I become a martyr."

"You ... you are impossible." She let out a low growl between clenched teeth. "I, for your information, have work to do. You and your psychodrama—your prejudice—will just have to wait for some other time, preferably long after you no longer work here."

They had never talked politics, never dared, but their arguments about technical issues were unceasing. They were two young polymaths who knew no boundaries to their own sense of expertise and who constantly criticized each other's work. She had a bachelor's degree in anthropology, a PhD in linguistics, and a second doctorate in social psychology. Her dissertation, "Social Network Theory and Media Incentivizing of Jihad," had brought her to the attention of CAASS. Ben regarded none of her work as real science and took pains to make clear the disdain he held for her research at the Center. He had once dismissed her methods to a colleague as "muddle-minded virtual voodoo." That Marwa had been within earshot was no accident. She, in turn, considered his mathematics research as obscure abstraction far removed from practical implications. That he was one of only two members of the group without an advanced degree proved to her that he could not possibly know what he was talking about.

▀▀ ▀▀ ▀▀

As the last of the crew filed into the circular meeting room, Woolyard and his Chief Scientist, Telly Athenasiou, stood in the center exchanging private last-minute comments, Woolyard's half-bald head of buzz-cut gray hair inclined within inches of Athenasiou's tied-back shoulder-length locks. The room, with its muted red carpeting, acoustic dampeners suspended overhead, and its circumference covered floor-to-ceiling with high-resolution displays, doubled as an auditorium for routine meetings and situation room for simulation exercises and live operations. To the lab crew, it was known as The Circus. Operation Flight Track was the first live challenge to allow them to use their tools for real-time analysis of complex data feeds. Woolyard likened their task to trying to identify and classify individual microbes in the stream from a fire hose pounding their faces.

Woolyard and Athenasiou were the only people in the room over forty. The rest were a disparate bunch of bright young misfits chosen because they didn't yet know that what they were being asked to do couldn't be done.

"We are tool builders," Woolyard had told them at the inaugural all-hands meeting months earlier. "We build mathematical and scientific tools that multiply and extend our awareness and intelligence. The best tools have specific functions but can also be readily adapted to new purposes."

He pulled a screwdriver from his back pocket and held it up. "A flat-blade screwdriver can tighten a screw or loosen it, but it can also pry open the lid of a paint can or, turned around, pound it closed. We're building such tools that can be used for ends and in ways we can't anticipate, that can be instantly reconfigured and repurposed to meet changing requirements. Even more important, we are not building individual tools but a software toolkit, a virtual garage stuffed with programmed tools that can work together, that can share data and augment each other. We want to be able to try new configurations on the fly, as quickly and easily as a recording engineer uses a sound board and patch panel to swap microphones, merge tracks, and switch reverb or auto-tuning in or out."

To drive home the point, he and Athenasiou had rolled out a cart loaded with equipment from Telly's own home studio. He demonstrated what he meant by taking samples of voices as the group called out suggestions for genre, rhythm, mood, and lyrics. He divided the group into sections and launched them into polyrhythmic clapping as he and Telly played guitar chords and mixed them with re-pitched samples. The result was hardly great art, but the demo made its point and earned them both a standing ovation. When they later presented everyone with autographed CDs of the remastered "CAASS: Chaos and Counterpoint," the group rewarded them with placards for their office walls declaring them to be "Officially Cool. "

— — —

For the launch of Operation Flight Track, the Circus had been hastily rearranged from its usual classroom-style seating. With everyone facing inward in a circle, it would be easier for them to see each other and keep tabs on the screens all around. On the small trapezoidal tables in front of each of them were identical networked laptops that gave them access to the display screens along with full remote control over their office workstations.

"This is not a drill, people," Woolyard announced as Athenasiou nodded, his pony-tail bobbing. "Pacificano Transocean flight PT20 left Singapore over three hours ago with enough fuel for a sixteen hour flight plus reserve. If this is anything like what happened with the lost Malaysian flight MH370—and preliminary indications are that this could be the case—we have maybe fourteen hours before it crashes someplace, maybe much less. It is possible that everyone on board is already dead; it is also possible they are alive and being held hostage.

"All right, let's find that plane!"

The blackened screens around the perimeter began to light up with images as the room filled with the clatter of seventeen keyboards and the chatter of overlapping conversations. Ben was seated with red-bearded Artyem Basilov, their spy satellite jockey, on one side, and Hector Guzman, the chunky signal processing guru, on the other. They were the point team in the scramble to locate the aircraft. With the regular transponders on PT20 out, the team had only a handful of pings—automated signals exchanged between on-board electronics in the engines and monitoring satellites—with which to try and triangulate locations and to relate to the last known position. They had to analyze time and angle of arrival of the signals at a satellite and combine this with other even less precise data to project a possible location and likely flight path. There was huge uncertainty in the track. Another ping, due any minute, could narrow the possibilities, as could any other data, soft or hard, exact or estimated.

On one part of the wall of screens was a map centered on southeast Asia and the Pacific with fuzzy green blobs and arcs super-imposed to represent the current best estimates of the present position of the aircraft. As new data and guesses came in from any source, these would be weighted and combined with previous predictions to spread or narrow the uncertainty. A civilian or military aircraft might report a visual contact with an unknown plane, a Pacific island cell tower might get a signal from a cellphone registered to a passenger, or radar might track an unknown object. Scattered over the map were bright red triangles representing unidentified airborne objects that would turn yellow and be flagged once identified unambiguously.

Ben was seated across from Marwa and her psychosocial team, as far away as he could get. Her primary data set was the passenger list and any accessible data linked with them directly or indirectly, including credit cards and recent purchases, emails, and telephone metadata, all being scavenged in real-time via the Internet or supplied by informants and collaborators secured through Parsons' team at the NTSB.

"Listen up, everyone." Marwa shifted forward in her seat. "We only got the verified passenger list and passport numbers fifteen

minutes ago, but we have been building a preliminary sociogram to map the relationships among passengers and between
passengers and other people not on the flight. It's not yet stable,
since our Web-crawlers are still fetching online data and our
programmed inference engine is still spinning hypotheses. Also,
Singapore has yet to give us the promised police and security
records, but we have found something interesting already."

She pointed. "If you look at the screen over there, you'll see in
the snapshot of the social network that one passenger seems to
be connected weakly with a few others, mostly by virtue of very
recent cellphone calls and shopping in the same stores in Singapore. More significant is the lack of other social connections, at
least in the data sets retrieved so far."

"So what." Ben leaned back and slouched. "So he's a loner.
Like some of the people in this room maybe?" That earned a few
snorted laughs and a couple of short hisses.

Marwa's hair flared as she shook her head a bit too vigorously. "Not the best guess. Even a loner ... like you ... makes calls,
buys things, lives somewhere. So far, this one guy shows up
hardly at all on the Internet landscape."

Woolyard took a half step toward her. "Okay, Fredericksen.
What's your best guess."

"His name, Brandon Zhang, is a pseudonym, backed by a
false passport good enough to fool Singapore airport security.
We're testing that assumption by looking for anything anywhere
on either the name or passport number. So far, nothing. It's as if
this Zhang guy suddenly sprang into existence in Singapore.
Whoever he is, he did not enter Singapore on this Hong Kong
passport."

"Right, so we might have a terrorist aboard. What about the
circle of weak connections among other passengers?"

"We're working on it."

Woolyard turned toward Liv Caswell, with her silver-studded nose buried in her laptop screen and her turquoise and violet gelled Mohawk poking above it. "Anything from your real-time text analysis that might suggest a hijacking or back-channel coordination or demands being communicated?"

Liv looked up and pursed her iridescent lips in concentration. "Nope. Nothing with any real confidence level, sir. Not yet."

"Location? Give us an update, Ben."

Ben straightened up. "Yes. As you can see from the tracking map, we are getting confirmed identities on a lot of aircraft, but we still have too many in the locus clouds—that's the blurred green overlays—for it to be practical to use satellites to image all of them. We are handicapped because most of the area of interest is still in darkness. In any case, the area covered by the locus clouds is orders of magnitude too big for high-resolution imaging. and wide-angle low-res wouldn't fully resolve any object as small as a plane."

"But you are starting the high-res search, right?"

"Yes, of course. We are looking for heat signatures and using infrared imaging where we can't do visible spectrum, but the resolution is lower. We have a routine that feeds tasks through our link with the National Reconnaissance Office to some of the spy satellites they operate. Basically, our scheme favors unknown objects closest to the spots with the highest probability of being the right location. But we don't queue up the requests; we wait for them to be completed and for the images to come back from NRO. That introduces delays on both ends, but saves us from ending up in a position where we can't follow up on new information because we have to wait for some satellite to complete a backlog of tasks."

Woolyard edged through a gap in the circle and took a few steps toward the exit. "Okay, I have some people to update and mollify. Meanwhile, Telly will coordinate here. Everyone, work together. Find that plane."

Chapter 5

ALON CHIANG PACED, back rigid, hands clasped behind him like some cinematic commander reviewing his troops. He turned from the wall of blue-tinted windows overlooking Singapore's New Phoenix Park where the Interior Ministry, the Singapore Police Force, and the Internal Security Department were headquartered. The cream of his ISD Counterterrorism Team were lined up on the other side of the oak conference table, sitting attentively, like judges in some edition of a Singapore Sing-Off. "We are going on the assumption that this is Malaysian flight MH370 all over again. We will not be as clumsy and inefficient as our neighbors to the north were, which is why you are here at this hour." He surveyed the team with his piercing blue eyes, a sign of the soupçon of French ancestry in his otherwise thoroughly Chinese face. His signature straight-edge mouth looked as if it were copied from a Ming-dynasty watercolor of a palace guard. "We start with the flight crew as our principal suspects. What do we know?"

Peter Ma, who looked as if he might be Chiang's younger brother except for the eyes, cleared his throat. "The plane was carrying a double flight crew. In charge as Flight Captain was Giancarlo Modica, an Italian, Singapore resident. He's been with Pacificano for three-and-a-half years. After coming here, he was promoted almost immediately to captain, supposedly on the basis of family connections. He had a spotty record and reportedly a drinking problem before moving here, but his work record has been clean since, and the police have nothing on him. He is married to a local Muslim woman, Jasmina Nesra, and they have one child, a boy, three months old. We already talked with the airline. A supervisor there reported Modica seemed to be tense and overtired when he checked in today.

"His first officer is Hazlina Osmon, a Singaporean, also Muslim. She has actually been written up in a news article as one of the very few Muslim women flying commercial aircraft. She is single, no children. She—"

Chiang interrupted. "Two Islamic connections." He glanced toward the end of the table. "No offense, Mahmoud, but circumstances require us to be suspicious." Mahmoud al-Hadj pursed his thick lips but shrugged and said nothing. "Any suspect activity, associations?" Chiang continued.

"Osmon recently returned from a trip to Qatar. We are trying to find out who she met and what she did there. Reportedly, she is secular. That's about it."

"Let's get more. You said a double crew, right?"

"Yes, the relief crew for the long flight consisted of Captain Dale Cornell and First Officer Kamal Singh. Singh is a Sikh, as his name suggests, born in Singapore, learned to fly in the military, worked his way up at Pacificano. Cornell has been with the airline since it was formed. He was flying cargo until they started their passenger service. He moved up the line and is now the most senior pilot at the airline. Even owns stock."

"Then why is he on the relief crew?"

"We were told it's practice on these long-haul runs to alternate as primary and relief crews. In any case, he seems as solid and straight-arrow as they come. His kids are both grown. One works for a rival airline, desk job; the other is at university in the UK. He's a widower—wife passed a few years back."

"You didn't say much about this Singh character."

"Not much to say. We're drawing mostly blanks when it comes to him."

"Well, let's start filling in the blanks. You and Mahmoud pay an evening visit to Mrs. Modica. Rajan, you take on our Sikh. The rest of you find out what you can about Ms. Osmon: mosque attendance, memberships, neighbors, dating, buying habits. I'll dig some more into Cornell, just in case. I'll also see if I can get anything from Interpol related to any of the crew." He paused, obviously mulling over something. "It's a real long shot, but I think we should look into possible connections with the crew of MH370. I never did buy the official findings coming down from KL." He closed the presentation folder resting on the table. "What are you waiting for? The plane is in the air and still flying, as far as we know. Let's sort this out. Any questions?"

"Do we know where the plane is?" Peter Ma, being senior, tended to act as spokesman for the rest of the team members.

"Somewhere over the Pacific, not where it should be."

"Are we doing anything to locate it?"

"The Americans are working on it."

Peter let his disapproval show. "Why are they involved?"

"The airline is part-owned by an American holding company. That's the official cover. The real reason is the US has the manpower and computing resources."

"Are we talking NSA or what?" It was a question aimed at placing his boss on the game board, ferreting out what he knew.

"Or what. But we're in communication. If we can find that plane before it becomes a piloted bomb or a flying tomb, that's what this is all about. We can sort out claims of credit—or screw-up—later."

-- -- --

Peter straightened his tie and buttoned his wrinkled jacket

before pressing the buzzer next to the apartment door. Mahmoud stood two paces behind him, right hand poised near the shoulder holster under his suit jacket. When there was no answer, Peter tapped on the door, then hammered loudly. "Police. Internal Security. Open up." He repeated the order in Chinese and Malay, but there was no response. Mahmoud stepped forward, ready to put a boot or a shoulder to the door, but Peter reached for the handle, twisted it, and swung the door open. In the entryway, three paisley fabric suitcases were lined up, bulging, ready to go.

Down the hall, a woman wrapped in a loose dark-blue dress just brushing the tops of her plain shoes stepped out of a doorway and hastily adjusted a gray hijab to cover her hair. When she saw the two men standing there, she caught her breath. "What is it?" She glanced toward the door from which she had just emerged.

"ISD. Are you Jasmina Nesra?" She nodded as her shaking hand tucked stray strands of hair under the edge of her scarf. "Is your husband Giancarlo Modica?"

"What is it? What has happened?"

"We want to ask you some questions. What—"

The sharp cries of a baby cut him off as Jasmina ducked back into the room and slammed the door behind her.

Part Two: Photography
Chapter 6

"Yes!" Marwa slapped her table in triumph. Everyone in the room turned expectantly her way. "We have what looks like a facial feature match between one of the passengers and an Interpol database."

Telly Athenasiou gave her a thumbs up. "Let me see if Parsons at ARRG can also get security cam images from Chengi Airport to triangulate." Telly, one of a rare breed who could actually multitask rather than just make extravagant claims, tapped out a message as he spoke. "Meanwhile, put what you got up on the big screen." Marwa swirled a finger on her touchpad to drag a snap of a passport photo page and the Interpol image side-by-side onto a part of the wall screen. Telly scowled. "Is that the right image?"

"Yeah, I know, they don't look exactly alike, but check out the metrics." She overlaid a pattern of lines and numbers on the two photos. "And if we fix the hairline like this ..."

"Okay, now I see the resemblance. Looks pretty good. If that's him, who is he? Not Dante Calabrese as it says on his Italian passport."

Liv Caswell jumped in. "If we are right, it would be Abu Omar, nom de guerre of a rather mysterious Islamist operative. There is some disagreement about his real name but not about how ruthless he is." She threw up a few graphic stills from YouTube videos of Abu Omar's handiwork. The grainy but gruesome images evinced groans from several colleagues. "Well, you get my point." She wiped the images from the wall screen.

Telly jabbed the air with his flattened hand. "Wait a minute. Marwa, where is he in the passenger sociogram? Put that up again. Which one is our guy?"

"That's him, circled. He's part of that lone-wolf cluster along with Brandon Zhang, the other guy with the funky passport."

"Okay, we may have some kind of a hijacking by a group of terrorists. Maybe as many as five, given the diagram. Let's go on that assumption. And see if we can get some matches with Abu Omar's known associates, if any."

Several minutes passed with everyone in the room busy tapping away on their keyboards. "And we have a plane." Ben held up a finger as if pointing to a plane circling overhead. "It's a sighting from a commercial flight en route from Honolulu to Sydney, Australia. The plane was spotted flying under the vertical separation limit and did not respond to radio contact. Hawaii radar did not get transponder data back from the plane. It's not exactly where our predictive model projected, but it's close enough. We are waiting for satellite images to come from NRO."

Artyem nodded to his right. "The sighting puts our target just at the edge of the daylight line. We have the first high-res sat photo coming in. ... Here it is now. It is definitely a plane. In that shot"—he jiggled his mouse pointer—"we are zoomed in and looking down at about fifteen degrees from the vertical. If we correct the color rendition ... there ... now. Although we can't actually resolve the markings, we can see the body colors are green, white, and red."

"Which are the colors of Pacificano Transocean?"

"Bingo."

"All right." Telly started typing again. "Let me pass this on to

Washington and see if Defense can scramble some jets out of Hawaii or someplace to go up and take a look. Do we have a flight path yet?"

"Yeah, just follow that dotted blue line just painted. It's headed toward Los Angeles. If this is PT20, it will arrive with plenty of fuel left."

"Oh shit. Are we seeing another 9/11 attempt?"

"It's not looking good, sir."

Chapter 7

As Woolyard marched into The Circus, the room quieted and team members straightened in their seats. "We have word from Hawaii. An F-22 Raptor out of Hickam Air Force Base on Oahu is closing on the position we fed them. Honolulu is trying to raise the plane by radio. We should have something within minutes."

"Do we have a feed from the F-22 or Honolulu ATC?" Arkady asked.

"We have the data feed from Honolulu, but not cockpit voice communications. The Air Force is squirrely about direct feeds from their planes, but Hickam will let us know as soon as they have anything. It will take some time for the F-22 to intercept."

The clicking of keyboards remained dampened and conversations were muted as the team held its collective breath for several minutes. The relative quiet was broken by a voice booming over the sound system. Telly tapped quickly on his computer to lower the volume.

"This is Colonel Garrison Sheldon, Hickam Air Force Base. Our pilot reports he has a visual on the plane and is trying to raise it on both military and civilian frequencies." A rush of static filled a long pause. "The pilot reports still no radio contact, but he can read the tail markings on the plane. We are confirming." There was another pause during which Telly muted the sound.

Several words were lost as Telly ramped up the volume and

Colonel Sheldon's voice was once again piped through the sound system. "… is confirmed as registered to Transporte Aéreo Rápido, a Mexican air freight service. Their filed flight plan makes them bound for Mexico City via LAX." There was another hiss-filled gap. "Our pilot has reached them by radio. They report intermittent radio dropouts and problems with their squawk. US Customs and Border Protection has been alerted to the irregularities and will meet the plane at LAX."

Ben leaned toward Guzman on his right. "Squawk?" he said half under his breath.

"Transponder or transponder code."

Telly flipped a cord-switch on the headset he was wearing. "Thank you, Colonel, for your assistance on this."

"Happy to oblige. Let us know if there is anything else we can do for you."

"Will do." Telly looked around the room at the despondent faces. "What's the matter? We cross one off and move on to the next on the list. Location, keep scanning. Psychosocial, keep digging. We're wasting time. Open-intel team, haven't heard from you for a while. I know you've been feeding your stuff to Psychosocial, but what's up? Anything to report?"

The open-intel team had been busy collecting and analyzing news media and other public sources for possible clues or connections. Kurt Masters, who led the team, was a recent recruit from Buzzfeed. A former pal of open-intel guru Aaron Zelin, he had come to the attention of CAASS based on his incisive blogs posted on jihadology.net.

"We don't have anything that rises enough above background noise." He took off his red-rimmed glasses and rubbed his eyes. "But there is one news item that I find interesting. It's a long shot—there's no semantic link—but it could be connected." Since coming to CAASS, Masters had developed a reputation as an analyst who combined dogged discipline with sideways leaps of insight.

"Shoot."

"Yes, wire services report a British MI6 counter-terrorism unit pulled two people off a flight leaving Gatwick for New York just minutes before it was to depart. The plane had already left the gate and was about to taxi for takeoff when it was pulled from the queue and directed to a remote area of the airport. The initial report cited mechanical problems and made no mention of MI6, but some passengers started tweeting and the story then hit the wire services. No details yet, but the event took place about the time our plane was pulling its vanishing act."

"Great. Let me see if our pals in DC can get anything fresh out of the Brits. Meanwhile, keep looking for other possible related stories within approximately the same timeframe." A rainfall of keystrokes pattered throughout the room again. "Oh, we ordered sandwiches for everyone. They're in the break room. Grab whatever you want and bring it back here. Take a bio break whenever you need, but keep it quick. And no more than one person from each team away from The Circus at any one time."

Chapter 8

THE SMALL INTERROGATION room at ISD headquarters seemed filled with Jasmina Nesra's panicky breathing. "Where is my baby?"

Across the bare table, Peter Ma pressed his thumbs together and took his time replying. This was the hard part for him. He knew his job, but the woman was not much younger than his wife. He considered his words. "He is being taken care of. You can see him again as soon as you tell us where you were going and why."

"I ... I was going to my sister's."

"Why?"

"Because ... because I am leaving my husband."

"And why is that?"

"Because he is Italian." She looked from Peter to Mahmoud. "And a Catholic."

"You are leaving your husband because he is an Italian Catholic? That makes no sense. Surely, this is not something you are just now finding out."

"No, but I am just now finding out what that means."

Both men waited for an explanation that was not forthcoming. Peter tilted his chair back and scowled. "It means ..."

"It means flying to America." She spoke, head down, talking into the table in front of her.

"To America ..."

"Do you know what whores there are in America?" She raised her head and looked into his face. "Do you know?"

"Your husband has been paying prostitutes?"

"No, he has no need of prostitutes, no need to pay. He has a planeload of whores that he flies with, and one of them he beds in America. First it was Los Angeles, and now it will be Chicago."

"He has been having an affair with one of the crew members?"

"Yes."

"You know this?"

"I am his wife. A wife knows."

Mahmoud stood up, head tilted and looking askance at her as he scratched at his beard. "Let me see if I understand this. You are leaving your husband, taking the baby, all on a hunch, some, ah—what do you call it?—intuition of the woman?"

"It is not intuition, it is ... knowing."

"He has admitted this?"

"No. He screams his denials. He yells his lies. It is the same as a confession."

Mahmoud threw up his hands. In a quiet aside to Peter, he switched suddenly into Singaporean Mandarin. "Muslim women are this way. I know."

Peter suppressed a smile. "And, Mrs. Modica, what else can you tell us about your husband? His politics? Other activities? Interests? Friends?"

"I've already told you about his activities, his interests, and his friends, if that's what you want to call them. And it is Nesra, not Modica. Jasmina Nesra. I kept my name. I am not some Italian girl." Her eyes angled upward as she thought. "He is not political, that I know. And not religious. Except about football. *Serie A*, Italy. He watches every Italian match he can—on television, on the Internet. That's his religion. He is a devoted

45

follower of Juventus—Claudio Marchisio is his patron saint—but he also sometimes prays before Milano. His brother lives in Milano. They are both Italian infidels."

-- -- --

"What did you get from her?" Alon opened the manila folder in front of him and prepared to make a notation.

"Nothing, really. Modica barracks for Juventus in the Italian premier league. Maybe he is having an affair with a stewardess. Perhaps he is upset that his wife accused him of infidelity and threatened to leave." Peter closed his notepad and slipped it back into his jacket. "Not much to suggest he might hijack a plane."

"Did you search the apartment?"

"Of course."

"And ... ?"

"And we found no flight simulator, if that is what you are asking, not like with the Malaysian pilot. The technical people are going over his computer. They'll let us know if they find anything suspicious. The rest? All routine."

"What about the other crew members?"

"Osmon is moving up our list. She flew first-class to Qatar on short notice, spent three days there, does not seem to have relatives in the country. Qatar is hardly a hotbed of Islamist recruiting, but it is a crossroads where many travelers can meet. We're trying to find out more.

"As of now, we are still throwing darts in the dark, looking for suspicious behavior or associates, conjuring up motives from nothing. Even if we consider Hazlina Osmon as having some jihadist leanings and reasons for pulling off a hijacking, it is hard to imagine a scenario by which this small woman could overpower the other three crew members—all men, all much bigger."

"What if she had a handgun with her?"

"What?"

"According to police files, she has a license as a member of a local target-shooting club."

"That is hardly the same thing as smuggling firearms on-board a commercial aircraft."

"No, but we have no idea what we are dealing with."

Chapter 9

BEN SCANNED THE LABELS on the sandwiches stacked in a row on the break-room table. Like the majority of Israeli Jews, he was thoroughly secular and largely unobservant. Still, he passed over the BLTs and the ham-and-cheese out of lifelong habit. He settled on a smoked salmon and avocado wrap and pulled a Coke from the cooler. He was at the doorway when his cellphone played the opening bars of *"Yerushalayim shel Zahav,"* a song that was to Israel what "America, the Beautiful" was to the United States: almost a second national anthem. From the ringtone, he knew that somebody in his immediate family was calling.

He thumbed the phone on and smiled. A pretty teen with mocha-chocolate curls and bright blue bangle earrings smiled back and greeted him in Hebrew.

"Not much," he replied. "And how about you, Shoshi? What is my little sister up to?"

"Me and Dad been talking since it hit the news. Like, we figure you're involved."

"Involved?"

"Well, with the missing plane. It was on the evening news. Another plane goes missing from Thailand or whatever—you know, one of those Asian countries. Dad's guessing you might be working on tracking it down."

"Aba is using his writer's imagination too much. I'm doing maths over here for one of the MIT research centers. I thought you knew."

"Aba says that's really just a cover for your, like, real work, which he figures is tracking terrorists."

Ben grinned and shook his head. "Well, both you and Aba ought to know that if I were doing anything like that I would not be able to talk about it."

"Ohmahgod, I knew it!" The image of her index finger grew to almost fill the screen of his phone as she extended it toward her webcam. "You just admitted it, Bini."

"I admitted nothing, Shoshi. Now it's your imagination that's working overtime. So, how are you doing? How is school?"

"Meh. Mostly. Algebra sucks. I miss you."

"No you don't. You're happy to be rid of me and to have Aba and Ima all to yourself. Are they around?"

"No, they just went out for a walk."

"How is Aba's hip?"

"Oh, it's fine ... I think. Doesn't complain, anyway, at least not about that. Everything else. Teenagers, the Islamic State in the Levant, my eye makeup, Netanyahu and the Knesset, rap music, indifferent American Jews, publishers and editors—the list is long. Trust me."

"Publishers and editors? Is he writing again?"

"Didn't you hear? He sold his first novel to an Australian publisher. Pikelet Press, I think it's called. He's been, like, walking tall and all ever since."

"Wow, no, nobody tells me anything anymore." He looked up as Liv Caswell bounced into the room. "Look, I gotta go. We're under a little pressure here."

"Yeah, I would guess so." Shoshi chewed on her lower lip. "Be careful."

"I will. But this maths business is dangerous work, ya know. Gotta watch out for division by zero and steer clear of outliers and singularities. Shalom."

She stuck out her tongue at him just before the screen went blank. Ben chuckled and tucked his phone back in the lower pocket on his cargo pants.

"Little sister?" Liv gave an interrogative tilt to her head.

"Yeah. She's been trying to figure out what I do here. And she worries about me."

"How old?"

"Thirteen."

"God, I hated thirteen. Well, and fourteen, and ..."

"I'm with ya."

"Really? But, I suppose ..."

"You suppose what?"

"Just funny how you and Marwa are always at each other. Seems kinda, well, adolescent at times."

Ben was about to protest, but Hector Guzman arrived in the break room. "Hey, we've been looking for you. You can eat that while we show you what we have." He snatched a foil-wrapped beef burrito for himself as he passed the table.

Chapter 10

HECTOR ALMOST DRAGGED Ben back to The Circus. "We got a break." He peeled back the foil from his burrito and took a bite as they crossed the room. "A sigint satellite operated by NRO was listening at the right frequency at the time of the last handshaking between the aircraft engines and Inmarsat. No accident, we assume. This allows us to triangulate, very roughly. We plug the numbers into our model and ta-da." He did a bow and palms-up gesture toward the main map projection on the wall screen.

Ben high-fived Hector. "That really does narrow it down. Now we have just those two regions as fitting all the data. I think we can eliminate the northern one for now, because somebody should have spotted the plane, given the air traffic around there. So the plane seems to be headed south now, but the uncertainty is still pretty big. That's a lot of empty ocean where we think it could be. Obviously, we can't send out search planes to cover that many square kilometers. Do we have any idea how high the thing might be flying?"

"Plugging in the rate of climb at the last secondary radar contact and the data from the Inmarsat pings would put it at between 43,000 and 49,000 feet. Operating ceiling for the 787-9 is 43,000. But it could have descended since. We would need a third receiver to triangulate in three-space in order to approximate the current altitude."

Ben turned to face Telly. "How about arranging for some ground-level listening post, preferably West Coast, to be ready for the next handshaking?"

"I'll see if DC can work something out, but it's not going to happen immediately. I doubt we can orchestrate that in less than an hour."

"Well, do the best you can. If you can arrange it, we'll have a better estimate of location and altitude as well as speed and direction from the current position. Of course, it costs us time unless we get a breakthrough from someplace else."

-- -- --

The hour passed quickly for some in the room, too slowly for Ben. "We have good news and bad news," he announced at last. "The good news is that the periodic exchange of maintenance signals between the plane's engines and Inmarsat finally made it possible to get a better estimate of the altitude of the plane. The bad news is the numbers. We were way off. We're now putting altitude at 17,000 feet, plus or minus 5,000. At this lower altitude, fuel consumption is higher. We have less time left than we thought and have updated the countdown clock accordingly. The nature of the data on which we are relying means the plane could either now be on a more northern track toward somewhere in California or south toward nothing."

"Thanks, Ben." Telly looked toward Marwa. "Anything to report from Psychosocial?"

"Our team is still in agreement that what we have is a cell of at least two, probably three, and possibly as many as five terrorists who have somehow taken over the plane. We are betting on the larger number. There is no smoking gun, but security camera images from Chengi support our identification of passenger Dante Calabrese as Abu Omar. We have additional links between him and another passenger, Brandon Zhang, traveling on what is probably a false passport, including security camera footage showing them emerging together from a restroom during the time the flight was delayed."

Ben opened his mouth wide. "Wow, now that's real suspicious: two guys taking a leak while waiting for their long-delayed flight."

Telly gave him a look that said to cut it out. "Okay, Marwa, what's the bottom line."

"A hijacking makes more sense if they are headed someplace. So, we would place our bets on the northern route, with a presumed target in Southern California."

Ben raised himself from his chair. "Then why hasn't any other plane spotted them? And why would they be flying so low? They would want to have the most fuel to reach their destination or do the most damage on impact if it's a 9/11 scenario. Even your own team and the open-intel folks have nothing to suggest a hijacking: no demands, no threats, no backchannel rumblings."

Marwa started to speak, but Telly held up his hand. "Just keep working the channels, crunching the numbers—"

"And making up psychosocial spy stories."

"Ben."

Ben would not let it go. "Not all guesses are equal here. What this side of the room is doing is based on numbers and mathematics, not yarn-spinning."

"Ben."

"Okay, I'll shut up. We'll task some satellites to try to get pics within both areas to see if we can settle it."

== == ==

The news and the mood in The Circus continued to cycle from good to bad and back over the rest of the afternoon. Repeated attempts to image the plane by high-resolution satellite photography had failed, and no further sightings materialized. The sense of desperation rose as the evening approached and the countdown clock based on the fuel estimate kept dropping.

Chapter 11

BEN TOOK A DEEP breath. "We have another set of handshake signals, but we now suspect the time stamp on one of the signals is skewed for some reason; we just don't know in which direction. If we take only the best data, here's what our models predict. The plane is currently over the Pacific off the coast of Peru, out of radar range and now flying at an estimated 13,000 to 17,000 feet on a bearing heading roughly toward the city of Santiago, Chile. Adjusting for the increased fuel consumption at this low altitude, if it doesn't change from its present course, it will run out of fuel and crash into the ocean somewhere in the area highlighted by the red circle, some distance off the coast not far from Santiago.

"As the plane should soon be close to entering Chilean airspace and the projected impact is within Chile's Exclusive Economic Zone, Washington has asked the Chilean government for assistance. They agreed to help, a bit surprising given that relations with the country in recent years have been rather ... chilly." Ben paused for an expected groan or two, but the only reaction was Guzman hanging his head. "Anyway, the Chileans are scrambling a couple of F-16 Falcons out of Los Cóndores Air Base in Iquique in the north."

Marwa cleared her throat. "What about the northern route, Ben, we haven't definitively eliminated that. We could be chasing a phantom off South America while the real bird is approaching San Diego."

"If the real bird were approaching San Diego, Marwa, we would have it on radar or would have at least one sighting, but we don't. Give it up. There may be terrorists on board, but the models say the plane is headed south-southeast."

Telly looked up from his laptop. "All right. We're about to find out for sure. The Fuerza Aérea de Chile, the Chilean Air Force, is patching us into radio comms with the squadron leader. It's all in Spanish, of course. I'm afraid my schoolboy Spanish is not very good. Hector, can you interpret for us?"

"Si. Sure." He smiled broadly as he put on a set of headphones, then cocked his head in concentration. "Okay, this South American accent is a little hard for me to follow, but I think the pilot is saying estimated range to reference coordinates, eighteen nautical miles, closing fast."

Chapter 12

COMANDANTE DE ESCUADRILLA Eduardo Fuentes had a passion for flying. He was particularly passionate about his fast and agile Víbora, Spanish for viper, the name by which the F-16 Fighting Falcons were known to pilots around the world. Fuentes had welcomed the orders to reconnoiter for the Americans. Government belt-tightening had sharply cut the number of military exercises in recent years until it had become difficult to stay in practice.

Nearing the rendezvous coordinates, coming in high for the best overview, Fuentes rolled his jet to get a better view through the bubble canopy. There was no sign of the missing plane. If the plane were there, he knew he or his wingman should see it or pick it up on their radar.

"Nada. There is nothing here, no plane. I am passing through the coordinates now. We will commence an outward spiral and keep looking for a while."

▬ ▬ ▬

In Cambridge, the mood dipped. Ben and Artyem were huddled around Ben's laptop, poring over every detail of their models and rechecking their assumptions.

Marwa watched, a smug expression on her face. "I told you. The hijack scenario, which is far and away the most plausible, points to the northerly flight track. We should be scrambling our own jets out of San Diego."

Ben held up his hand. "Just give us a few more minutes here."

As Artyem and Ben worried away at the model, Hector continued to translate the negative reports from the F-16s.

"Wait a minute." Ben interrupted him." I think we have it. We've been modeling the flight as if it were trying to conserve fuel, flying more or less normally. But what if we're wrong and they want to use up the fuel? What if they're flying lower than the expected altitude, say at the lower limit of our estimates but still within the probable error of our signals analysis? Let's see where that puts them." He moved sliders and entered new parameters. "Look at this, guys. The new projected impact is farther north, near one of the deepest parts of the Pacific, an area of the Atacama Trench known as the Richards Deep." He right-clicked to bring up a reference menu, then whistled. "Deep is the word. Our atlas puts the floor of the ocean there about five miles down. If that's the impact area, off the coast from Antofagasta, Chile, they would currently be right ... there." He tapped the return key and a highlighted cursor appeared on the map. "Telly, have them pass on these new coordinates to the pilot, and tell him the plane is probably going to be lower than we had expected."

— — —

Fuentes was flying at 5,000 meters between two sheets of gray, with near-solid cloud cover above and the darkening sea below. A blip appeared on his radar. He squinted against the diffuse glare of the low sun as he scanned the region where the radar said the quarry should be. Against the backdrop of choppy blue-gray sea below, it would be hard to pick out any aircraft, but at last he caught a glimpse, a tiny flash of color in a shaft of sunlight. "There it is." He signaled his wing man.

"We see it," he said over the radio. "Well below us. We are dropping to 4,000 meters."

"Okay, Viper One, approach and slow to keep pace with the

aircraft. If you can, contact the pilots by radio."

"Roger." Fuentes and his wingman throttled back as they neared and came alongside the plane. "I am closing on the aircraft, but ..."

"Is there a problem, Viper One?"

"I have not actually seen this new type of Boeing in flight. It looks right, but I cannot be certain. There, I now see it does have the Pacificano markings."

— — —

In Cambridge, Hector Guzman translated the exchange. "Okay, it sounds like they're close enough to see that it's a commercial airplane. The base wants absolute confirmation. Now something about Saturday. Soccer maybe, Valencia versus Barcelona. No. it's phonetic alphabet. They're repeating it. *Nueve-Valencia-Valencia-Barcelona-Sábado.* Sounds like a tail number. Is that the right registration number, 9-V-V-B-S?"

"Yes! 9V-VBS, a recent Singapore registration. We have it." Telly shook his fists in the air and the room erupted in cheers.

Hector continued his interpreting. "They are pacing the plane, trying to get a response by radio."

— — —

Fuentes eased forward until his canopy was just even with the cockpit of the DreamLiner and then held steady. "I can see into the cockpit. I see two people. They are slumped in the seats. They have not responded to radio. I will pull forward so I can be sure they can see me and do a wing waggle. If anyone is awake. No. No reaction. No response. But I see two more at the back of the cockpit, the same, slumped over."

There was a pause from Los Cóndores, then another question. "What about passengers?"

"Some of the windows in the passenger cabin are ... They are turned black. I can see in some, but no movement, even when I

59

waggle my wings. Somebody should notice. The windows on this plane are quite large. I can see some passengers that look as if they are bent over. Not moving."

"And on the other side?"

"This is Viper Two. It is the same here. Nothing. No sign of life."

"Roger. Viper One, Viper Two, return to base. We have done what the Americans asked. It is a flying coffin that will soon crash into the sea. There is nothing more we can do."

■■ ■■ ■■

Hector relayed the news to the CAASS team. "The pilots have just been told to peel off and head back to the base."

Both Marwa and Ben let out a loud "No!" at the same time.

Ben pointed a demanding finger toward Telly. "You need to ask them to stay with the plane."

Telly's hands hovered over his keyboard. "What can we do at this point? This is not like in the movies, like *Executive Decision*, where Steven Segal can board the plane in flight."

"No, but we need to learn as much as we can while it is still in the air and to pinpoint the impact exactly."

Marwa nodded vigorously. "I agree. In fact, I want to be with the pilot the whole way. I want to know exactly what he sees, and I want to talk with him."

"I don't think we can do that."

"Then you relay the message. Tell them this is important."

Ben was out of his seat, standing now. "Yes, and if we can get them to pace the plane right down to the deck, we will know more about exactly what is happening. Is it a dead-stick glide? Are the control surfaces fixed, free, or still under program control? Everything could be relevant, not just crash coordinates but angle of impact, how it breaks up if it does, how long it takes to sink. The more we know, the more likely we are to be able to make sense of what happens and maybe pull off a successful re-covery.

"In fact, now that our model has been confirmed"—he sent a triumphant glance toward Marwa—"we should try to get Chile to start search-and-rescue ships steaming to the general area of the expected impact. And reconnaissance planes. Who knows, maybe someone is alive. Or they might have a chance to recover the Cockpit Voice Recorder and Flight Data Recorder."

Telly looked unconvinced. "All I can do is ask."

"Then ask, as nicely as you can. And tell them what we just told you, why this is important."

Telly typed away, then waited several seconds for a reply. "Chile said no, the jets are already headed back to Iquique. I'm sorry."

"No, that's not acceptable."

Telly laughed. "Not acceptable? What can I say? That's what's happening. It's beyond our control."

"Then get that guy in DC, the NTSB magician. Get him to try."

"I ... That's Woolyard's bailiwick."

"Goddamnit." Ben stood up and stomped out of the room. Within some seconds he could be heard yelling at Woolyard. The yelling stopped and soon Ben re-entered, shoulders slouched.

Artyem looked up at him. "What's the problem? He said no?"

"He already tried. The fighters only have a limited range, less than 300 nautical miles on a roundtrip mission. They've already flown two legs of a triangle. Their Air Force says it can't be done, to follow all the way and return."

Guzman held up his hand. "Wait a minute. We still have the audio patch with the radio comms. The pilot is arguing with the base. His F-16 is equipped with drop tanks, which were full on takeoff. They extend the range. He is volunteering, insisting he can continue to pace the plane and still make it back to base.

Now he is being given a direct order to return. He acknowledges and says he is heading back, but he is still arguing." Hector laughed.

"What is it?"

"There is some salty language in the background. It seems someone higher up has directed that the Air Force do everything in its power to comply with our request." He laughed again.

Telly wagged his finger. "For such a grave situation, you seem to find a lot of humor."

"Well, see, the pilot was just ordered to turn around again and catch up with the 787 once more. But he responded that he was already chasing the plane again."

Laughter and fist pumps rippled around the circle. Telly pivoted in his seat and gave everyone a sour look. "Need I remind you that this is not success. This is defeat. We are soon to witness a planeload of people crash into one of the deepest parts of the Pacific. There are 273 passengers and thirteen crew members on that plane."

Chapter 13

Commander Fuentes acknowledged his new orders. "All right, I will report what I see, everything."

To get more room, he rolled away from the plane as it neared the coordinates the Americans had given. "The plane is starting to lose altitude, but ... Yes, I can see. The control surfaces are adjusting. Still under control. Autopilot, I suppose.

"I am dropping, parallel with it. 3,500 meters now. I will call out altitude every 500 meters as we go down." He dropped back just enough to be able to watch the plane without turning his head as much.

"The plane is now nosing down somewhat more. Both engines are out now. 3,000 meters.

"I will follow as far as I can." He knew the F-16 could pull 9gs and shoot straight up if needed, and he knew his limits as a pilot. "Nearing 2,000 meters. On my mark ... mark.

"It is nosing into a much steeper dive now. 1,000 meters. Mark.

"500 meters coming. Mark."

Fuentes pulled back on the side-stick and cut in the afterburners. His 7g pullout bottomed out at less than 100 meters above the water. His vision darkened as he climbed quickly through 2,000 meters before leveling off to circle back and check the site.

"I saw the plane dive at a steep angle and flip on impact. The wings sheared off and the fuselage broke up into ... it looks like at least three pieces. The debris field is spread in the direction of impact but is not large. From this altitude I can't tell if there are bodies in the water. I'll drop down and make as slow a circle as I can to get a closer look." He checked his fuel reserves. "One pass, then I have to head back."

Fuentes took in as much as he could as he made a low-altitude turn around the crash site. "Either one of the sections of the fuselage is already sinking or I did not count right. I see only two pieces and one wing now. No sign of inflatable rafts or bodies with lifejackets.

"I am ... sorry. There was nothing I ..."

== == ==

In The Circus there was stunned silence as Guzman finished his translation. "The pilot says the flight data from his plane can be forwarded to us for analysis. Now there is some argument back and forth. More cursing. It seems we will get access to the data, but it will be passed through channels. The pilot apologizes again. Now he is saying goodbye and he is sorry—in English."

Chapter 14

THE HALF-HOUR BREAK that Telly had mandated stretched into an hour. Conversations trailed off as everyone trooped back into the room to sit in silence. As Dr. Woolyard took his seat, Marwa rose and walked to the center of the circle. She clicked on a remote and hundreds of images of faces sprayed themselves in a massive moving collage around the room. "We put this together from what we had pulled off the Web and from the scanned passport pages. We got nearly all of them. Across the top you see the seventeen flight and cabin crew members. The text crawl across the bottom carries the names of the passengers and crew.

"Oh, I almost forgot, we have music." She looked toward Liv. After a few seconds, the haunting opening horn passage of Ravel's "Pavane for a Dead Princess" drifted from the speakers overhead. "Always loved that piece," Liv said quietly.

Marwa glanced down at her notes and continued. "The crew ranged in age from twenty-three—that's the handsome flight attendant on the far right—to sixty-one, Co-Captain Dale Cornell. The youngest passenger was a little girl who had just turned three and the oldest was eighty-seven. For most of them, we know very little—well, except for our cluster of suspects—but here are some random excerpts we scrounged off the Web." She lifted her iPad and started reading.

"Here's a posting from the JobSeek-Singapore website: 'Bruce Sundstrom brings a passion for precision to his work in x-ray photolithography. With a BA in Physics from the Singapore Institute of Technology and thirteen years of experience at Fil-Micro Industries, he is ready to help take your company's thin-film micro-fabrication program to the next level.'

"And this next piece is amazing, from *The Straits Times*: 'Diminutive Hazlina Osmon is a Muslim martial arts expert—and an airline pilot. She is not only the first woman to reach the rank of First Officer with Singapore-based Pacificano Trans-ocean Airlines, but she acknowledges that there are only a handful of Muslim women around the globe who fly commercial aircraft. "I was always independent, marking out my own path. My father encouraged me to be strong and to succeed. I think he wanted me to be a boy," she adds with a husky laugh.'

"And here's a note from the Yuan family Facebook page: 'Pic of Penny on her third birthday—deliriously happy as usual.'

"There's so much here. An older couple from Tel Aviv were on an around-the-world junket. They'd posted regular updates to a personal blog." She looked over at Ben. "I ... I can't read it all, but we started a wiki for everyone to read and contribute. We ..." Marwa's voice broke. "We thought maybe a moment of silence ..." There were nods around the room as the music faded out and everyone paused in thought.

Telly and Dr. Woolyard waited before rising slowly from their seats and converging in the center. They each hugged Marwa, then turned to face the group, with Telly starting a slow clap as he gestured around to the entire team. "You did good, people. You worked hard and pulled off something amazing." He put an arm around Marwa's shoulders. "All of you deserve a pat on the back and more. It's been a long day. Many of you have been here for some fourteen hours. What do you think, Doc?"

Woolyard nodded agreement with the unstated premise. "I think everyone can call it a day. We'll save the postmortem debriefing until tomorrow. All-hands meeting at thirteen hundred hours. We got word that there are ships headed to the crash site and the promise of reconnaissance planes at daybreak. We'll know more in the morning. Go home, everybody. Get some sleep."

Around the room, people started gathering papers, shutting down laptops. Ben closed a few programs, then stood up. "Shouldn't we keep working on the models. We still don't know what really happened. I mean, not like the crash itself but I mean who ... what made the plane change direction in the first place and ultimately crash. We still don't know everything about that suspicious cluster of passengers. Maybe Psychosocial could find some more connections, develop more elaborate profiles."

Marwa looked both puzzled and pleased. "I'm willing to stay. Anyone else?"

Despite several volunteers, Woolyard put up both hands and spread his fingers. "No, it's time to call it quits. Tomorrow, everyone, tomorrow."

Part Three: Archeology
Chapter 15

I<small>T WAS THE KIND</small> of muggy morning in Singapore when the air was saturated with street smells and even in the air-conditioned ISD headquarters, Peter Ma was sweating. He stood just outside Alon Chiang's open office door, waiting to be acknowledged and invited in. Alon finished typing his case note and closed the Word file before looking up. "Sit. What's the story?"

Peter took a seat on the straight-back metal chair facing Alon's desk. "Well, you know we lost the plane. That is, they found it just about the time it ditched in the ocean. No survivors. That means our investigation changes course. We have provisionally eliminated most of the cabin crew as suspects. Co-Captain Cornell and First Officer Singh both appear to be non-starters. Captain Modica was having marital troubles and may have been having an affair, possibly with a crew member, but there is hardly reason to believe he would take a plane down because his wife yelled at him. First Officer Osmon is the only still-active suspect among the crew, and that is only by virtue of an absence of exculpatory information. That and the fact that she is Muslim. We'll be following up on contacts and associates. We are also still trying to find more about her recent trip to Qatar. That's about it."

"And the passengers?" This was always Alon's way: clipped questions, like a schoolmaster administering an exam.

"We got some help from the Americans on that. They pointed

the finger at five passengers, one of whom they claim was Abu Omar, the notorious and rather mysterious Islamist suspected of involvement in at least half a dozen terrorist operations. Traveling on a false passport, needless to say. They connect him with another passenger allegedly traveling on a false passport. We are not waiting for more from the Americans but are following up on all of these leads ourselves."

"What about the plane?"

"Brand new. This was its maiden flight. We secured from the airline copies of the maintenance records, such as they are at this early stage. Pacificano is being completely cooperative. Boeing is in the loop and a rep is on his way. The whole file is in the case folder."

"What do we know about the airline? Not exactly top tier."

"No, but it's been profitable over its entire thirty-year history, largely because management is willing to take chances on opening promising new routes. This non-stop service to the capital city of the American heartland is an example. They signed up early for the extended-range aircraft that makes it possible and economical."

"The owners?"

"Italians, Americans, Singaporeans. It was started by the Cusamano brothers. According to a story about them in *The Straits Times*, the two—one who had immigrated here, the other still back in Sicily—had been feuding over something for years. With the help of some cousins from America, they got together, pooled their resources, and started an air-freight business. The *Times* article said the word *pacificano* means 'we reconcile' in Italian."

"Mafia connections?"

"Not that we know of. We have an inquiry in with the Italians."

"Anything link flight PT20 with Malaysian flight MH370?"

"Haven't found any yet. Different plane, different everything, except for the almost identical initial flight paths toward Beijing. And, of course, the rerouting and ultimate fate. I did learn that the Boeing 787 flies under the same type certification as the triple-seven, which Malaysian Airlines was flying, if that means anything."

"Anything could mean anything at this point." Alon drummed the desktop with his fingers. "I have a meeting in twenty minutes with people from the Civil Aviation Authority that is leading the technical investigation. It would be easy to think that the pressure is off, since the fate of the plane is already settled. That would be a mistake. We can't leave this test with so many question boxes not ticked. We are not Malaysia, we are Singapore. We must show the world that we know what we are doing. Understood?"

"Yes, sir." Peter stood and barely stopped himself from raising his hand in salute. "We will spare nothing in the investigation."

Chapter 16

THE LIGHTS WERE ALREADY on when Ben let himself into the Center at his usual time in the morning. He looked around warily. "Hello?" There was no answer except for the buzz of the bad fluorescent. He stopped first at the Director's office on the guess that Woolyard might have come in early to get a head start in prep for the meeting, but the office was empty.

As Ben approached his own office, he saw that the door was wide open. Marwa was at her desk, chin on her palm, studying a sociogram on her monitor screen.

"Well, good morning, Marwa. What suddenly possessed you to actually start work at a reasonable hour?"

"I've been here since six."

"Why?"

"Getting a jump on you. No, actually it's because I can't let go of this. I feel we should have been able to find that plane faster, and my team should have been able to figure out what was going on."

"We'll know more when we get the black boxes. And I'm sure the Singapore intelligence people—and our own—are working on the case. Something will turn up."

Marwa swiveled her posture-chair to face him squarely. "But that doesn't mean we'll hear about it. We're just geeks, real-time data analysts. This is no longer a real-time situation, and they need feet in the field not Web jockeys. We're going to be pushed aside, and it'll be back to business as usual: programming software, building models, and playing games with simulated situations."

"You liked the pressure of the real thing, didn't you."

"Yes, just like you. Well, like most of us."

"Not everyone. I thought Artyem was going to have a coronary at a couple of points. Not everyone seems to thrive on adrenaline." Ben sat down and woke up his computer with a shake of the mouse. "For me, I appreciate having this chance to go back and take a less-pressured view of the data and the models. And I admit that I really can't let go of it either."

Marwa turned back to her computer. Ben shrugged and began launching software. The two worked in silence, lost in their divergent worlds for the better part of an hour, until Ben interrupted the quiet. "Interesting."

"What's interesting?"

"Take a look at these plotted descent paths." A graph with three downturned curves was displayed on his screen. "We got the flight data on the F-16 pace plane forwarded overnight from the Chilean Air Force. I found it on the Center's dropbox. The starting point with the little plane icon on the left is the 3,500 meter reference point from the pilot. Other inputs include flight parameters for the 787-9 with the reported take-off weight minus fuel because it was flying on fumes at this point. The red curve, A, is what we would expect if the plane were flying on auto-pilot, which would be attempting to stay aloft by default. The orange line, B, is what the plane would do if it were in completely uncontrolled free-fall, with unchanging control surfaces. The green line, C, is a guess at what a really skilled human pilot might try to do with this aircraft if he were ditching without power and attempting the softest landing possible. It's based on a reconstruction of the flight path of the US Airways

Airbus 320 that was so expertly flown in a dead-stick ditching on the Hudson River back in 2009. "

"What about our plane, which one was its path?"

"Great question? And the answer is … ta-da … D, none of the above!" He tapped the spacebar and a black line appeared on the screen that curved downward much more steeply at the end than the other plots.

"What? Are you sure?"

"I'm sure. It's a high-confidence curve fit. I mean, it's not exact. I could display it as a box-and-whisker plot to show the variance, but it would not be as pretty. A box-and-whisker plot is—"

"Duh. I know what a box-and-whisker plot is. So this implies the plane was deliberately crashed."

"Yes."

"Someone crashed it? After fifteen hours of flying it, they decide to ditch it?"

"Someone … or something. As if they wanted to crash it at a particular spot."

"Like one of the deepest points in the South Pacific."

"Right, one of the deepest points, with a nose-down crash that was most likely to take the plane to the bottom."

Her mouth hung open as she considered the implications of what he was saying. "They aren't going to find much debris when they reach the site, are they." It was said almost without inflection, as if the answer were already obvious.

"No. In fact, the news services are now reporting that the first reconnaissance planes have arrived over the area and have not found a debris field."

"It's like that Malaysian flight. They never did find the debris."

"The difference is that we are already on the spot after mere hours, not weeks later. And instead of thousands of square miles to search, we know exactly where the thing went down."

"You don't think someone onboard was still alive to fly the thing, do you?"

"It doesn't seem plausible. In which case, there had to be some very sophisticated programming of the autopilot to pull off that crash. Hell, the whole flight had to be programmed just right."

"Who would do that? Why?"

"That's a question for you. You're the Psychosocial Lead."

== == ==

Woolyard arrived at the Center shortly before noon and peeked into their office. "I thought I told everyone to sleep in. Meeting's not for another hour."

"We've been doing some follow-up analysis on flight PT20. Let me show you what we found."

"Save it for the meeting. I need to get on a conference call with NTSB and the brass in DC at ..." He glanced at his watch. "In six minutes. So, later." He strode briskly away.

The rest of the staff trickled into the office over the next hour. By the time Woolyard and Athanasiou entered The Circus, the chairs and desks had been arranged back into neat rows and all seventeen analysts were seated in their customary spots—with one exception: Ben was next to Marwa, and the two were talking, heads inclined, in low voices.

Woolyard stood facing the group and cleared his throat. "We have been gazumped. Another agency has taken over the investigation. We are standing down. The same applies to our partners at the NTSB."

Mouths opened and brows creased as his words sank in.

Ben broke the silence. "What does that mean, standing down? Marwa and I are in the midst of a new analysis. We have evidence of intelligent control in the last minutes flying. We—"

"It means what it says, Ben. We are not working on that flight any longer, and we are not interested in any further fantasy re-constructions. We will be moving on to other projects as of to-day, as of now. Telly will give all of you your new assignments." He gestured to Athenasiou as he backed away and started to-ward the door.

Ben was on his feet before Telly could say anything. "That's bullshit. What's going on? I, for one, intend to keep working on this situation." He looked toward Marwa, who nodded and said, "Me too."

Woolyard stopped at the door and half turned toward the group. "No, you won't, neither of you. We have our orders, and you have yours. That's it. No more work on flight PT20."

"Orders or no orders, I am going to finish what I started." Ben took a few steps toward the door and stopped when Woolyard didn't move aside. Tension spread over the room like a darken-ing sky before a summer storm.

"Markham, don't do anything foolish. Let's talk in my office." He held out his hand toward Ben.

Ben's cheeks puffed out as he considered his options. He let out the air in a puff. "Okay, sure, we can talk. Then I need to get back to the analysis I was working on."

"We'll see." Woolyard led the way as Ben followed him out of the room. Marwa leaned forward is if to rise and join them, but Telly started talking and she changed her mind.

Chapter 17

WITH HIS ARMS AROUND an empty ten-ream copy-paper carton, Ben kicked his office door fully open and pushed past Marwa.

She turned from her work. "That was a long meeting with Woolyard. What's the bottom line?"

Without answering, Ben pulled out the center drawer of his desk, dumped its contents into the box, and proceeded to do the same with the top right drawer.

"What are you doing?"

"Clearing out my things. My research fellowship has been canceled."

"What?"

"I've been made redundant, that's what. Fired. Sacked. Terminated. What's that other American expression? Ah yes, canned."

"I don't understand?"

Just then, Victoria showed up at the door and did a good imitation of a soldier standing at parade rest. "I'm here to escort you out of the building."

Ben glared at her. "I always knew it. You really are with the CIA."

She laughed and shook her head but didn't say anything.

Marwa stood up and put her hands on her hips. "Will somebody tell me what is going on?" She looked from Ben to Victoria. Victoria only shrugged.

"I'll tell you what's going on, somebody is so determined we not find out what actually happened with the Pacificano flight that they would rather dump good people than risk that we put two and two together and get wherefore."

Victoria laughed again. "You're one clever kid, Markham. Two and two equals wherefore. Not Shakespeare, but cute. Wherefore? Therefore. Let's just finish up here so I can see you out and get back to my work."

"Your work? You mean watching the door or keeping an eye on the others so they don't get bright ideas?"

The exaggerated expression of amazement on Victoria's face would have done justice to a sitcom supporting actress. "You are some freakin' genius, Markham. How did you ever put that one together?"

Ben reached to the back of his desk and picked up the Lucite picture frame with the photo of Karl and Shira at the beach on one panel and Shoshi after her bat mitzvah on the other. He collapsed it and laid it carefully in the carton, which he hefted onto one shoulder. He took a step toward the door.

Victoria blocked his way. "Mind if I take a look?"

"Be my guest." He shoved the box at her.

She pawed through it in a perfunctory manner and handed it back to him. "I'll need your ID badge. Needless to say, we've already deleted your entry code, biometrics, and passwords from the security database."

"Needless to say." He juggled the box, unclipped the badge from his belt, and slapped it into her outstretched palm.

"After you, Markham." She gestured for him to lead the way.

Three paces down the hall, he spun and pushed the box into her hands again. "Forgot my keys in the rush. They're on my desk." Before she could say anything, he stepped around her and re-entered the office. He jerked the thumb-drive key fob from the USB slot on the back of his keyboard and palmed the whole thing in one sweep. He emerged from the office jangling the keys and made an overhand toss into the box that Victoria now carried. "Nothing but net," he declared in triumph. He took the carton back from Victoria and hurried ahead of her.

Both Dr. Woolyard and Telly Athanasiou were waiting in the reception area. Woolyard took a step toward Ben. "I am sorry it has to end this way. I must admit, I am rather surprised. You were in the military. I would have thought you understood about orders and chain-of-command."

"Israeli military, sir. It's a little different. We understand about orders and the chain-of-command, but we are also expected to weigh the moral and ethical issues in our own actions."

"That's one way to look at it." Woolyard held out his hand. "I wish you good luck in any case."

Without setting it down, Ben reached under the box he carried and awkwardly shook the Director's hand.

"I hope you remember, Ben, that personnel records can be amended. This does not have to be the final word on the matter."

Telly held out his hand and waited for Ben to take it. "No scorched-earth scenes, Ben. Okay?"

"Hey, slash-and-burn agriculture served generations of rainforest farmers quite well. But don't worry about me, Telly. I had paratrooper training in the IDF. I know how to land on my feet." He waited for Victoria to open the outer door, then turned back for one last look. Marwa was standing by the reception desk, watching, her eyes filled with questions.

■■ ■■ ■■

In the Director's office, Telly looked agitated. "He's persistent as a beaver. He should be watched."

"That he should. We certainly have the resources to track him. The question is who should become the tracker?"

"Someone from Psychosocial. Fredericksen is both connected

and combative with him. She could do it."

Woolyard doodled on his desk pad with a closed ballpoint pen, adding to the filigree of grooves in the green pad. "Perhaps. Yes, you may be right."

— — —

Ben was still stuffing and shuffling his personal junk into the blaze-orange panier packs on his bicycle when he heard the door of the express elevator open. He glanced up to see Marwa step out. "What are you doing here?"

"Going for lunch."

"They serve lunch in the parking garage now?"

"No, but my car is here." She paused as if weighing something in her mind. "Wanna join me? I'm headed for The Kabab Factory up near Harvard Square."

"Now there's a name to inspire confidence in the cuisine. They serve assembly-line Middle Eastern fare, I suppose."

"Indian. But don't let the name fool you. It's this little hole-in-the-wall place that serves some of the best curries in the area—and at reasonable prices."

"Never heard of it. Where near Harvard Square?"

"Beacon and Washington. Right across from Dali."

"Dali? Never heard of it either."

"You have lived a truly sheltered life, Markham. How can you not know Dali? With the lavender painted front and the big wooden double door on the corner? No? It has absolutely awesome Spanish cuisine. We'll have to go there for drinks and tapas after work sometime." She bit down on her lower lip. "Oh, I forgot. They really did fire you?"

"Really. The General was resolute."

"The General? You mean Woolyard?"

"Yeah, I found out yesterday that he's military. Retired, I assume. Anyway, they can kick me out, but that doesn't stop me from digging into this. I mean, that plane was under control at the end, and it was deliberately ditched at a precise spot, one of the deepest points in the Pacific Ocean." He paused for effect. "Something really fishy is going on."

Marwa groaned. "Do you never stop being flip?"

"Never." He flashed his best silly grin at her. "And I'm persistent in pursuit. I'll find that thing and figure this out."

"I don't think anybody is going to find that plane. The reports so far are that there is almost nothing in the debris field. The fuselage and wings went down even before the first ships could arrive. They're bringing in special towed sonar gear to search for the audio pings from the black boxes, but the boxes could be at the bottom of the Atacama Trench." She fished her keys from her purse. "Anyway, let's go get some lunch. My car's over there, the yellow VW."

== == ==

Marwa had to drive around for nearly ten minutes to find a parking place on a narrow side street. They walked back and joined the line outside the glass storefront of The Kebab Factory. "Second wave, late-lunchers," Marwa said. "Can I ask you a question?"

"Sure, shoot."

"Are you going to be all right? I mean, you lost your job. Are you going to have to leave the country?"

"No. I'm a citizen."

"But I thought you were Israeli."

"I am. I was born in Israel, but my mom is American. I have dual citizenship, and I entered the country on my American passport."

"That's handy. If there were a Palestinian state, I'd have dual citizenship, too."

"I'm with you, believe me. I wish we all could find a way

forward to a two-state solution, but I certainly don't have any new ideas."

"Me neither."

"So you grew up in Israel? But your English is so good—and no accent."

"My mother worked hard to send me to the best schools. I lived with cousins in Toronto where I went to high school my junior and senior year, then on to Cambridge and ... You don't want the whole résumé, do you? Anyway, I'm good with languages, accents. I think it comes from being a singer." The line inched toward the door. "Oh, I probably should have asked you about any, you know, dietary restrictions."

"If you are asking whether I keep kosher, the answer is no. I eat anything."

"Even pork? Shellfish?"

"Not back in Israel, but here I'm pretty open. Well, not pork chops, but seafood is pretty much okay. My family is not religious. My dad is—well, it's complicated. I would suppose you could say he is Jewish by osmosis. My mom is a bit of a mystic but mostly a rational, secular Jew. My little sister is maybe the only one who could conceivably end up observant. She loves ritual and has talked about becoming a rabbi. Then again, she has also talked about becoming a pop singer. Or a neuroscientist like her idol, Mayim Bialik. That was last year when she was twelve, of course. You never know with her."

"What about you? Your people have pretty much the same food taboos as we do."

"Yeah, but I'm vegetarian, which keeps things simple. This way I don't have to worry about finding halal meat. It's more about health and habit for me anyway. My favorite veggie dish in this place is an eggplant curry from Hyderabad. It's got this long name I never remember."

"What's this really about? You didn't ask me to lunch to discuss Indian food and dietary rules. So, what's up?"

"Nothing, really. Just being friendly to my officemate. Well, ex-officemate."

"Uh huh. And you expect me to believe that? After a long history of word warfare, suddenly you want to be friendly? I'm touched." He bowed slightly with his right hand over his heart. "Maybe there is hope for peace in the Middle East."

Her dark eyes locked with his and her mouth opened as if to say something. Ben waited impatiently, then apologized. "I'm sorry. I'm trying to come to terms with being out of work. And my head is spinning with ideas of how to proceed with solving the mystery of that plane."

"I want to help."

"Not a good idea. There's no point in both of us being booted out. Besides, I have more experience in this sort of thing. I ... I wouldn't want anything to happen to you."

"This sort of thing? What are we talking about, Ben?"

"I mean like cover-ups, agencies that do their real work in dark and dirty alleyways—that sort of thing." She gave him a scrunched-face look of skepticism. "No, really. I've been around that scene most of my life. My father was a Mossad agent, although he was killed when I was very young. By the time I was twelve, I was part of a network of teenage computer hackers that helped expose a terrorist plot against Israel. And a few years later, my team was instrumental in foiling an attempt to take down the US power grid."

"You're kidding me. You mean like real-life 'Spy Kids' and all?"

"Sort of, I suppose. My uncle Lev and aunt Anat were both also with Mossad, and I was with military intelligence, Unit 8200, when I served in the IDF. It really kinda runs in the family. My dad—stepfather—is a tech blogger and writer who has gotten himself entangled in a whole series of espionage escapades. So, yeah, it's for real."

"And here we are—for real," she said, as they entered the café at last. A busy waiter whizzed by. He gestured them toward an open table for two against an upholstered banquette along the opposite wall. Iconic Indian paintings, carved elephants, and assorted kitsch artwork looked down on a room filled with the pleasant static of dozens of overlapping conversations and the sweet scent of chiles and cardamom, garlic and ginger.

After looking over the menu, they both took the simple way out and settled on the lunchtime buffet. Once their plates were filled with a sampling of the aromatic dishes, they returned to their table.

"So," she said between bites, "there's more to you than meets the eye. Here I thought you were just another smart-ass Israeli male with a chip on his shoulder."

"And here I thought you were just another prickly pseudo-liberated pampered Palestinian woman with an antagonism for Israeli Jews."

She stiffened. "Stereotypes."

"True, but stereotypes come from somewhere; they have roots in reality."

"Now you're treading on the edge of a minefield, Ben."

"Okay, let's bring in the minesweepers and clear a path. I'll start by admitting that Israeli men—many, anyway—do have a real attitude when it comes to women. It—"

"Just like Arab men. It has the same historic roots in restriction and oppression of women rationalized by religious argument. We—"

"Exactly. So, let me understand. You are some sort of Islamic feminist, like, burning your hijab and marrying a—"

"Watch it, Markham, your foot is hovering over an antipersonnel mine—or at least halfway into your mouth. Same difference."

"Sorry, I didn't mean anything by it." He held up a forkful of Goan Fish Curry as if to study it. "I guess what I really meant was, well, just basic curiosity. I've been trying to figure it out—you married to a priest, I mean."

"Minister. Seth was ordained as a Lutheran minister, but he's not a pastor. He works in social services."

"How ... ?"

"How did we end up married? Pretty much as anyone does. People fall in love and people fall out of love. It happens. It doesn't always make sense."

"But I thought it was haram, forbidden, for a Muslim woman to marry a Christian. Something about a non-Muslim husband not being able to properly guide her and guard her soul."

"Yeah, as we were saying, centuries, millennia of so-called protection, a patriarchal patter to justify maintaining male domination."

"And Seth? He's different? I certainly have known Christian men who hold onto male privilege just as tightly."

"Seth is also a feminist, that I will give him. Believe it or not, we met at Harvard, at a colloquium on 'Faith, Feminism, and Falafel: Changing Roles in Middle-Eastern Culture.' He can be very charismatic. I liked the way he talked; he talked a good line. Ministers are good at that."

"You make it sound like it was a line, just a line."

"Look, this is getting a little too personal, especially since we are here to talk about what happened to flight PT20 and the people who are now, presumably, at the bottom of the sea. What do you propose to do?"

Ben finished chewing his fish, then ran his tongue over his teeth. "I don't know what we are going to do, but I do know what

I am going to do. I'm going to start thinking the way my father and uncle and dad would. I am going to do some serious archeology, keep digging."

"What about your aunt? Didn't you say she was with Mossad, too? You left her out of your list."

"My, you are the fanatic feminist, ever vigilant for subtle signs of sexism. I didn't mean anything by it. I—"

"No, men never mean anything by it. They just keep doing it."

"Oh, for Christ sake. I—"

She covered her mouth and laughed.

"What now?"

"A Jew invoking the Christian savior. Funny."

"It's just an expression. I didn't mean anything by it. I ..." He started to laugh with her. "Okay, men are funny. We can't help it. We are the morally inferior sex."

"Inferior, anyway." She winked at him. "But back to your agenda—our agenda. How are we going to work this?"

"As I said, we are not going to work anything. I don't need any help."

"Yes you do, my overconfident colleague. You need somebody on the inside to keep getting you access. I may not have your spy-versus-spy experience, but I am smarter than you, better educated, and ..." She held up a hand like a crossing guard to keep him from interrupting. "Just wait. Besides, I know stuff you don't, just like you know stuff I don't. Put the statistics and the socio-tech insight together, and we have a much better chance of getting to the bottom of this— even if the bottom is a deep ocean trench. So, unless you want to find out what it's like to be on the wrong side of a Muslim feminist with advanced degrees and a grudge that will never give up, you better agree to work with me."

He laughed again and extended his hand. "Agreed, then. I

yield to superior forces." She took his hand and held it with a long, firm squeeze.

Chapter 18

SAM PARSONS STORMED OUT of Keating Summer's corner office at NTSB headquarters in downtown Washington. The news from his boss was not what he had expected. As he cut the corner at the turn toward the elevators, he ran smack into Lottie Schoeneberg. "Oh, I am so sorry. I ..." He took a step back. Even after six months, he could still become tongue-tied by her Teutonic good looks. She was a tall, twenty-first-century Marlene Dietrich, with an athlete's body and an accountant's mind. "What are you doing here?"

"I work here, remember, just like you." She gave a look up and down the hall before leaning in to give him a quick kiss. "I heard what happened," she said in a lowered voice. "We can talk about it when you get home tonight."

"No we can't. It's classified."

"And I have clearance. Plus, I already know what has been going on." She surveyed the hallway again. "There was something funky about that airline hijacking, and now it's being left up to Singapore and Santiago, as if they'll be able to figure anything out. My own guess—"

He put a finger on her lips. "Don't let loose lips sink ships, especially if the ship is ours. We'll talk back at the apartment." He nodded and raised his voice a few decibels. "Nice to bump into you, Miss Schoeneberg. See you around." He continued toward the elevators as a knot of office workers approached from the other direction.

== == ==

The day dragged on as Sam shuffled papers, read reports, and pretended to find pleasure in preparing to wrap up the work that had been his baby for two years. He was torn between just dropping his sources and co-conspirators, leaving them in the dark about what had happened, or doing something more pro-active and provocative. He could expose them, although there was nothing particular to be gained by burning his contacts. He could string them along, although that would be hard to sustain for very long. He could create an audit trail by documenting the network. If he left things as they were—an invisible network that existed largely in memorized names and numbers and re-membered exchanges—it would slowly wither and die like a ne-glected house plant. As far as Sam knew, he could contact all of them, but it would be harder for most of them to contact him.

Then there was General Woolyard and his team up in Cam-bridge. They would not just go away. He assumed they would be shuffled off to other assignments, maybe gradually defunded, perhaps absorbed piecemeal into the NSA or some other agency. He almost reached for his cellphone to give Woolyard a call, but then realized there was little cause other than curiosity and some risk of stirring up the hornets at this point. Play it cool, he had always told himself. Keep your head down and your wits about you.

== == ==

By the time Marwa and Ben left The Kebab Factory, the wait staff were giving them looks of polite impatience. On the walk back toward Marwa's car, Ben confided in her. "I have some things going for me that ... well maybe I shouldn't have."

"Like what?"

"For starters, I have a flash drive with backups of all my files from the Center and some that are not mine."

Marwa's mouth formed an O. "Definitely not kosher. We're not supposed to make backups or take—"

"I know. Years of hacking into other people's systems taught me to always have insurance. And my dad taught me that rules are always subject to interpretation."

"How did you pull it off, this insurance?"

He grabbed his keys from the pocket of his pants and dangled the attached thumb drive. Marwa looked puzzled. "But I thought all the USB ports on our computers were disabled."

"All but the ones on the back of the expanded keyboard I had special ordered and delivered directly to me. Everyone thought all those color-coded programmable keys were so cool. No one looked at the back of it where two USB slots lurked under the overhanging edge."

"You are devious, Markham. I am beginning to believe your claims to be a spook."

"Well ... I am not sure whether I should trust you, but ..."

"Maybe you shouldn't trust me."

He ignored her remark. "Let's just say I got a glimpse of a fax to Woolyard before we started working on PT20. I have a name, a contact at the NTSB that could be a, shall we say, tunnel into the citadel, a way around those who want to stop what we are doing or suppress whatever we found."

"How are you going to contact this person without being discovered?"

"I'm going to pick up a cheap burner phone and a prepaid calling card at that pharmacy across the street, then I'm going to call this guy in DC. I noted his mobile number on the fax, and I never forget a number."

== == ==

Sam didn't recognize the number on the caller ID, but he swiped his thumb across the face of his smartphone. "Yes?"

"T. Samuel Parsons?"

"Yes. Who's calling?"

"Would you maybe like to know what really happened with Pacificano Transocean flight 20?"

"Who is this?"

"Do you want to know or not?"

Sam's mind was pawing through piles of people who might be on the phone. "How did you get this number?"

"Let's just say access to a database."

"How do you know what happened?"

"I know. Do you?"

"It crashed in the ocean."

"Everybody knows that, but I know how it crashed, what made it crash. If you want to know what I know, meet me at ..."—Ben fluttered his tongue as he struggled to recall a name—"uh ... Luigi's Little Napoli in Washington, tomorrow night at seven."

Sam tried to weigh the risks and the potentials. "Okay. I'll be there." Whoever was calling hung up without responding.

-- -- --

In Cambridge, Marwa shook her head in confusion and disapproval. "How are you going to meet someone tomorrow in Washington. We're in Massachusetts. And how do you know about a restaurant down there?"

"My dad told me about it. I think he ate there once when he was at this computer games conference, covering it for his publisher. But that's another story. It's just a name that stuck in my mind because I thought it was funny. I remember odd bits like that—and numbers. As to how we'll meet at the restaurant, there are such things as trains and planes and automobiles, ya know. How would you like to drive to DC tomorrow?"

"Drive? You want to drive all the way to Washington, DC?"

"Sure. It's only four hundred and some miles, I think. Take us maybe, what, seven or eight hours? I don't have a car, but we can use yours. We can spell each other."

"Wait one minute, here. We can use my car, huh? I have to work. I still have a job, you know, not like you."

"When you go back this afternoon, tell people you are not feeling well, leave a little early, then call in sick tomorrow morning. You can pick me up at my place at eight. We'll hop over to get on the Mass Pike and be in DC by four tomorrow afternoon."

"My, you do push ahead, don't you."

"My dad taught me that the longer you wait on things like this, the more likely somebody will trace something or smell something or see something. You have to keep ahead of the other side. Speaking of which ..." He twisted the back off the cheap cellphone he had just used, removed the battery and SIM card, and tossed it in a trash receptacle by the sidewalk. "One use, that's how it's done. I'll dump these somewhere else." He stuffed the card and battery in his pocket.

Marwa was staring at him. "I can't just pick up and—"

"I'll see you at my place at eight. The address is here on my business card. And now I think I'll walk on up to Harvard Square and catch the T back to pick up my bike. Better we are not spotted together back around MIT. See you in the morning." He started walking up Kirkland toward the Square.

Marwa stared after him, shaking her head. She pocketed the business card and turned the corner toward her car. As she approached it, she let out a groan. There was a bright orange parking ticket tucked under the passenger-side windshield wiper.

▬▬ ▬▬ ▬▬

The sound of Lottie's hip-check against the warped apartment door to coax it closed alerted Sam that she was home. It was unusual for Sam to be home ahead of her. She was one of those smart and effective functionaries who did her job well and finished at five sharp. Sam was the type who could get caught up in work until she texted him from home that it was after nine and she was getting hungry.

She walked over to the kitchen area of the compact apartment, hung her trench coat on an open peg on the wall, and tossed her keys into the bowl on the side table. "What are you cooking?" She came up behind him and rested her chin on his shoulder as he shelled pistachios.

"Persian pilaf."

She lifted the cover on the heavy skillet. "Mmm, smells good. Cinnamon?"

"And garlic and some other stuff my mother used."

"Is it really Persian? I thought your mother was Turkish."

"She was, and so is this dish. It's like French fries, which are not French. It's a Turkish lamb and rice dish, probably originally an Ottoman interpretation of a Persian concoction. Anyway, this is how my mother made it."

"You on a nostalgia trip tonight?"

"I suppose—a search for stability in a shaky world."

"How bad is it? I only heard that your program might be defunded."

"Yeah, but 'might' is not the operant word. The only thing holding back the axe is that they don't yet know what to do with me. Once they find some safe slot to shove me into, ARRG will be history, forgotten history."

"Why? I thought you had been doing some good work. TWA 800, Malaysian Airlines 370, and now the real-time work on Pacificano 20. You even tracked and found that thing before it went down."

"Well, NTSB didn't exactly find it, but some of the larger network did. You know, the thing I don't get is why the hurry. I understand about cover-ups—been there, done that— but this is like the guillotine. Slick, slam—everything is cut off."

"Do you want me to see what I can find out at work? I mean, the one good thing about Budget and Accounting is that we have fingers in everything."

"Sure. You do that. But remember, not everything shows up in budget spreadsheets. That team of techno-wizards up at MIT that helped on the Pacificano tracking gets millions without any oversight or accountability."

She started rubbing his neck and shoulders. "You would be surprised what a persistent Prussian can do with a database and some due diligence. There is always a trail, however faint. Even black ops buy staples and paper." She inhaled deeply. "How long before that is ready to eat?"

"Why don't you go take your shower. By the time you are out and dressed, it will be on the table."

"Sounds good, smells yummy." She kissed him on the neck.

While Lottie showered, Sam tried to decide how much to tell her and what to say about the telephone call and the meeting. Let her do some of her due diligence, he told himself. It can't hurt. On the other hand, there was no point dragging her in any deeper than necessary. He knew from experience that people who knew too much could disappear, a lesson worth remembering, a lesson that should be kept in mind, always.

Chapter 19

INBOUND MORNING COMMUTERS clogged the Massachusetts Turnpike but traffic out of the city was not nearly as heavy. As they approached the slowdown at the Weston tolls, Ben turned toward Marwa. "I wasn't sure if you'd show up this morning."

Pulling out of the tolls, Marwa signaled and shifted lanes to pass a slow-moving produce truck. "I wasn't sure either, but I've never been to DC, so I figured what the heck."

"And your husband didn't mind?"

"My husband is in Vermont, in Burlington, where he works for Lutheran Social Services of New England."

"Oh, I see. I didn't ..."

"You probably don't see. Jobs in his profession are scarce now in Massachusetts, and I didn't want to leave CAASS. It's a long-distance marriage. We spend most weekends together, usually at our Danvers apartment."

"That must be tough, being apart during the week."

"Not as tough as being together on weekends. We're both stubborn and probably will stick it out anyway."

Ben looked over at her, then out the side window. "I didn't mean to pry."

"You didn't pry. I just told you how things were. What about you? Girlfriend? Fiancée?"

"Nope. Nothing serious, anyway ... so far."

"Well, don't go all long-winded on me. I don't need that over-sharing sort of detail."

"What can I say? There really isn't anything to talk about."

"And besides, you're a guy. So, we switch topics. That's what guys do. So, dude, what's this trip really about? How is it you know this guy down in DC?"

"I don't know him. I found out about him by reading some correspondence that I shouldn't have. My instincts were right about him. I mentioned his name to my dad when we Skyped last night, and he told me to be careful, wouldn't say more. So, I got online and did some research. Our dinner date was the lead field investigator on the Sadler Creek pipeline explosion down in West Virginia a while back. His team at the NTSB produced a report that got a lot of press and sent a lot of conspiracy theorists off speculating about what really was going on."

"What really was going on? I don't remember the story. What did your dad tell you?"

"He told me nothing beyond the warning, but that told me a shitload. Dad used to confide in me when we were, like, working together sometimes, but he has gotten less and less talkative in recent years. He and Ima got a real scare on a trip to Madeira awhile back. He ended up pushed off a cliff and had to be medivacked to Florida for hip surgery. I knew he also had something to do with the pipeline story—he recognized this Sam Parson's name—but he never said anything about it. I was in the army at the time."

"You weren't bullshitting about this cloak-and-dagger background, were you?"

"No, it's all true. It runs in my family, as I said. We are a suspicious and self-protective bunch. Anyway, right after this Parsons is paraded before the press as the investigative hero of these pipeline explosions, he seems to have dropped off the planet, only to rematerialize now working on airline crashes and hijackings.

"So, it seems I do have a nose for trouble. Maybe Woolyard was right not to trust me. I do have to keep in mind that he has something on me."

"Something on you?"

"Well, I did intercept a confidential fax to him, and he caught me. Which means he knows I know about Parsons. If he is as smart as he claims to be, he may even figure I would try to get in touch with Parsons." Ben worked his jaw as he stared off in thought. "We do need to be alert." He looked to each side, then twisted to check out the rear window. "How long has that Chevy been on our tail?"

"What?"

"The green Chevrolet."

"I don't know a Chevrolet from a Chevalier, but I think that big green car just came in after the Newton tolls."

"Well, switch lanes and slow down a bit to see if he passes us."

"You are nuts. Or paranoid."

"Just do it. And keep your eyes forward; don't acknowledge that we know he's there."

The Chevrolet soon passed them. It was driven by a woman; there was a child seat in the back behind her.

Marwa forced a laugh. "So much for your CIA tail. Or would that be FBI? You know, by the way, they always drive black sedans, never green."

"Scoff if you will, but I for one intend to pay closer attention to what and who is around us."

Marwa floored her VW to speed up again. "Speaking of closer attention, did you catch the news story about the Canadian intercept of a couple of terrorists about to cross over into Detroit? And there was a supposed drug lab shootout in Texas that ended badly when the place blew up and incinerated the suspects?"

"What the hey do these have to do with us or each other?"

"Timing. They all happened at virtually the same time, which was when MI6 was pulling US-bound passengers at Gatwick and Pacificano flight 20 went incommunicado."

"That's nuts, like numerology. You can always find some association. Pick any time on any day. There's always stuff going on someplace around the world that will make the news."

"I didn't say it meant something, but it could. That's the kind of connect-the-dots game I've been trained to play."

"Reading tea leaves."

"Scoff if you will." They both chuckled.

      -- -- --

After missing the turnoff for the Tappan Zee Bridge and ending up driving through Manhattan in heavy traffic, they reached Washington much later than expected. Ben was driving as they entered DC. Neither of them were aware that they had picked up a tail—in a black Lincoln—on the outskirts of the city.

Chapter 20

IT TOOK THEM TWO turns around the block to locate Luigi's Little Napoli and then twenty minutes to find parking. Luigi's was smack in the middle of the block, a place you could walk right by without realizing it was a neighborhood restaurant. A wrought-iron railing set off the concrete steps leading down to a dark-paneled wood door with a simple sign. Inside it looked like an Italian movie set dressed for a mafia shoot-out scene. Worn red leatherette covered the benches along the walls. Fake LED candles flickered in ruby-glass bowls on the tables, and blood-red napkins were folded like tents at each place. It was deserted except for a busboy arranging cutlery and a somnambulant maître de who said nothing as he widened his eyes in inquiry.

"The name is Hampton," Ben said. "We have reservations ... for three. We're early but ..."

"Of course, Mr. Hampton. Do you wish to wait at the bar until the rest of your party arrives or would you prefer to be seated right away."

Ben hadn't noticed the four-stool bar to the side of the entrance where a bartender polished glasses and watched a silent soccer match on a screen in the corner. "You can seat us now, thanks."

"Very well. Right this way."

As soon as the maître de left, Marwa leaned toward Ben. "Hampton?"

"Yes, I'm Leo and you're my sister, Mia. Remember that."

"Okay, Leo, but I think this is silly." She looked up to see a tall, swarthy man enter. "Could that be him?"

Ben glanced over and nodded. "Could be. He looks different than in the news coverage of the pipeline investigation. I think it's the beard. Anyway, he's coming our way."

The man stopped a few feet short of the table. "Pardon me, but are you two from Cambridge?"

"We are. Please join us." Ben gestured toward an empty chair. "Parsons, right?"

"Yes, Sam Parsons." He extended his hand for a handshake. "And you are?"

"Leo Hampton. And this is my sister, Mia."

"No you're not. You're Binyamin Markham."

"How ... ?"

"Chuck—General Woolyard—told me about giving one of his people the boot. And let me guess, this is probably your co-worker, Marwa Fredericksen." He held out his hand to her.

It was her turn to be surprised. "How did you know?"

"Lucky guess. Plus, I reviewed a roster of the Center staff before coming tonight." He repositioned the chair to be facing both of them and seated himself. "Shall we order? Despite appearances, this place is reputed to have pretty good food. Never been here myself, but I checked Yelp. It does seem to have known better days, though."

A waiter in a classic Italian black wrap-around apron brought menus the size of small billboards. As the three studied them, Parsons plunged ahead without making small talk.

"So, you wanna talk about PT20. I don't know if you kids realize how hairy this sort of thing might get. If my group gets defunded and yours gets sidelined at one stroke, that says some people with real clout do not want the investigation continued.

And then you go and get fired, Markham, which puts the exclamation point at the end of the paragraph. The news media are saying that the US is offering unspecified technical help, but the search is now in the hands of the Singaporeans and the Chileans. Yeah, right. That looks to me like letting the whole thing die from chronic bureaucracy and acute ineptitude. And who knows why?"

"We do," Sam said without looking up from his menu. "At least we know some of the story."

"So you said over the phone. Are you going to tell me or not?"

"Sure, but let's eat. It was a long drive and I'm running on nothing but two grande lattes and a blueberry scone."

Sam ordered veal scaloppini and both Marwa and Ben opted for a baked eggplant parmagiana with toasted walnuts and classic béchamel. "It's comfort food," she said when Sam inquired. "Simple, satisfying."

"And you're vegetarian, right?" Marwa gave him a look of mild annoyance. "It's the halal thing, isn't it? Remember, I looked through the personnel records for the Institute. Marwa Khalidi Fredericksen. Not too hard to figure that one out."

"Not too hard. I see you like figuring things out."

"I spent years doing field investigations on gas pipeline incidents—sort of engineering detective work."

"Then you crawled your way up from underground pipes to high-flying airplanes, huh?"

"Ooh, slam! Got booted up—or out, really."

Ben suddenly became interested. "That was the Sadler Creek investigation, right? The news media made you out to be some kind of hero, tracking down shoddy products from China or Japan or something."

"Shoddy programming from a German supplier. Alleged, I should say. And there was more ... Well, let's just put it this way:

when it comes to the government, it seems there is always more to the story, as Snowden and Manning showed us."

"Are you saying the real story is something different?"

"I am not saying anything, would not be allowed to say anything. You understand."

Ben tilted his head as he nodded slowly. "I get the message. So, do you think maybe Marwa and I should move into some other field, like maybe gas pipelines?"

"Not pipelines, you might get burned."

Ben snorted a laugh. "And not aircraft, you might crash."

"Touché. And in your case, the plane crashed, and you got burned. So, I'm still waiting to hear what you have."

Ben pulled out his smartphone and showed screen shots of his final descent models.

Sam scowled as he studied the images. "It does look suspicious, but the autopilot could do that."

"Possibly, but only if deliberately given some elaborate and rather exact programming. At least that's what I understand. I don't know, you tell me. You're the one with the NTSB. I could have a better idea myself if I could get access to something more than a laptop and a browser, some real computing power that wasn't inside some agency of one government or another. Years ago I could have conjured up a small army of bots, but that was back in my hacker days."

Marwa leaned forward and tapped a finger on the table. "And I could use Internet access that wasn't being watched too closely. I would like to follow up on some suspect news stories and continue tracing some passengers."

"Let me think." Sam rubbed his beard-covered cheek. "You know, there is somebody you might want to meet, CEO of a security software company. Something tells me he might be of some help." He pulled a smartphone from his pocket and dialed a call. "Hi, I should have known you'd pick up right away. This is Tank Parsons. Remember?" There was a pause. "That's right. Only now I'm with a team on the civilian aviation side, at least for the time being." Another pause. "Ain't that the truth. Look, I have some people here you might like to meet. They could use some of your expertise and maybe some technical support. Any chance you might have some space in your calendar tomorrow?"

Both Ben and Marwa were looking perplexed, but Sam kept talking. "Nine? Sure, sounds good. See you tomorrow." He tucked the phone back in his pocket.

"We won't be here tomorrow. We have to head back."

"You haven't even eaten yet. What are you going to do, drive back after dinner? All the way to Cambridge?"

"Well, Marwa has to be at work tomorrow. We figured she would take the first leg, then I would drive through the night while she slept. Take her right to the office."

Sam smiled warmly. "I'd forgotten how crazy we are when we're young. Look, get a room, stay over, and head back after meeting with this guy."

Ben gave Marwa an inquiring look. She shrugged. "That could be expensive. And I would have to call in again."

Ben's face lit up. "Sam, do you know a hotel called—it was like a girls' name—uh, like Miranda or Madeline or ..."

"You mean the Meredith? "

"That's it."

"Yeah, near the Convention Center. Nice place but pricey. Out of my range."

"My dad stayed there when he was working a video games conference. Ran up one heck of a tab and ended up getting a voucher for a couple of free nights. I can check with him and see if it might still be good."

— —— ——

By the time they finished dinner, Ben had a message from Israel with a QR code for the voucher. Sam looked over and saw the image. "Amazing technology. A bunch of little squares will get you a room at The Meredith now. Do you need directions?"

"We'll find it." Ben waved his phone.

"Of course. I'll pick you up about eight tomorrow morning, then. Once we're out of DC traffic, it will be an easy shot out to Reston where this company is. See you tomorrow. Sleep well."

Chapter 21

MARWA STEPPED OUT OF the revolving door at the entrance to the hotel and gave the three-story lobby with its twenty-foot crystal chandelier a long, touristy look. "Your father gets to stay in some pretty nice digs. I hate to think what this would cost a night if we had to pay for it."

"But we don't. Even after all these years, the hotel had a record. Apparently, Dad was paying for not one, but two rooms for an extended stay."

"Is your dad one of these wealthy Israeli high-tech entrepreneurs?"

"No, he's just an underpaid writer who has a way of getting drawn into doing somewhat risky work on an expense account. Ultimately, it was the citizens of Israel who footed the bill for this."

"How do you figure?"

"Well, when my friends and I were running the bot network, Mossad was getting the benefit. I assume they paid for this. Let's check in."

There was some debate at the front desk over whether the voucher for two-free-nights would cover two rooms for one night. When Ben asked to speak with the night manager, the clerk at the desk disappeared for several minutes before returning with a manufactured smile on his face and an apology on his lips. "No problem with the two complimentary rooms—on our concierge floor, of course."

When the formalities were completed, Ben turned to Marwa. "It's too early to turn in. After you get settled, you want to meet me down here for a drink?" He put his palm to his forehead. "Oh, I am so sorry. I forgot."

"What? You forgot that I'm Muslim? And you assume I don't drink. Are all Israelis observant? Do all Jews keep kosher?"

"No, of course not. But I thought, you know, that Muslims can't drink."

"We can. Anyone can drink, but most of Islam does not. I've tried alcohol. Yes, that's right, I did. Didn't do much for me. Astringent and uninteresting."

"Oh, 'astringent and uninteresting'? As if all alcoholic drinks were the same. Like all Jews and all Muslims." He winked.

She laughed. "It was vodka with a beer chaser, a high-speed high. I was at university—Cambridge—away from close super-vision for the first time, feeling all grown up and ready to take big bites of fresh experience. I was being seduced by a teaching assistant with a goatee and a most charming British accent. The alcohol didn't work and the seduction was even less effective than the drinks. Never touched another drop."

"You know, we Jews have a very different approach to alcohol. Wine is rather central to celebrating the Jewish Sabbath, and we're actually required to overdo it once a year, at Purim."

"Really? I always thought that was just another ethnic slur."

"Really. But to me, it's not so much about some physiological reaction but about the experience of sharing joy with family, with friends. Wine can be such a rich and gentle pleasure. There's this wine bar not far from my place in Boston that has a huge cellar of wines from around the world. Last week, Hector and I tried a late-picked grüner veltliner from Austria with touches of grapefruit and white pepper that ... I'm sorry."

She was laughing. "No, go on. You make it sound, well, almost transcendent."

"Oh, it can be that. Aba, my dad, introduced me to wine at a very early age, starting every Friday night. At first I was, like, what is he talking about? It all just tastes like, you know ..."—he made a face—"ew, wine. But I began to catch on to the nuances, as different as one person from another." He looked at the ground. "And as temporary. I ..."

"What is it?"

"I was thinking of my Bubbe, my grandmother. We lost her last year."

"I'm sorry."

"No, don't be. She lived a full life, well-loved and active to the end."

"I lost my grandmother, too, but it was many years ago. She was not quite fifty. She was in Gaza City at the wrong intersection, with Hamas and Shin Bet converging—before the withdrawal."

"Now I am sorry. I—"

"You? You think you are everything, responsible for everything. It's one of the many problems with you Jews. It's either all your fault or all somebody else's. Back there, in the Middle East, there is more than enough blame to spread around and so little ever changes. I hated the hot-heads of Hamas as much as I hated the coolly cruel Shin Bet. But I hate neither my people nor yours. And now I think I could use a drink. Are you ready to introduce me to the transcendence of fermented grape juice?"

"Sure, but let's get settled in first. I'll meet you down here in, say, forty-five minutes. We can check out the lobby bar. That way we don't have to find our way back to the hotel."

== == ==

Ben looked up to see Marwa enter the bar section of the lobby.

She had put a headband in her hair, and it fell in cascades over her shoulders.

"You look great. Wait a minute. That's not the same blouse you were wearing. How ..."

"Magic. No, I just slipped down into the shopping area on the lower level and picked up a few things."

"I'll have to do the same."

"What's this?" She pointed to the array of wine glasses on the table. "You going for some kind of record? How many glasses do you need?"

"It's called a flight of wines. Appropriate, I thought. These are samplers that will give you a chance to compare and experiment, to see what appeals and what doesn't. That flight is called 'Southern World Whites' and includes three rather exotic varietals: a vermentino from Australia, a viognier from South Africa, a torrontes from Argentina."

"And what are the red ones?"

"This is 'Merlot Mash-up': three very different wines from the same grape, starting from a light and easy drinking California merlot and finishing with a big Australian merlot-shiraz. I fig-ured we could just have fun with this."

"And what's on the plate?"

"Nibbles. Crackers and assorted smoked seafood. I thought if you were going to sin, I should be a sport and sin with you."

Marwa responded with an open-mouthed smile. "It's only a sin if you believe it is. I don't believe anymore. I don't pray five times a day, and I haven't been inside a mosque in years."

"Then why the halal thing?"

"I'm still Muslim. It's not something you can put on or take off like a scarf." She looked over the glasses in front of her. "Where do I start. Is this arranged like Hebrew and Arabic in our honor or just the lazy American left-to-right?"

"Start with the Australian white on the left. But don't just drink it; get to know it first, like this." He demonstrated how to hold the glass up to the light, to swirl the wine and smell it before drinking any.

"I see, it's a whole ritual." She accepted the glass from him and copied his movements, lowering her nose deep into the wineglass.

"Now, when you take that first sip, suck some air through it and swirl it around in your mouth to get the full experience on the palate."

She started to giggle. "Really? All this just for a glass of wine?"

"It's not just a glass of wine. It's a glass you are sharing with me. And it's your first. So, savor it. Notice the hints of peaches and lemons in the nose. See what I mean? Now take that first generous sip. There's a touch of grassiness, almost like fresh hay, along with tropical fruit notes."

She couldn't keep from laughing. "Are you all like this?"

"Who? Jews?"

"No, wine fanatics. What do you call yourself? A wine-iac"

Ben had to laugh. "I call myself Ben. Just give it a try and see how it goes."

They shared each wine from the first flight with both of them favoring the viognier. "I do see what you mean by how different wines can be," she said. "That middle one has a solid fruitiness to it, like a peach that is almost but not quite ripe. Now what about those others?" They finished the flight of reds but disagreed vigorously, with Marwa liking only the first merlot, which she described as soft and fruity, like ripe cherries. Ben dismissed it as too simple and too sweet. She called the merlot-shiraz that he favored harsh and fuzzy.

Marwa licked her lips after extracting the last drop of viognier from the glass. "Can we get more?"

"Are you sure? First time out, you know, don't want to overdo it."

"I won't."

Ben nursed the last of the merlots while Marwa downed two additional rounds of the viognier and finished off the rest of the smoked oysters and scallops. She leaned across the table and put a hand on his shoulder. "I do think I rather like wine. And I do think I rather like you for that."

"I'm not sure whether that will ease my conscience a bit for having led you astray or is more likely to make me feel all the more guilty." He twisted his wrist to sneak a look at his watch. "I do think it's time to call it a night. Shall we meet for breakfast? Say seven?" She closed her eyes and nodded.

He steadied her with an arm around her waist as they made their way to the glassed-in elevators. On the concierge floor, he walked her to her room, which was two doors past his. She slid her keycard in the slot but the little light blinked red and the door wouldn't open. She tried again with the same result.

"Here, let me try." He took the card and unlocked the door. "Gotta put the right spin on it."

She turned around in the open doorway to face him. They stood smiling at each other, nodding.

"Yes, it was good," he said, "a good evening, good wine." The scent of her winey breath was intoxicating . "I ..."

She took his hand and kissed him, a light, almost sisterly kiss, then closed her fingers around his and drew him into the room. The lights had been left on by the housekeeper, and the bed-covers were already turned down. Marwa stepped out of her shoes and started undoing her jeans as she backed toward the bed. She reached out and covered his face with kisses as she pulled him down on top of her. "Ben, oh Ben. I want you so much."

Chapter 22

A LINE OF SUBTROPICAL greenery in massive terracotta planters marked off the atrium café from the rest of the hotel lobby. At the entrance, Marwa stood on tiptoes to scan the morning crowd. A hostess at the podium spotted her. "May I seat you? We do have some open tables."

"Er, no thank you. I'm meeting someone for breakfast. He's here somewhere." She craned her neck. "Ah, there he is. I see him way over there. Thanks." She glanced at the clock on her phone as she negotiated her way between tables toward Ben's spot by the windows. "I'm really sorry for being so late," she said as she set down her purse. "All I need is some coffee, then we can go."

"No problem." He carefully folded his comp copy of The Washington Post. "It was ... quite a night."

"I ... I don't remember all of it. I ... I am not sure if ..."

"We didn't." His smile was gentle as he pushed the newspaper to one side. "I tucked you in and went back to my room."

"I don't know whether to be relieved or disappointed. Or maybe insulted."

"Definitely not insulted. But it would have been so wrong. You were drunk. I'm not that kind of guy. Plus you're married. I'm not that kind of guy either."

"I remember you letting me into my room. I remember ... I'm sorry. I ..."

"Nothing happened. Forget it. Maybe The Prophet was right about alcohol. Anyway, let's get some coffee in you and then go out front to wait for Parsons." He flipped over the mug at her place and filled it from the insulated carafe on the table. "Do you need some more cream or is there enough left?"

"I take it black." She warmed her hands around the mug before taking a sip. "We really should talk."

"No, we shouldn't. There's no need. As I said, nothing happened, so there's nothing to spoil a good friendship."

"Is that what it is? Are we friends now?"

"Seems like it. Who would have thought? We did spar like a couple of welterweights right from that first day." His body bounced as he smothered an inward laugh. "You were such a bitch."

"I was such a bitch? What about you? This arrogant smart-ass, this damned ... cute Israeli. And I knew right away I had to keep you at a distance."

"Distance can be good ... sometimes."

"I don't know. I think I've had enough distance in my life. I have a long-distance marriage, and home is always a long-distance phone call at international rates. I study people at a distance. Maybe it's time for something less distant."

Ben looked around awkwardly. "Yeah, well ... I'll get the check. You go ahead and wait out front in case our ride shows up early."

— — —

Ben emerged from the hotel just as Sam pulled up at the front in a silver BMW M3 with the top down. "Good morning, you two. Hop in."

Ben held the door for Marwa, then realized he should have slipped into the back first. He took a couple steps back and executed a clumsy vault into the rear seat. "Sorry about that. But you did say hop in." He stroked the black leather upholstery.

"Sweet wheels. Very sweet."

"It's my girlfriend's. I drive a dorky Chevy sedan, but she lends this to me now and then. I hope you don't mind the breeze and the noise, but the day is just too nice to waste. We won't be able to talk much on the way, but, given the kind of work we all do, we probably wouldn't have all that much we'd be allowed to talk about anyway." He pulled out of the semi-circular drive, gunned the engine to slip into a spot between two trucks inching along, then hit the brakes as traffic came to a standstill.

It seemed to take forever to get out of the city, but once they crossed the Potomac and picked up the Parkway, outbound traffic started thinning. Within a half hour they were pulling up at the gate at Scenaria International's headquarters in Reston.

Ben craned his neck as they passed by the company's green-and-cream logo. "Why didn't you say where we were going? I know this company."

"Who doesn't. They provide software security solutions for governments and critical industries around the world."

"No, I mean I know it. I actually worked with them—along with my dad—when I was a kid."

"When you were a kid? Are we talking about the same company?" Sam swung the car wide and slipped into the last visitor parking space.

"I know it seems wild, but I was this nerdy teenager who kept poking into dark places on the Internet. I don't think the full story has ever been told about some of the stuff I did."

"Maybe someday you can tell me, but right now let's go meet the CEO."

They entered the main building, where alternating bands of creamy travertine and deep jade marble girdled the lobby. Behind the reception desk, a world map highlighted countries where Scenaria security solutions were in use. After signing the visitor log and being given badges, the three of them were escorted into a spacious outer office and told to wait. They sat in silence for several minutes until a pencil-thin man in a silver-gray custom-tailored suit entered the room. His button-down dress shirt and plaid tie with matching pocket square were coordinated shades of lavender. "Mr. Botteneau will see you now." He opened the door to the inner office where a middle-aged man with an adolescent face was studying something on a tablet computer.

Douglass Botteneau's eyes widened in surprise as he looked up. He stood, buttoned his suit jacket, and came around from behind a massive cherry-wood desk that looked as if it had been custom-built in that very room. "I can't believe this. Look at you, Bini. You were just a kid when I last saw you, and now ... Forgive me, but how you've grown." He grabbed Ben and gave him a bear hug and a back slap.

"And look at you, DB, how you've shrunk," Ben teased.

"Yeah, I was kind of hefty back then." He took a step back, spread his hands, and gave a half turn to show off his slimmed-down profile. "Taking over the company has been a challenge, a good challenge but exhausting. Our new corporate gym helps. As you can see, I've moved up some from database programming. I've shed a lot of pounds and most of my old wardrobe, but I'll probably never outgrow the old nickname." He turned toward Marwa. "Forgive me. I'm Douglass Botteneau. Just call me DB. And you are?"

"Marwa Fredericksen. I work with Ben here."

"Lucky you." He looked toward Ben and raised an eyebrow. "And lucky ... ah, Ben." He finally extended his hand to Sam. "And Tank Parsons. It's great to see you again. Here, everybody, have a seat." He gestured toward a round conference table of inlaid wood that matched the desk. "Fill me in. What's up?"

"I'll let Ben and Marwa give the details, but their group and mine were both working on that Pacificano flight that disappeared earlier this week, then ditched off the coast of Chile. We were crunching data in real-time, trying to locate and track it by integrating feeds of satellite data and radar with other sources."

"Wow. How could I help with that? You do know, we don't do airplanes. Practically everything else. We have good penetration in most critical industries, but strictly on the ground, I should say. We're particularly strong in the electric power sector, ever since thwarting that power-plant software attack a decade back—thanks in part to Ben and his dad, by the way."

"Maybe you can do something to help these two," Sam said. "They need some computing power and secure Internet access. I figured you would have plenty of both."

"So do you, I would imagine. Doesn't the NTSB have computers anymore?"

"Of course, but there are an awful lot of eyes in the shadows at the NTSB, especially looking over my shoulders right now."

"I see. And let me guess: where these two work, the management is not exactly supportive of whatever they are up to."

"Your guess is good. So, can you help?"

"Quite possibly. But first, can anyone tell me the specifics of what this is about?" He listened patiently as Ben and Marwa brought him up to speed on Operation Flight Track. When Ben explained about the models of the final crash, DB suddenly straightened up.

Ben stopped his explanation. "What is it?"

"Run that by me again."

"The plane was under control when it splashed down in deep water. From what we've been told, it went straight to the bottom. What are you thinking?"

"I'm thinking you should talk with your father about this. He might know something."

"You're being cryptic."

"Damn straight I'm being cryptic, and with good reason." He looked at Parsons. "Did you tell them about your zigzag career path?" Parsons responded with a tiny, rapid shake of his head. "You want me to do the honors?" There was no response. "Okay. I'll just plunge ahead by saying that each of us at this table knows some things we are not supposed to know. The first question is whether we are going to come clean with each other. The second question is, if we put what we know out on the table, whether we will be able to figure out how it all fits together."

Ben squinted. "If it fits together."

"Oh, it fits, that I'm damn sure of. It's all puzzle pieces that spilled out of the same box." The phone on his desk started beeping; he glanced over at the caller ID. "You'll excuse me while I take this outside. I'll be right back."

It was a few minutes before DB returned, a serious look on his face. "That was my head of security. The guard at the gate noted a car stopped down the road. When he sent someone to check it out, it sped away but came back sometime later and stopped at a different spot. Looks like you got shoes on your trail. One of you must have led them here." He looked around the table.

Parsons looked at Ben. "I swapped cars today with my girl-friend and brought a burner phone with me."

"I used a burner phone to call you yesterday. One use. And right now the battery is out of my own phone." Ben gave Marwa a disapproving look.

"What? I haven't used my phone."

"But it's on?"

"Well, yeah, but ..."

DB and Parsons eyed each other. Ben leaned forward. "She's not used to this game. We all have more experience. But she's a fast learner, and I'm sure it won't happen again."

"And how did you pay for tolls on the way down here?"

Ben slapped his own forehead. "We didn't. We sailed right through the toll plazas on EZpass all the way. I guess we might as well have been wearing orange suits and driving a stolen car."

"Well, let's hope you're a fast learner, too, Ben."

"Well, I better be. Is there any way we can find out who they are, who's watching us?"

"My security guy is guessing FBI."

Parsons nodded. "Probably a good guess. Let's hope it's them and not somebody less savory. Whoever they are, they can now link all of us together."

Ben was making a time-out sign with his hands. "Suddenly we are acting like we are on the dark side. Will one of you tell us what is going on?"

DB stood up and took off his jacket. "We don't know. I don't know, anyway, except that we—some of us—have grabbed onto something too hot to handle. So, what haven't you three said?"

Ben shook his head. "You both already know what we got. Your turn, Parsons."

"Well, the NTSB is dismantling my group. It was always a quasi-unofficial operation, so it will probably just quietly sink back into the bog of government bureaucracy. But, it's another cover-up, that's clear. The reasons for the cover-up are not clear." He looked from Ben to Marwa and back. "Trust me, I know about burying the goods. I was complicit in covering up the real story about those pipeline explosions, but I knew why the deception was necessary, or at least why the Whitehouse and the State Department thought it was necessary. I'm in the dark on this one. Why would our government not want people to know what happened to this flight? What's our stake in it? It wasn't even one of our airlines."

DB loosened his tie and unbuttoned his shirt collar. "Well, gang, I don't know about you people, but I'm wading out of my depth. This is beginning to sound more like the stuff your father—or his friends—would know about, Bini. You do remember, Parsons, that Karl Lustig has a long history of entanglements with Israeli intelligence."

"My dad? You think he knows something about this?" Ben said.

"Karl knows ... something, maybe ..." He stopped as if censoring his words. "But you should really be asking him yourself."

"You know my dad, so you know he is not one to betray confidences, even to me. Why don't you just tell us what he told you? Let us suss it out from the same starting point."

DB sat thinking while the tension at the table rose. "You're right, I suppose. You probably will figure it out, so I might as well tell you what I put together out of some broad hints from Karl. It might save us all some time.

"Your father once did consulting work for a company called IsTac, Israel Tactical Systems. Ever hear of them?"

"Sure. They make high-tech military gear, drones, avionics chipsets, that kind of stuff."

"That's the outfit. Supposedly their specialized computer microchips are the best. Their chipsets are widely used in both military and civilian aircraft around the world."

"I remember IsTac. My dad actually got some patents out of his work with them. So what does this ... ? Wait, are you suggesting the downed plane might have used IsTac microchips, that they were defective or something? But I think I remember reading that we ... Israel uses those chipsets in the avionics systems of our F-16i fighters, maybe other combat aircraft."

"And so does the US. And China. And Saudi Arabia, and France, and ... the list goes on. As I said, they are widely used."

"And you think some of these are being used in commercial aircraft, that they might have been installed in the plane from Singapore? That's a testable hypothesis. It should be possible to find out what chipsets were being used in the triple-sevens and 787s. If they're not IsTac chips, we can toss this sci-fi scenario into the trash bin, at least for now."

DB leaned back and stretched to snatch the phone off his desk. He punched two numbers. "Avery, can I get you to do some research for us? Aviation industry, Boeing 777 and 787. Find out about the suppliers for their avionics systems and what chipsets were being used." He waited. "Okay, get on it and let me know what you find as soon as you get it. Great." He returned the handset.

Chapter 23

THE METICULOUSLY DRESSED Avery knocked and entered without waiting to be acknowledged. He handed a manila folder to DB, who gestured like a vaudeville magician introducing a comely assistant. "Everybody, this is Avery Foreliss, my administrative assistant, good right hand, and trustworthy confidant. You met but probably were not properly introduced. He has many talents, including making himself all but invisible. Avery, this is Sam Parsons, NTSB, and Ben Markham and Marwa Fredericksen from ..."

"CAASS, Center for Advanced Adaptive Systems Studies," Marwa said.

"Right, CAASS. We're working with them on ... a Special Executive Initiative." The pitch of his voice rose on the final words as if to put them in quotes.

Avery nodded twice in acknowledgement, shook hands with each of them, then excused himself and slipped quietly out of the room.

"Avery is whip smart, whip thin, and as quick and efficient as a sideshow bullwhip artist snapping cigarettes from a stooge's lips." DB opened the folder. "Let's see what he found." He ran a finger down the page. "Nope, no IsTac chips and no IsTac as subcontractor, at least as far as our industry databases reach."

Sam leaned forward. "My sources might be able to reach a bit further. Can you get me a secure VOIP phone?"

"Is the pope Catholic? We're a security company, remember." He walked around to his desk and extracted a handset from the middle drawer. "Pick a protocol and dial away. Goes through our own servers, no telco or ISP records. Even the guys next door at Langley would have trouble listening in or finding a trace. Of course, there is no stopping the snoops over at Fort Meade."

Sam checked his watch. "It's a long shot at this hour, but let me try." He thought for a moment, then dialed a number.

"Parsons here. Can you talk now? Any chance you can get me a copy of the maintenance records on the downed Boeing 787 from Pacificano flight 20? Splendid. This next is a tougher one. How about the maintenance records for the triple-seven on the Malaysian Airlines flight 370 that disappeared in March 2014? What? How clever of you. So, you were already looking into a possible connection. Excellent. If you could forward them to the regular dropbox that would be great." He smiled at the others around the table. "Yes, of course. If we come up with anything we'll share it. Cheers." He laid the handset down on the table and addressed the group. "A colleague in Singapore is forwarding photocopies of the maintenance logs. I should be able to retrieve them in a few minutes. Can we get some coffee, DB?"

■■ ■■ ■■

Parsons borrowed DB's own tablet computer to pick up the images of the maintenance records from the private dropbox and project them on the office wall. "Well, I'll be ... See, right there, the very day of the flight. 'Avionics field upgrade, modules CO9-A216 and CO9-A217 replaced.' This delayed the departure of the flight. Now we look at the bill-of-materials for the upgrade, and here we are with the manufacturer of the replacement boards, Endyne Aviation Solutions. So, now we browse to their website, go to the About page and—trumpet fanfare—it's a subsidiary of Israel Tactical Systems."

Ben put his fists together beneath his chin and adopted a studious expression. "What about the other plane you asked about, the Malaysian one."

"Well let's see. Oh, the record is a mess. It's not all in English and some of the entries are unreadable, but there is an entry in early 2014 with two very telling part numbers on them." He moved the mouse pointer to a scribbled line with two numbers: CO9-A216 and CO9-A217.

Ben was now on the edge of his chair. "You're suggesting that both planes could have been deliberately sabotaged with defective chipsets used in these replacement avionics boards."

"That's what it looks like—if DB is right about the microchips."

"I'm right. And your father knows about this, Ben."

Ben looked about, like a squirrel caught in the passing lane during rush-hour traffic. "But why? What's the motivation? It still doesn't make sense to me that the Israelis—or the Americans—would deliberately equip their own military aircraft with defective electronics. And it doesn't really fit with the scenario for how that plane was flying at the end, when it crashed. As if there weren't enough holes in this fantasy, what possible reason would there be for anyone to bring down two fully-loaded passenger planes? No group has ever come forward about the Malaysian hijacking."

"That's what you have to find out." Parsons pointed at Ben and Marwa in turn. "That's why I brought you two here to meet with DB. It's obvious we're on our own and have to do an end run around official channels that seem to prefer that the questions remain unanswered."

Ben nodded toward Marwa. "This is clearly where she comes in. It has to have something to do with who or what was on those planes. Now we have some clues, a pattern from the technical angle, but next we need to figure out the people angle."

"Wow, thanks for the endorsement," she said.

DB spread his arms. "Okay, I'm in. Whatever you need to figure it out, the facilities of Scenaria are at your disposal. I'll have Avery get you set up in a conference room with whatever you need in the way of computers and access. He'll have our tech support people brief you on how to negotiate our network and use our special software."

Marwa looked skeptical. "Why are you doing this?"

DB hesitated. "Let's just say I'm driven by a need for closure, for follow-through. Like, I love playing Clue, I'll admit, and I crave intrigue—as long as it doesn't get dangerous. I don't do the danger thing, not anymore." He gave Ben a knowing look. "Only in first-person-shooter games. I still enjoy an occasional match, although there's not much time for simulated thrills in my life now."

He was clearly warming to his own storyline. "Of course, it's also my business. Anything that might give the company a leg up on the competition in a new arena, that's always worth something." He looked in Ben's direction with his eyes focused somewhere else. "If all that is not enough reason, then factor in your dad, Ben. Karl is a friend. And I still think you should have a chat with him about all this stuff."

"My dad always told me to keep an eye on all the other players. So, what about the FBI outside?"

Parsons answered before DB could respond. "I might be able to do something about that. Let me use your magic phone again, DB, and call another friend."

Marwa flashed Parsons a wry smile. "You have a lot of"—she made finger quotes—"friends."

"I'm a friendly sort of guy. And it's my job. I'll see what I can find out."

DB slid the handset toward Sam ."There you are. I'm going to go talk with Avery and check in with some of my crew." He got up from the table.

Sam rose and stretched. "And I'm going in search of a men's room."

DB gestured with his thumb. "There's one just off the outer office or you can go past Avery and down the hall to the left."

— — —

Sam scrolled through his contact lists as he continued past the toilets. It had been long enough since they had last spoken that he had forgotten the telephone number. He copied it into his burner phone. He had decided against using the VOIP phone because he didn't want to risk leaving a record of the number even in a local call list.

A woman with a trace of a Georgian drawl in her voice answered on the second ring. "FBI Cyber-Crime Unit, Agent Rivers speaking."

"Hello? I was trying to reach Arkady Pohl, but I seem to have the wrong number."

"Right number, but Pohl has been reassigned. He's at another extension. Can I help you?"

"You can if you can give me his extension."

"I can if you can tell me what this is about."

"It's about old friends. I'm in town and wanted to say hi."

"In that case, he's on extension 6036; I can transfer you. What did you say your name was?"

Sam glanced around for inspiration, then noticed the watercolor wildlife prints hung along the hallway. "Mallard."

"Mallard. Right. And do you have a first name, Mr. Mallard. And don't tell me it's duck, either."

"Close, Duke. Duke Mallard. And I swear to God, if I hear one more crack today about my name, I will literally scream."

"Well, Mr. Duke Mallard, I wouldn't want to have you screaming in my ear over the phone. Besides, I take some kidding about my name, too."

"And what's that, Ms. Rivers? Not Joan, I hope."

"No, much worse: Flo. And it's not short for Florence either. I'm transferring you now. Do you want me to stay on the line for your migration?"

"Oh, you are terrible, Flo. No, not necessary. Just let it flow through." There was a click and then a long series of rings.

"Counterterrorism Unit, Pohl speaking."

"Everybody in Washington must be swapping desks and shuffling units. Counterterrorism fits you, Arkady."

"And what fits you? Who is this? Wait a minute. Tank Parsons? Pipelines?"

"Good one. But Sam fits me better than Tank these days, and I've been promoted out of pipelines. In fact, I'm about to be, er, promoted again. So, how the hell are you, Arkady? And how is Agent Delacroix? You still working with her?"

"I'm good. And Barbara Delacroix is doing even better. She retired about the time I moved over to Counterterrorism. Is there a reason for this blast from the past."

"There's a reason for everything. How about a drink? After work today. Pick a place." Sam was hoping Pohl would read between the lines and agree to a rendezvous.

"I ... We really have our hands full right now."

"Me, too. I've been busy chasing planes falling out of the sky. That's why I'm calling now. It's important we talk. Right away."

There was a long pause. "You still got my cell number?"

"I never throw away anyone's number."

"Okay, call me in fifteen." Click.

Parsons strolled slowly down the hall as if he were deep in thought. Near the end of the corridor, he spotted a supply closet with a simple cylinder lock which he quickly picked. Slipping in before anyone saw him, he pulled out his burner phone again and dialed the number he read from his other phone. Arkady finally answered. "So, what's up, Parsons?" He sounded a bit out of breath and the rustle of wind could be heard in the background.

"Like I said, I'm trying to make sense of planes falling out of the sky. What about you?"

"I'm trying to make sense of a wave of killings and disappearances that have only one thing in common: timing."

"And I think I know when they happened. Early Tuesday morning, right?"

"What? Did you read about them in the papers?"

"No, but I'm getting an uneasy feeling that your interests and mine are very much connected."

"If you are talking about that Singapore Airline hijacking, I doubt it."

"It wasn't Singapore Airlines, and it wasn't a hijacking."

"They found the black boxes?" Arkady sounded surprised.

"No, they didn't find the black boxes, and they aren't going to find them, but I know some people who know something about what happened."

"And what does this have to do with the FBI and my interests? Maybe you should be talking with the CIA. I can help grease the skids through the Bureau's CIA liaison."

"Arkady, I'm telling you the Bureau is already interested in these particular people and is tailing them. There must be a reason. That's why I think our paths may be crisscrossing again."

"Names?"

"I need honesty. Can I trust you to keep this just between us?"

"No, you can't. There, so at least you got the honesty you wanted."

"Okay. Then how about this: can you tell me if you have agents on stakeout at a particular location?"

"You know better than that. I can't tell you where we have anybody posted or who we might have under surveillance." The sound of a deep breath came over the phone. "I suppose I could tell you if we don't have anybody someplace. But you realize, then we might have to send somebody there."

"Fair enough. Reston. Scenaria International."

"Ohmagod, not Scenaria again. That company is so much friggin' trouble. Okay, I'll look into it. Call you back."

Sam was on his way back to the DB's office when the burner phone rang. "They're not ours," Arkady said, "at least not my division. I don't have access to everything in the entire Bureau."

"Okay, thanks."

"Be careful, Parsons. You're not trained for this."

"Maybe I didn't attend the same academy as you, but there's a lot to be said for on-the-job training. Anyway, you be careful, too."

▬▬ ▬▬ ▬▬

Ben and Marwa spent the afternoon with their noses to computer screens. Even with the material he had stored on his key-fob thumb drive, Ben had trouble getting the borrowed system to work the way he wanted. In the meantime, Marwa started by trying to reconstruct from memory as much information as she could. It was random bits and pieces recovered by free association: the names of some of the passengers, the number of special meals delivered from the flight caterers, the fact that one of those connected in the cluster with Abu Omar was traveling on a Somali passport and another had made a cell phone call to a number in Portland, Maine, just before takeoff.

She accessed public domain resources to gather data on selected names from her newly constituted list and used some open source tools to analyze the content of news stories. Both she and Ben persevered, but neither of them made any great breakthroughs. When DB looked in on them late in the day, they were frustrated and ready to quit.

Marwa made fists and pretended to pound at her keyboard. "If I had access to my databases at CAASS, it would be a different story."

"Could be arranged." DB lowered his voice. "We have a lot of talent here."

"What are you saying?"

"Knowing how networks and systems can be compromised is our business."

"You actually think you could hack into the CAASS computers. I doubt it."

"No guarantees, but I would lay odds that we'd have a solution by morning if I turned loose some of our ex-black-hat hackers from down in The Vault."

"The Vault?"

"Yeah, Ben remembers, I'm sure. That's our high-security isolation room where we study malicious software and build countermeasures without contaminating the rest of the company's computers. You are coming back in the morning, aren't you?"

Ben looked at Marwa, and they both shrugged. "Not sure it makes sense. In the end, we didn't accomplish much today."

"I should have asked earlier. Where are you two staying?"

"We're not. We really need to head back. And we can't afford the prices around here. Do you know what they wanted for an extra night at the Meredith?"

"I can imagine. It's downtown Washington. But you might as well stay out here. We have a deal with the Hyatt Regency. I'll have Avery book you a couple of rooms through the weekend." He stopped their objections with a warning finger. "No, no. It's on the company, a justifiable corporate expense. And you'll need a car."

"I've got a car, just not here. My VW is still parked at the hotel, running up parking fees. I figured we would be back to pick it up after our meeting."

"I'll have Avery make arrangements to retrieve your car. If the Bureau is already tracking you, why make it easier? Avery will get you a company car. It won't be fun like Sam Parson's little ragtop, just something that won't draw attention."

Part Four: Ethnology
Chapter 24

ABDI FARAH HATED the car. It was a junker, an old blue Ford restored to temporary function by Abdi's friend Cali Muhammed, who could breathe life into a dead inkjet printer or fix a busted blender with equal ease. And now the Ford, with its doctored license plates and overheating V6, sat silent and steaming beside the road just a few miles short of the finish line. The drive down from Maine and the bland, regimented buildings of Portland's public housing at Kennedy Park had been long and nerve-wracking. Cali had taken too long to ready the Ford, and the departure from the Somali neighborhood had been hurried, with no time for goodbyes. Abdi would not have dared speed even if the old car had been capable of it, yet he feared even more that he might arrive too late.

Abdi did not look his twenty-seven years. With his acne, sparse beard, and big brown eyes, he could pass for an unthreatening teenager on a joyride. Abdi had never been to Gloucester, but he knew the seaport town well. The facts and folklore he had learned from Wikipedia, its people he had met through reading the online edition of The Gloucester Times, and the streets he had memorized by walking them using Google Maps Street View. He knew the waterfront boardwalk, the stacks of lobster traps behind buildings, and the brick-paved sidewalks on Main Street. And he knew precisely where on the way out Eastern Point he needed to be and exactly when he must arrive. He was not going to make it.

He cursed, then immediately offered a quick apology. He was certain he would not live long, and he wanted no more sins on his head before the moment arrived. He held out his thumb in the vain hope of hitching a ride. Acutely conscious of the weight of what he carried in his gym bag and sweating from the warm autumn afternoon, he almost wished not to get a ride. That way he could say he had tried, that the failure was not his, but Allah's will. In any case, the others, whoever they were, wherever they might be, would surely succeed, and the knife would slice the arteries of both Israel and America with one stroke.

The horn blast shook him out of his thoughts. "You want a ride or not, kid?" The yellow and black Jeep was pulled over, but the shoulder along this section of Route 133 was too narrow and cars were already backed up behind it.

"Yes, I do want a ride. I must get to Gloucester." He climbed in and held the black-and-white gym bag in his lap.

The tires squealed on the sun-warmed pavement as the driver pulled out. He posted a middle finger for the motorist behind who had just given him another blast on the horn. "What's the hurry, kid?"

"A job, I'm applying for a job."

"Oh, yeah? Where? I've been looking for work since May. Who's hiring? You think they might have something for me? I've been a lobsterman. And I can paint, do light carpentry, even some electrical if no one is asking about a license."

"It's a cousin, at a restaurant. The ..." He fished for a name buried in mental files of falsified memories. "It's called Jalapeños."

"Oh, yeah, I know it. Mexican joint on Main. Never tried it. Stuff's too damn hot for me. Gives me gas. I'll take a good fish chowder, a burger—hold the mustard, though—or baked mac-

and-cheese. Now that's real eating." He considered the boy's dark skin. "You Mexican?"

"No, I'm from Portland."

"Naw, what I meant was ... aw, forget it. Where do you want to be left off? Front of the restaurant? Main is one way the wrong way from this end. Gotta go down Rogers and head back."

"You can let me off anyplace downtown." He glanced at his cheap watch. With the ride, he would make it, but he would have to walk the rest of the way. He needed an extra margin because it was Friday. "Maybe the other end of downtown, near the Walgreens. I ... I need to pick up something."

"Sure, buddy, whatever. You got a name?"

"Bill."

"Well, ain't that somethin'. I'm Will." He took his right hand off the wheel and offered it to his passenger. "Here we are, Will and Bill, both William, huh? What are the odds?"

Will spun the wheel and angled into the parking lot adjacent to the Walgreens. "Good luck, kid." He waited for Abdi to climb out, then sped off.

Abdi watched the Jeep until it was out of sight before crossing the street and heading toward the turnoff for East Main. There was just time for the trek out Eastern Point Road, past the docks and shops along the marina to the wooded private roads that were not covered by Google's Street View. But his cousin, who was indeed from Gloucester but had never set foot in a Mexican restaurant, had made Abdi feel as if he knew the whole city. Getting back out of the isolated neck without a car would be difficult, but Abdi would try, and the risk would be worth it.

Abdi knew that every workday evening except Friday, Abe Sackman would leave the office of his non-profit foundation in Rockport at 6:30 to drive to his home near Niles Pond on Eastern Point. On Fridays, he left for home early. The home was only worth two-and-a-half million, but Abe was worth closer to a hundred times as much, and his foundation was worth double that. Much of the effort of Abe and the Sackman Foundation was spent in aid of Israel. Abe was active in a long list of pro-Israel organizations and a highly visible supporter of Zionist causes.

Abdi smiled to himself. When Sackman and the other rich and powerful pigs of American Jewry were all executed within the same hour, who would then dare support Israel? Who would send money? Who would have the courage to cajole congress?

When he was first recruited for the mission, Abdi had realized its brilliance: to spill the blood of those who were the life-blood of Israel, the many moneyed American Zionists whose wealth and influence sustained the oppressor, a nation too weak and inept to stand on its own. Without the American money and support, the evil State of Israel would crumble like the fabled walls of the city his people knew as Ariha, and his brothers in Palestine would then be free to take back the land that was theirs, that Allah had decreed should be in Muslim hands for the rest of time.

Abdi trekked out the winding one-way road to find the sheltered spot that his cousin had described, where the road turned and the brush alongside was thick. He knew the deep blue Mercedes he would be looking for, the license number, and the color of the driver's hair. He knew when he should fire from behind the bushes as the car rounded the bend. He bent low to ready the assault rifle in his pack, then crouched and waited.

Chapter 25

AS THEY RODE UP the elevator in the Hyatt Regency, Ben asked Marwa what she wanted to do for dinner.

She exhaled slowly. "I don't know. I know it's Friday night and all, but I don't really feel like going out, if that's what you're asking. I need some down time to process everything that's happened today. I'll probably just order room service."

Ben hid his disappointment. "I'm with you. Would you like some company? Unless you really want to be alone, we could do room service together."

"Do you think that would be such a good idea? I mean ..."

"I'll be a perfect gentleman. Promise."

"You are a perfect gentleman, Ben, but you forget there are two of us."

Ben smiled. "I'm flattered. I'm not sure I fully understand, but I'm flattered."

"Forget I said that. I think I'll just order a sandwich and go to bed early. Do you really want to go back in to Scenaria in the morning."

"Yeah, I want to try to finish what we started. But it doesn't have to be too early. Maybe ten or so? Meet for breakfast at nine?"

The elevator doors slid open. Marwa looked at the number on her key folder. "Oh, here we are. Wow, the concierge floor again. I hadn't noticed. Your old friend is taking good care of us. And yes, breakfast in the morning." She turned left out of the elevator.

"Laila tov," Ben said as he turned right. "Good night, sleep well."

— — —

Ben was finishing a turkey club sandwich in his room when there was a rapid tap on his door. He checked through the peephole, then let Marwa in. She put her arms around him and rested her head on his chest without saying anything. "What happened, Marwa?"

"Too much. I got a call from Seth. He was not happy with me staying down here. Big surprise. We argued, kept at it until I had enough. I hung up. But then I made the mistake of turning on the news. Did you hear? There's all this stuff happening. All over. I just have this feeling it's all linked, and I don't know how. It's a little freaky."

"You? Freaked out? By what?"

"Turn on CNN. They loop the headlines. You'll see."

Ben found the remote hiding under a room service menu on the night table. He tuned to CNN Headlines.

Ben muted the sound and scanned the headline crawling across the bottom of the screen. "What does this stuff about a resurgence of ISIS units operating inside Syria have to do with us? Or with the plane crash?"

"Just wait. I think it'll be the next story." They stared at the text crawl until the next story started. Ben thumbed the mute button again.

"An alleged terrorist lies in critical condition in Boston's Mass General Hospital after being wounded in a shootout with State troopers and local police from Gloucester, Massachusetts. The name of the patient has not been released, but sources say he is dark-skinned, in his twenties, and a resident of a largely Somali community in Portland, Maine. Police were called to the seaport town of Gloucester after a prominent philanthropist from the area, Abraham Sackman, and his driver—who has not been identified pending notification of next of kin—were shot and killed on their way home. Neighbors in the exclusive Eastern Point section reported hearing rapid gunfire before the car in which Sackman was being driven crashed into a stone wall. Our reporter on the scene said the car was riddled with bullet holes, reportedly from an AK-47 style assault rifle. The alleged assailant fled on foot and was quickly located by police.

"Now, we go live to CNN correspondent Judith Silber Adams outside Mass General Hospital."

Ben muted the TV. "What on earth does this have to do with flight PT20."

"One of the five passengers in the suspect cluster was from Somalia."

"OMG, Marwa, that's like numerology. It's a coincidence, nothing more."

"Then why did one of our passengers, a different member of the same group, make a cellphone call to a number in Portland just hours before the plane left?"

— — —

Arkady had heard the news on All Things Considered as he was driving home. He knew he shouldn't text and drive, but he also knew he needed to act quickly. The message he awkwardly thumb-typed on his phone was full of typos, but it didn't matter. His brother would understand and get back to him. That was the one thing he could trust about Dima—he would respond. There was little else trustworthy about the man.

Arkady was stalled in heavy Friday-night traffic when the reply arrived on his burner phone. It was not garbled. He read it and immediately started pounding the phone to pieces against the center console. He considered throwing it out the window, then thought better of it. He could dump it at the airport. He looked at his watch. There was just time to take the next exit, detour back to National Airport, and catch a flight to Boston. There was no need to let Dima know what flight he was on. Dima would know, as he always seemed to, and Dima would meet him, as he always did.

Chapter 26

UNDER THE UPSWEPT CONCRETE canopy of Terminal C at Boston's Logan Airport, passengers flowed like twigs in a fast brook around Dmitry Pohl. Oblivious to everyone but alert to everything, he leaned casually against the sign at the foot of the escalator leading up to the passenger bridge for Central Parking. His hair was bleached, and he sported a dirty-blond goatee. Even so, the family resemblance was there for anyone to notice on a second look. At one time, they could have passed for twins, Dmitry and Arkady, but now Arkady's face had softened and rounded while Dima's had grown weathered and toughened. As schoolboys, Dmitry had more than once taken a test for his younger, less gifted brother. Then they had gone separate ways: Arkady to America and into the FBI, Dmitry to Israel and into Shin Bet. After a few years in the domestic security service, he had switched to Mossad—and beyond. He made no effort to move as Arkady approached the escalator.

"What are you doing in Boston, Dima? I thought you were back in the Middle East."

"I'm working, defending the homeland."

"So now New England has become an enemy of Israel?"

Dima laughed as he stepped onto the escalator. "We're Jews. We have enemies everywhere."

Arkady followed him. "And what work is it this time?"

"You've heard of the Boston Harbor Cleanup?"

"I see: cleanup. Dirty work."

"Somebody has to do the dirty work."

"And let it be you. Admit it, you relish these jobs."

"I relish a safe harbor and a clean environment."

"Who is your target this time? Another young couple like the last time our paths crossed?"

"You know that I can't say. You'll hear about it soon enough afterwards. But you didn't text me and fly up here to chat about cleaning up environmental hazards."

"No, I came up here to tap into your expertise on microchips and tea roses."

"Neither are in my line of work."

"But you know about them, how they're used—and misused."

Dima didn't respond, but his brother could read his face from long practice. They reached the top of the escalator and stepped off.

"Shall we go, Cub? There's still time for a late dinner. The Boston area has so many possibilities."

Arkady flinched at the childhood nickname he so hated. "Your choice. I didn't come here for food, I came for information."

"Good information is more dear than good food, even at Boston restaurant prices." At the end of the enclosed passenger bridge, he stopped at the parking kiosk to prepay his ticket. "One more way to be tracked." He patted the machine. "We leave digital footprints wherever we go, as if we were always walking on a layer of fresh snow."

"I doubt your credit card is anything that can be traced back to you or your pals." He snatched the card from Dima's hand before it could be inserted in the machine. "Who are you today? Ah, nice to meet you, Mr. Philip Pressman." He handed the card back. "What's your game, Mr. Pressman?"

"You play the same cat-and-mouse games as I do."

"No more. I drive a desk these days. What do you drive?"

"A rented Mustang. It's on the top level, outside, the only place I could get a spot. They never have enough parking spaces here because they keep expanding the parking garages instead of making it easier to get to the airport. You'd think they'd learn. 'Build it and they will come.' They keep building, and the cars keep coming. Always more."

Arkady was beginning to wonder why his brother had agreed to meet if he was going to offer nothing but movie quotes and platitudes. As if his mind were being read, Dima turned to him. "After we eat, we can discuss the cultivation of roses. After."

"So be it. And have you decided where we will eat."

"Yes. It's a special place near Central Square: very trendy, very good, and very near impossible to get into, but ..."

"But you know the chef and can work something out."

"I do, and I can, at least Philip Pressman can. Ah, here's my chariot. Let me text Tony and let him know we are on our way." He thumb-typed a message with lightning speed before using his key fob to unlock the black-and-yellow Mustang. "Right. So, we are on our way to Craigie on Main. I would recommend the tasting menu: locavore heaven, and you will hardly be able to walk when we leave."

-- -- --

A succession of eight small-plate courses and a bottle of Rioja later, Dima was patting his belly as they left the restaurant. "And so, dear brother, what is your conclusion about the place?"

"I have never before eaten so much treif food in my life. You didn't say it was a place that elevated pork and shellfish to the level of high art."

"Perhaps it was a test."

"A test. I guess we failed as Jews. It's a good thing we are not haredim. So, what do I think? The food was excellent, varied; the

139

conversation more bland and lacking a certain substance."

"You want me to tell you what *HaVered* is up to."

"Of course."

"And I would tell you there is no such organization. The Rose? What an absurd name for an organization, much less some secret society of avenging paladins. A ridiculous fantasy."

"Then why did you agree to meet if you were merely going to flash your credit card and play word games? I thought you would actually share some information."

"You are as naïve as ever, my wolf cub. I agreed to meet because of the information you were going to share with me."

"You have it backwards. And your hidden rose garden is very close to being exposed in any case."

"You don't say. Really? Rose bushes have nasty thorns, you know, and they make an excellent, almost impenetrable hedgerow."

Arkady turned abruptly around and headed toward Mass Avenue and Central Square.

"Where are you going?"

"Home. I'm wasting my time. I thought ..."

"You thought because I once said something to you and did you a favor, that I would do so again. Now is not then, and you have no idea how big this is. That you are my brother buys you no immunity. None. You are alive only because I have said nothing about you. A word—one word—and you would be gone. The same for anyone connected with you, however weakly. Old pals, new acquaintances"—he snapped his fingers—"gone."

Arkady stood in the middle of the sidewalk, at a loss for words, shivering in the chill autumn air. Dima thrust his hand into the pocket of his coat and took a step forward. Arkady stiffened as Dima's hand came out. "Relax. Here, it's a CharlieCard, for the T. It's still got enough on it to get you to the airport."

"Thanks. Thanks for dinner."

"Forget it. I mean it ... literally. Forget this whole evening and anything you think you might know about roses, domestic or wild."

Arkady looked down at the card, studying it, suddenly inspired. When he looked up, Dmitry had already slipped away into the side-streets of central Cambridge.

Chapter 27

"ARE YOU STILL IN Singapore?" The animated lips of the avatar were out of synch with the processed voice.

Dexter Nelson tried to hide his annoyance. "No, I was never in Singapore. There was no need."

"How did you ...? Never mind. I won't ask. Where are you now?"

"Saint Paul."

"Why?"

"A break from the heat for a few days. The op is complete."

"No. We missed a cadre."

"Another? How the fuck ... ? Where? Who did they hit?"

"The entire family of liquor mogul Freeman Brownsteen in Toronto. That was a bomb in a stolen delivery van that pulled into the circular driveway at the Brownsteen mansion. Stateside, a meeting of the Board of Directors of The American-Israeli Business Forum at the Radisson Blu Hotel in Minneapolis. There, a returned Somali jihadist dressed as a room-service waiter blew himself up along with all six members of the board. Two pro-Israeli lobbyists and the head of the arms-industry group that pays them died when their DC-bound private plane crashed on takeoff from Atlanta. The pilot is believed to be Somali with connections to radical Islamists. A little later, philanthropist Abe Sackman and his driver were ripped to shreds by automatic weapons fire on their way home in Gloucester, Mass. Police spotted a Somali immigrant trying to flee the area on foot, there was a shootout, and now the gunman is in critical condition in a Boston hospital."

"How the fuck did we miss all these bastards?"

"Homegrown. The only teams not converging from outside. We were too busy watching the borders, preventing entry. Too easy to lose them, lose track once they're in the US. This bunch were all Islamist Somali immigrants recently radicalized or returned from jihad, scattered. They must have networked on their own after someone was recruited to the mission. This would have been a small, widely dispersed cell. They were flying beneath the radar, the few hiding among the many, terrorists mixed in with the good Somali citizens of Portland, Toronto, the Twin Cities, Atlanta."

"Anything else?"

"Isn't two dozen bodies enough? Despite all our planning and coordination, their public service message was delivered and will no doubt be heard—loud and clear."

"Maybe not. Look at the brighter side. Only four targets, and one of them was in Canada. Americans don't give a shit about what happens in Canada. Hell, the news media probably won't even connect the dots. This whole business will be dismissed as isolated extremists because US intelligence services will skew the narrative. They will not want even a hint that they might have missed something bigger. It will all blow over in a few weeks. Flight PT20 is already dropping down to a couple of column-inches on the inside pages."

"You always were the optimist, a dreamer. But it's time to wake up and get back on the job. Two alleged accomplices in the hotel bombing have been taken into custody in Minnesota. The Mounties are still out beating the bushes, but if they bag anyone, we will have to move quickly to get someone over the border.

According to the news, authorities in Georgia and Massachu-setts are working on the assumption these were lone-wolf opera-tions. We know better. The cell may have been isolated, but then again, some of the players might know something of the other cards on the table. We can't risk anything coming out about the larger op. If the scope of their operation becomes known, the extent of our interception is likewise exposed. We cannot risk that. We must take out every last link.

"Unfortunately, having failed in blocking the borders, now we have to do our work inside the country, which is always trickier, always more dangerous."

"Which one do I take?"

"Minnesota, obviously. You still have a kit stored there from last year, don't you? Massachusetts is already covered. Be creat-ive, be quick. If nothing else works, be Jack Ruby. Just don't be taken into custody."

Dexter stared at the screen to keep from blinking nervously. "I'll be Sergi Cardona again, thank you."

"You will be whoever and whatever we need you to be." The avatar abruptly blinked out.

Dexter Nelson was already getting once more into the mind-set of the Spanish business traveler, preparing for the hours of reconnaissance and fabricated business chats. He had to find a way to get to the accomplices. Alleged accomplices, he corrected himself. Not that it mattered. They were dead men.

Chapter 28

PETER MA COULD NOT contain his impatience. He fairly danced in the doorway to the office. "Excuse me sir, but we have a lead. We found somebody, and we need to act."

Alon Chiang looked up, his mouth down-turned even more than usual, with added disapproval narrowing his eyes. "A moment." He signed the paper on his desk with an exaggerated flourish, then slowly and carefully folded it, creased it, and slid it into an envelope. "What?"

Peter swallowed and took a breath. "A man claiming to be a relative of one of the passengers had made an inquiry after the plane vanished but before it was located. An airline representative took down names and telephone numbers of those who didn't stay at the airport to await word. They neglected to turn over the list until now."

"So?"

"The man was inquiring about Dante Calabrese."

"An Italian passenger?"

"No, from his passport and security camera recordings, we now know it was Abu Omar, a Palestinian terrorist. It was thought he was in the West Bank, but instead—"

"What about the so-called relative? Where is he now?"

"Here, still in Singapore. We have an address on him. I thought—"

"Yes, I want to be in on this. No tactical team. This is not Los

Angeles. Or Kuala Lumpur. We don't make attention-grabbing assaults for the benefit of the media. Massive but quiet: that's what we will do. Have them seal the building, then wait for my arrival." Alon opened his desk drawer and removed his Heckler & Koch. He checked the pistol and inserted a 15-round magazine, then slipped an extra magazine into his jacket pocket."

"Shouldn't we wear vests, sir?"

"On the way, we'll get the body armor on the way. Let's go."

━━ ━━ ━━

Peter and his boss stood to either side of the apartment door, guns drawn, as Mahmoud al-Hadj joined them. "Alive," Alon said in a whisper. "We want this man alive. That's why we do not trust this to a Special Team. If you kill him, your career is over."

Mahmoud moved into position between them and kicked the door in. The lock gave, but a chain held, and it took a second boot to the door for it to swing wide. Gunfire erupted from the apartment, and bullets struck the opposite wall of the hallway. Mahmoud crumpled as dark crimson spread through the front of his shirt. Peter pulled him aside.

Alon crouched and dove through the doorway, opening fire as he stretched prone on the rug just inside. His first shots hit the man at the window in the thigh and groin. Alon calmly raised his aim to the arm that now pointed a SIG Sauer P226 directly at him. They both fired at almost the same moment. Alon took the shot in his left shoulder as the man's hand spasmed open and the pistol dropped. Unarmed and badly wounded, the suspect stumbled toward the door. Alon grabbed an ankle with his good arm and brought the bleeding body sprawling down on top of him.

"Get the damn EMTs here. Now!" he screamed as Peter and a uniformed officer dragged the suspect off of him and out the door. "Take care of him, then Mahmoud. I can wait."

146

-- -- --

The morphine and his own adrenaline kept the pain in check as Alon walked slowly down the stairs. His shoulder was bandaged with his arm in a sling taped to his side. He stopped outside the basement interrogation room. "Help me get my jacket on over this before I go in." He struggled into one arm of his sports jacket and waited for the two uniformed officers to open the heavy door.

The prisoner sat on a stool in the middle of the room. It was the first that Alon had really noticed the man's face. At the apartment, Alon had never looked higher than the man's shoulders. The cheeks were sunken and pockmarked, the skin worn and weathered like old canvas. Spicules of gray mottled the beard. The man stared into space, clearly in pain but trying to hide the fact in an artificial calm.

"Who are you?" There was no answer. Alon crossed the room and stood over him. "You are Fareed al-Masri, Abu Omar's lieutenant. See, we already know, so your silence is symbolic at best, self-defeating in the end." There was no response. "Right now you are strong, even though you have lost blood. But you will weaken. And you will tell us who you work with and everything that they are doing or planning."

The corner of the man's mouth twitched, but he said nothing. Alon circled behind him and bent to speak directly into his ear. "We are not the Americans, and this is not Abu Ghraib. We will not strip you and humiliate you. We are more serious here, more physical, more direct. We were trained by the Israelis, by Shin Bet. Ah, I see from your reaction that you know them. Consider us their most distinguished graduates. We will pull what we want to know from you. In the end you will beg to tell us. Better to talk now, and it will be easier on you. And on these men here, who will sleep better knowing what they did not need to do to you."

Al-Masri tried to spit, but only air and a few drops of congealed blood escaped his mouth. Alon's right hand struck the side of the prisoner's face with a loud crack that almost knocked him from the stool to which he was shackled. Alon straightened up and addressed the waiting men. "Do it. Do whatever you need to get him talking." He adjusted his jacket and left.

— — —

Alon looked up from reading the transcript. "And the prisoner?"

Peter shook his head slowly. "He … as it says, he took his own life in the holding cell after … after the confession."

He flipped pages of the report. "This is well written, well enough edited. The interrogation certainly didn't take long."

"Our interviewers were efficient. They were trained in what the Americans so euphemistically refer to as 'enhanced interrogation' techniques."

"To be expected. We were trained by the best, you know."

"Yes, and we were also fortunate that this was Abu Omar's lieutenant, a recent replacement at that. I would expect Abu Omar himself would not have so quickly yielded such information. Al-Masri was not a very sophisticated subordinate; it was quite stupid of him to inquire at the airport regarding his boss. But then, he was new to his role, promoted only months ago after his predecessor was killed in an American drone strike. There is always a replacement, not always a good one."

"You said he took his own life, correct? Then prepare a suitable coroner's report and get someone to sign it for when we have to deal with the press or some board of inquiry. And speaking of Americans, let's take a clue from their expeditious handling of bin Laden. Cremate the body immediately and have an explanation ready."

Peter dipped his head in agreement. "Do you think the

Americans will believe this?"

"Do you think the Americans will be told? This still does not explain the crash of the plane, only that some co-conspirators went down with it. If we tell the Americans anything, they will want to know how we got the information. For now, we—you and I—do nothing. The decisions and disposition will have to be passed higher up. We did our job."

"As you say, sir. And it has been a long and difficult day. I'll be heading home now."

Alon was already preparing for his next meeting and said nothing. Dismissed with silence, Peter backed out of the office and headed for the exit. His stride was lengthened, his footsteps loud. Alon Chiang—always unbending, always in absolute control— stood between Peter and his ultimate objectives. Loyalty was expected—demanded—but never rewarded. If there was a future for Peter, he knew it was not here, not in servitude under Chiang.

Outside the building, Peter picked up his pace and turned immediately toward the entrance to the MRT. While on the subway, he used his phone to prepare a message with an attachment. When he reached the station nearest his apartment, he sent the message as he rode the escalator to the surface. There was nothing outwardly suspicious about either the contents or the destination, but Peter nevertheless looked around nervously as he started down the block toward his building.

Chapter 29

SERGI CARDONA KNEW BETTER than most that some problems could be resolved at a distance; others required closer, more intimate intervention. The Twin Cities suspects in custody could not be dealt with remotely nor could the matter be deferred. This was his specialty: quick, decisive, and creative action, as with the problem in Singapore. The challenge Sergi faced this time was how to get close enough to do anything at all. The prisoners were being held in downtown Minneapolis at the Hennepin County Adult Detention Center in the Public Safety Facility, a spare and ugly modern building across the street from the massive heap of gray stone that was the old City Hall. While they were in jail, only a bunker-buster bomb could reach them. After arraignment in the courthouse around the corner, however, they were to be remanded into federal custody. There would be a handoff and a transfer to an unspecified facility. They would no doubt be stubbornly silent at first, but there was no guarantee how long they would hold out. They must not be given enough time to talk with the authorities.

From his motel near the airport, Sergi headed uptown, straight for the vicinity of the jail, an area with block after block of dull and imposing government office buildings. As he strolled casually across the semicircular plaza outside the Federal Courthouse, he noticed something he had missed on his first turn around the block. Just beyond a parking garage on the corner where he remembered police sharpshooters had been stationed on a previous high-profile prisoner transfer, there was another building, taller by a few stories. The angle was not good, and it was almost too far away, but the roof would look down on any police tactical teams as well as provide an unobstructed view to a good share of the courthouse plaza.

Sergi walked under the glass-enclosed pedestrian bridge that spanned South 4th Street and entered the lobby of the venerable Hotel Minneapolis where he booked himself into three nights on the concierge floor. He retrieved his gear from his parked rental car and dumped it in the room. Returning to his car, he circled the block for one last review before driving south to Bloomington and The Mall of America. Once the largest indoor shopping mall in the world and a tourist destination for visitors from Japan and elsewhere, it was one place where he knew he would be able to get all the items on his list in one trip.

By the time he returned from his shopping spree, he had assembled an outfit that would pass for one of the black uniforms of the local police SWAT team. Close up, it would fool nobody, but, from a distance, it was insurance against being spotted on the roof of the hotel. Anyone not in the know would just assume he was part of the security detail.

While he waited for the concierge lounge to close, he treated himself to room service: a pulled chicken sandwich and spinach salad from Max, the restaurant on the corner that the concierge in the lobby had praised. He finished neither the salad nor the sandwich.

Once the hallway traffic thinned out, he scouted the stairwells for roof access, carefully jimmying the locks he picked so he could make his way quickly and quietly back to the roof when needed. Returning to his room, he stretched out on the still-made bed to catch a few hours of sleep.

— — —

Sergi sat bolt upright. It was ten minutes after three in the morning, time to make his way to the roof. It would be a cold remainder of the night spent huddled on the roof, but he couldn't take a chance on being spotted on the way up during daylight.

Once on the roof, he zipped up the black jumpsuit over his down jacket, slipped on his padded motorcycle helmet, also black, and curled up on the lee side of the service entrance. He slept fitfully and awakened with stiff limbs and fingers in time to peek over the edge and watch the sharpshooters deploying themselves on buildings overlooking the plaza.

Sergi mounted the scope on his Israeli-made M36 rifle and set it up with the bipod on the edge of the roof. As he waited, he followed pedestrians through the scope and timed them as they crossed the plaza. His field of view was limited by the glass pedestrian bridge and the parking garage where one sharpshooter was already positioned below him. There would be little time. The prisoners would be surrounded by police and would be moving targets as they were hustled quickly across the street and the open plaza. He decided he would wait until the prisoners were being escorted back from the courthouse, counting on the security detail being a tiny fraction less alert on the return after an uneventful delivery to the building.

Sergi considered worst-case scenarios and concluded that he might have as little as four or five seconds to take out both targets. The guards would probably not react when the first bullet struck—it would be traveling at more than twice the speed of sound—and his compact rifle was equipped with a reasonably effective suppressor. If they heard the shot at all, they would hear it a little over half second after the bullet struck. By the time they finally reacted after another three-quarters of a second or so, then took effective action, a couple of seconds would have passed, long enough for Sergi to get his second shot off. He rehearsed the precise and minute moves he would need to make in going from one shot to the next. The M36 was a semi-automatic; if necessary, he could immediately get off a second round before moving to the other target. A second shot would be needed in either case only if he bungled the first; a 7.62x51 NATO round to the head could not be survived at this range.

He had checked out the wind pattern between the closely spaced tall buildings of the area while walking around the day before. The morning had dawned with typically still air, but the wind was already picking up, generating streamers and swirls in the light dusting of overnight snow. Sergi checked the direction, made a quick estimate of wind speed, unchanged from yesterday, and consulted the app on his smartphone to compute a firing solution that even took into account the temperature and atmospheric pressure it read directly from the phone's built-in sensors. Despite the modest 250-meter range, with a small, moving target and so little time for a clean first shot, he knew he could not rely on just his experience-honed instincts. He was finishing the last adjustment on the rifle sights when the patrol cars arrived to block off the streets around the jail and courthouse. He would recheck windage when the prisoners first reemerged from the courthouse. He looked up from his adjustments in time to spot the group crossing the street.

There was a problem. Only one prisoner was huddled in the middle of the circle of officers. A second group started across a few seconds later. The prisoners had been split up. If they emerged from the courthouse separated by this much, it would be very difficult to take out both targets.

He watched the two groups enter the heavily guarded entrance to the courthouse. As the second group disappeared inside, he checked his watch. Fifteen minutes for arraignment, twenty if there were hiccups. He waited.

Forty minutes passed with no signs of the prisoners leaving. What if they were led out another way? No, the sharpshooters were still in place. Just wait, he told himself.

Sergi jumped to full alertness when the first group came out of the courthouse and started moving quickly across the plaza. He followed them through the scope with his other eye open to spot when the second group emerged. The first group was almost across the plaza and would be out of his sight in just seconds. He had to take the shot or scrub the whole operation. Just as he prepared to squeeze the trigger, the second group appeared—from a different door. He took the shot, pivoted the rifle, and shifted his body, but from his vantage point, he could not get the second target's head in the crosshairs.

The guards in the first group were now crouched on the pavement and looking up in his direction. They started firing, and Sergi ducked before realizing they were firing at the police sharpshooter positioned below him. The sharpshooter was yelling at them to hold their fire, that he was police.

At the same time, the officers around the other prisoner made a mistake. Instead of ducking back into the building, they hustled the prisoner in a direction away from Sergi's position. Sergi cradled his M36 and ran with it along the edge of the roof to get a better angle. The police marksman below heard his running steps and turned toward him. Just as Sergi reached the corner, the policeman commenced firing. Sergi felt a sting in his side as he flattened himself on the roof. He calmly thrust the rifle in front of him, panned to lead the running prisoner, and squeezed off two shots.

Chapter 30

THE LARGE-SCREEN TV in the Hyatt Regency lounge was turned up too high for Ben and Marwa to ignore the morning news.

"... and in a bizarre twist that brings to mind the killing of Lee Harvey Oswald by Jack Ruby, police in Minneapolis were escorting two suspected terrorists from court early this morning when they were fired upon by a sniper. Both suspects were killed outright. Police returned fire, and the sniper, shooting from the roof of a nearby hotel, was shot and killed by police marksmen on another building. Police do not know the identity of the assailant, who was staying at the hotel and had paid for the room with a corporate credit card that police say has been traced to a shell company in the Cayman Islands. The FBI is taking over the investigation because the prisoners had been bound over into federal custody at the time of the shooting.

"Authorities have yet to disclose the identities of the two prisoners, both residents of the Cedar-Riverside area of Minneapolis, also known as Little Somalia. They were being held in connection with the suicide bombing earlier this week at the Radisson Blu Hotel in downtown Minneapolis. An FBI spokesman would not speculate on motives for either the bombing or the shooting today. The suicide bomber has now been identified as Ahmed Ibrahim, a resident of Riverside Plaza. Six members of the American-Israeli Business Forum were killed in the blast; a seventh person, a middle-school student attending the meeting as a guest observer, is still in critical condition at the Pediatric Trauma Center in the Hennepin County Medical Center."

"Now, from Boston, this story: Abdi Farah, an unemployed truck driver from Portland, Maine, has died, presumably from gunshot wounds, in Boston's Mass General Hospital. Farah was captured yesterday after allegedly shooting and killing philanthropist Abraham Sackman and his driver in Gloucester, Massachusetts. That shooting took place within fifteen minutes of the time of the Radisson suicide bombing. Authorities declined to comment on any possible connection. A spokesman for the hospital said that the patient had improved since admission, and his status had been upgraded from critical to serious, but he died suddenly while still in intensive care. The immediate cause of death has not been determined; an autopsy is planned."

Marwa grabbed Ben's arm. "See? It's the Somali connection, a common thread that somehow ties these two simultaneous attacks to the downing of the plane and ultimately to a notorious Palestinian terrorist."

"The ties are awfully tenuous."

"Not if we could actually get access to the cell phone metadata and find out who our passenger called in the United States."

"It's not all Somali's anyway. Some of this news is about the Somali's being killed. It doesn't compute. Unless ..."

"Unless?"

"Unless the Somalis knew something, and these latest killings in Boston and Minneapolis were intended to keep them from talking. Let's finish up here and get over to Scenaria. Maybe their hotshot hackers have gotten access to the CAASS system. If so, we can plunge ahead with these leads."

—— —— ——

Ben and Marwa were back in their temporary office at Scenaria when there was a triple knock on the door jamb. The Chinese-American who entered sported a shaved head and eyebrows like two wooly-bear caterpillars. "Hi, I'm Dune Huang. I used to head one of the teams down in The Vault. They found a way into the system up at your Center and set up a tunnel and a proxy you can reach at this address." He handed them a strip of paper with a string of numbers on it.

"How in hell did you manage that. The Center uses the best firewalls and security software that taxpayer money can buy."

"Exactly. That means they use our security software. Nobody knows that system better than our software engineers. We recently found a new vulnerability, a way to bypass it. It's a previously unknown and never-used exploit, something left over from some very old code that dates back to the early days of the company and somehow never got patched. We'll quietly release an upgrade to fix it in a few days. In the meantime, make yourselves at home in their network but try not to do anything to call attention to your presence. If they spot you, it'll be easy for them to pull the plug, maybe to track you back to here. That wouldn't be good for any of us."

"We'll be careful. It'll be a read-only break-in. Thanks."

"You're welcome. But try to limit how much you use the access. Big data going through the tunnel could attract attention, too. Good luck." He smiled and left.

They were testing out the backdoor access to the CAASS computers when Sam Parsons arrived. Ben scowled and shook his head in confusion. "What are you doing here, Parsons? Doesn't the NTSB give you weekends off?"

"It's my own time. I thought I'd help by kibitzing and sharing a couple of pieces of information."

"Share away," he said.

"It's not the FBI on your tail."

"No? How do you know that?"

"Inside sources."

Before Sam could say more, DB showed up outside the door wearing cargo shorts and a company logo tee shirt. "Did I hear somebody say something about the FBI?"

"You heard me saying that the guys in the black sedan yesterday were not from the FBI, according to my sources there."

"Well, whoever they are, they're back today. I think it might be time I call in some muscle to get to the bottom of this. The last CEO inherited a Rolodex when the founder left for parts unknown, and he passed it on to me. I think I know just who to call on. I'll be back to check in on you all later."

== == ==

The call was answered with a curt "Saltmarsh."

DB was thrown off. "Is this Brian Mallory?"

"Who's asking?"

"You may not remember me, but I used to work for Richard Talpa when he was running Scenaria. The name's Douglass Botteneau. Everyone called me DB back then. Still do."

"Oh, yeah, I remember. You were into first-person shooter games, if I recall. Developed quite a knack for quick reflexes and accurate shots under pressure. Where are you working now?"

"Still at Scenaria, only now I run the place. I took over as CEO after Harry Krebber had his heart attack."

"Good for you. What can I do for you?"

DB explained his surveillance problem.

"You want me to stop them or just find out who they are?"

"Let's start by finding out who they are, then we can decide whether to stop them."

"Sure thing. You know, Talpa had a special billing arrangement with Saltmarsh Services."

"Whatever it was, we'll work out something equivalent."

"Our services are not cheap."

"I assumed so. Talpa was not one to spare the expense when it came to protecting himself."

"No he wasn't. I'll get right on it but can't promise when I'll have something."

"I understand. You know where to find me."

"I do. That's my job."

— — —

DB was in his office reviewing year-end financial projections when the weekend Security Coordinator came rushing into his office. "Mr. Botteneau, there's something going on out front that I think you should know about. Police cruisers are blocking both ends of the road, and they got guys with their guns drawn approaching that black sedan that's been hanging around since yesterday."

DB and the Security Coordinator arrived at the front entrance in time to see the sedan, it's tires smoking, pull out and swerve around one of the officers. The car fishtailed as it sped toward the building. It skidded into the Scenaria parking lot and headed for the closed rear gate, crashing through it and speeding out onto the dirt service road beyond. Within seconds, the two police cruisers tore across the parking lot in pursuit and plunged into the dust cloud stirred up by the fleeing sedan.

"Well, I guess that's conclusive: definitely not FBI."

"What did you say, sir?"

"Nothing. Get someone to take care of that busted gate right away."

Back in his office, DB tried to concentrate on the forecasts, but his mind was shuffling through possible scenarios. The phone startled him, and he took his time answering.

"It's Mallory here. Just wanted you to know it was my boys out front, not the cops. They already nabbed the Ford Fairlane. It was driven by a couple of rent-a-cop types hired by somebody to keep an eye on your guests. Clueless amateurs. And they don't know who hired them. It was a cash deal from a walk-in. I'll have my guys follow up, but don't get your hopes up. Those clowns were amateurs, but I have a hunch their client is not. I'll keep you posted."

— — —

Brian Mallory did not belong behind a desk. A big man, proud of his mixed Irish-American and Native-American ancestry, he had started his own agency after retiring from the FBI. Saltmarsh Services LLC was a one-stop-shopping security group staffed by ex-warriors and field agents: graduates of the FBI, the CIA, and veterans of any of a long series of bungled American interventions beginning with Vietnam. Brian himself had been on one kind of battlefield or another ever since enlisting as a college dropout to serve in Vietnam, where he had lost his right thumb. That had earned him the nickname Lucky Duck because the land mine that had cost him his thumb had left his platoon leader legless. Now Brian knew he was in his last battle—and the cancer was winning.

Scenaria, or at least a succession of its top managers, had been among the agency's best clients over the years. Saltmarsh had provided protection, had carried out investigations, and had located resources that could not ordinarily be obtained on the open market. Brian Mallory was not one to judge the politics or the ethics of his clients, as long as he and his men—and all but a handful of his crew were men—stayed clean and safe.

He scanned the folder on the new CEO to jog his memory. Along with several black question marks, there were two red bullet points in the executive summary on Douglass Botteneau. He had been implicated in some shady commercial dealings by the company founder, Richard Talpa, but neither had ever been charged. Mallory knew Talpa well, having saved his life in Vietnam and covered his ass on multiple occasions since. The second red flag noted that Botteneau had once been in a fire-fight with a bunch of eco-terrorists who ended up, surprisingly, getting the rough end of the deal. That, too, had been quietly papered over. Brian, who had done work for both of Botteneau's predecessors, knew the man to be a choir boy by comparison.

He handed the folder back to Suze Kerchoff, one of the few of his distaff field staff. He wished he could recruit more like her, but it was not easy finding women with the talents and tenacity his agency required. "Make this current, flesh it out, and see what you can dig up about any of the highlighted links. And remember, Botteneau is our client; we always protect our clients."

Suze, who stood a half inch taller than Brian and could some-how look sexy in fatigues, was a former MP who had seen two deployments in Iraq before being assigned to a Stryker brigade in Afghanistan. There she was wounded at a temporary Detainee Collection Point she was overseeing when the DCP was overrun by Taliban-affiliated tribal forces. Given that she was a good ten years Brian's junior, she could quite probably best him in a mixed martial arts match. Brian had always liked her and now was beginning to regret that he had never put the moves on her.

"I'll take care of this, sir," she said, "and I'll take care of our chubby client."

"That's an old photo of him. By now he might be morbidly obese—or slimmer than you. Who knows? Just find a way to keep an eye on him while you are following these other tracks. I'm going to work another angle from here. I'm wondering why Botteneau thought those clowns were FBI. I'm going to have to get back in touch with some of my old Bureau buddies."

-- -- --

Arkady Pohl slipped his cellphone back in his jacket pocket. Two calls in two days, and both of them linked to Scenaria. The call from Tank Parsons had been a surprise; the call from Brian Mallory was a kick upside the head. Arkady twirled his rollerball pen like a propeller as he tried to decide what to do next.

He could not just let it all drop. If his brother was somehow involved, the matter was neither simple nor small. With this latest call, he had agreed to meet Brian for a drink; to do otherwise would have been unthinkable and might have triggered some of Brian's investigative instincts, which were formidable. Arkady did not want the Indian-Irish Bulldog, as Mallory had been known when he was with the Bureau, chewing at his leg.

Raise the stakes, he told himself. He checked his watch and made a call. "Brian? It's Arkady Pohl again. Listen, can we change the venue? The Bureau is sending me out to Dulles this afternoon. Do you know a bar called The Sting? Right, that's the one, just outside Reston. I'll meet you there, five-thirty, might be a little later, but I'll be there."

Arkady knew the bar was a favorite watering hole of several top Scenaria people. It would push the topic to the fore and maybe create some opportunities for chance encounters that were not entirely chance. He decided to place another call and better the odds.

Chapter 31

BEN STOOD, STRETCHED, and walked around the conference table to stand behind Marwa. As he approached, she quickly switched from an email window back to a graphic application, covering the screen of her laptop with a spider-web of crossing lines connecting tiny colored triangles, diamonds, and circles. As he watched, she dragged shapes around, occasionally stopping to right-click for a popup form that she filled with notes. "More sociograms?" he said.

She looked up at him. "Yeah, but this is not very scientific."

He laughed. "And that's something new and different?"

She reached back to give him a playful whack on the arm. "Yes, this is, like, it's all fudging the data and, well, futzing around with it. Trying different ways to picture it and tease out patterns."

"Dr. Woolyard would approve."

She stiffened. "What do you mean?"

"I mean he liked your sort of stuff, that's all. Have you heard anything from him or anyone else at CAASS?"

"Uh, not really. I guess they are wondering where we are, what's up."

"Mmmm. What exactly is up? What are you trying to do with your boxes and arrows?"

"I'm attempting to track Somalis, see what's with the Somali connection."

"Aren't you making too much of the Somali thing? It's not like Somalis are the enemy. They're not all radical Islamists."

"I know, I know. We all know. " Her voice mixed fatigue with mild mockery. "I'm sure most Somali immigrants are peace-loving, law-abiding, and non-violent. So are most Palestinians, most whatever, but we don't hear them, do we; we hear the extremists. Do you know the song 'Parallel Lines'? No? It's by Blue-Green Algae Invasion, a rap-metal group of Palestinians and Israelis from Jerusalem," She tapped out a hip-hop rhythm on the conference table, closed her eyes, and started rapping:

> Parallel lines:
>> parallel lines of opposing signs,
>> a shouting match of repeated attacks.
> And in the middle, between,
> Too subdued to be heard above the slogans and
>> screams,
> The voices of the many all murmur a dream.
> A fanatical few invoking The Name:
>> faithful fundamentalists and true reactionaries,
>> orthodox extremists and revolutionaries,
> True believers all distinctive
>> but all sounding the same.

Marwa stopped abruptly, opened her eyes, and looked around with an expression of acute embarrassment. "Well, you get the idea."

"Wow. No, I never heard that one. Never was too big on punk poetry, but there's a lot of truth there. You know, you really have the touch, sound like the real thing. Maybe you could have had a career in pop music."

"Ugh, not pop. Punk maybe. I was so into that scene when I was in college that I considered dropping out to become lead vocalist in a metal-core band started by an ex-boyfriend. Anyway, by definition, it's the extremes of the distribution that we're interested in. The average citizen doesn't crash planes or assassinate prisoners."

Their discussion of politics and poetry was interrupted by Sam Parsons returning after the excitement out front had died down. He was followed a minute later by DB, who apologized as he entered. "Sorry about all the disruption. It seems whoever was keeping an eye on us—or you—is definitely not the FBI and is now heading cross-country.

"I also apologize because I think I interrupted Sam earlier. You were about to say something?"

"Oh, right, I was. I got a text message from Singapore, a contact who was helping with Operation Flight Track. The message had a link to a YouTube video of two kittens playing with a paper bag."

Marwa gave him a raised-eyebrows look. "What?"

"Ben has probably already guessed this one."

"Yes, I have. I'm guessing video steganography. The real message is hidden in altered pixels of the video."

"Right, and it took a bit to extract the message in code, which included excerpts from a transcript of the interrogation of a prisoner. I'll spare you the rather unpleasant details, but before the prisoner allegedly committed suicide while in custody, he spoke of plans to attack targets in the United States."

"Passenger planes?"

"No, people, prominent people, rich and influential Jewish supporters of Israel. The man—"

Marwa cut him off. "Ohmagod, the Somali jihadists, that's what they were up to; that's the thread that links them. Who was this prisoner?"

"Abu Omar's right-hand man, an Islamist named al-Masri."

Marwa was triumphant. "That proves the connection with the flight."

Ben squinted. "I'm not sure it qualifies as proof, but I would call it very suggestive. So, did they miscalculate? Were they hoisted by their own petard? Or maybe the group on the flight was supposed to be part of this operation, but they didn't make it. Instead, their plane ends up crashed into the ocean, hijacked by someone else."

Marwa nodded in grave assent. "And maybe they were not the only team that didn't make it. There was that pair coming from London that—"

Sam plunged in. "What ever happened with them, anyway?"

"I don't know. I've been too busy to check all my news feeds." She started tapping on the laptop keyboard, then scrolled down through a series of headlines and summaries. "Here it is. 'Suspected terrorists shot and killed during escape attempt outside London.' Escape attempt. Yeah, right. Okay, here's the synopsis. 'Members of a previously unknown terrorist group were being transported to the Vauxhall Cross headquarters of the SIS for interrogation when, in an apparent attempt to free the prisoners, an unmarked lorry cut off the van carrying them. In the ensuing gun battle, the prisoners were caught in the crossfire and suffered fatal multiple gunshot wounds. During the melee, the occupants of the lorry fled on foot and have somehow eluded all attempts to locate them.'" Marwa sneered. "Somehow?"

Sam sat down across from Marwa. "It does sound like a setup of some kind. But if these were attempts to stop terrorist teams from entering the country to carry out a mission, that leaves us considering the disturbing notion that an entire planeload of people was wiped out to thwart the attack. And it didn't work. A bunch of wealthy targets were taken out, anyway."

"All by Somali radicals," Ben added. "Or at least as far as we know, which means it could have been one small group, a single domestic cell of homegrown terrorists. But let's follow the implications. If this screwball theory about PT20 is true, what about the Malaysian flight a while back? It makes no sense at all. It happened long before these incidents."

Sam leaned back in his chair and clasped his hands behind his head. "Exactly. As if it were a trial run."

No one spoke until DB grunted. "Who would kill hundreds of innocent people just for a test?"

"Terrorists." Ben answered quickly. "How many died in the Twin Towers? Terrorists behead journalists just to make a point, they slaughtered thousands who happen to pray in the wrong way. Why not wipe out a planeload for a trial run?"

There was no answer. Marwa broke the silence. "Maybe we are going about this all the wrong way. Ben and I have been awash in rivers of data and buried beneath mountains of models, digging, digging for something to answer our questions. Maybe we need to step back and reconsider what questions we're asking and how we're trying to answer them. We need to get our noses out of our screens and start scribbling questions on a whiteboard."

Ben walked over to the whiteboard on the far wall, picked up a marker, and drew several squiggly red question marks. "Done."

"Ah, Ben, what are we going to do with you."

DB pushed himself back from the conference table. "Well, with that, I'll leave you three to have at it. I still have a company to run and a report to get out by Monday."

Ben put out his arm. "No, please don't go just yet. Don't you remember, the power plant attacks. It was working together as a group that solved the problem. It took more heads knocking together to figure it out. We should do some brainstorming. Here, Marwa, you're better at this stuff than I am." She took the marker from him and they swapped places.

"Okay, let's start back at square one with flight PT20," she said. "What, if anything, is unusual about this flight? I mean, besides that it went missing."

Ben kicked in the first idea. "The plane was on its first scheduled flight."

Sam followed. "It had just had two of its computer boards replaced."

"Okay, I'll play," DB said. "It left hours late."

"That much is not unusual," Sam said.

"Yes, but it was late because it had unscheduled maintenance and had taken on last minute cargo." Marwa underlined it as she wrote the idea down.

"I'm still playing," DB said, "but I don't know your rules. Can we ask questions here? Do we know what the cargo was, who or where it came from?"

"Sure, questions are good." She wrote 'What? Who? Where?' after the cargo item.

"Yeah, and we have been entirely focused on who and what were on the plane rather than who and what were not on the plane."

"What do you mean, Ben?"

"You said it yourself, Marwa, when you went over the passenger manifest. Wasn't there a no-show, and the luggage had to be pulled at the last minute?"

"I did, you're right." She wrote 'No-show?' on the whiteboard.

Ben rose and drew a sloppy triangle that joined three of the questions. "Look at this, three last-minute events, anomalous actions. New cargo, new computer boards, and a passenger who came and went. What if these go together?"

"What do you mean?"

"I don't know. Yet. Can we get more information on the shipment and the passenger? Is Singapore following up on either of these?"

Parsons slipped his jacket back on. "If you all will excuse me, I can send a text to Singapore. The day hasn't even started over there, but the message will be waiting when they get up."

\-\- \-\- \-\-

Peter Ma heard his phone buzz on the nightstand beside his bed. He picked it up and slipped out of bed without awakening his wife. In the kitchen, he read the message from his NTSB contact. He already knew the answer to the first question but not the second. He was embarrassed to think that he had not followed up on the passenger who had checked in but failed to board the flight. If he answered only the one question now, he would lose face. It would look like he didn't know his job and had failed. The contact back in the US would not expect a reply for hours. He could go into the office early and work on the no-show passenger. It was so obvious, how had he missed it?

Part Five: Cryptography
Chapter 32

DB WAS NURSING A Haymaker as he sat with Maude Girard, who was two drinks ahead of him, and Dune Huang, who was not drinking and never did. Dune had taken over as Chief Technical Officer when DB had moved up to become CEO. Maude, the only woman in the nerdy Threat Analysis group was now temporarily leading the team. As the only current employee in Threat Analysis with anything approaching management potential, she had DB's attention, and he was keeping an eye out for the right time and slot to move her out of The Vault.

The Sting was crowded and noisy, with a honky-tonk player pounding out ragtime at the upright piano across the room and people talking over each other and the music. In the midst of too-loud shop talk about the recent Black Hat hackers convention, DB noticed a woman at one of the tables eyeing them. She seemed to be interested in Dune, but it was hard to tell. Poor girl, Dune was as gay as mardi gras. It would be fun but cruel to let it play out. DB took another sip of his drink as Maude and Dune debated how best to gain remote access to a police cruiser through its onboard computers. When he looked up again, the woman was approaching.

"Aren't you Dune Huang?" she said as she slipped into the middle of the huddle. "I recognize you from your picture in Beltway Bytes Weekly. You recently got promoted or something at some computer company around here, am I right? Forgive me for being so forward, but I really liked what you said in that interview about preventing an escalation of cyber warfare on the Internet."

Dune smiled at her and glanced past her to DB. "Well, thank you. Yeah, you're right, that interview was last year. I'm now CTO at Scenaria, just down the road."

"Well, I'm Suze Kerchoff." She took his hand and held it as she talked. "I work in IT, too, but nothing glamorous: accounting. Mind if I join you?"

"Er, no, sure. Pull up a stool. This is Maude Girard, one of my brilliant software bug-and-virus people, and behind you is my boss, Douglass Botteneau."

Suze nodded to Maude, gave a perfunctory greeting to DB, and zoomed in on Dune. DB was wondering how long it would be before Dune let her down easy. He didn't have to wait much. With the woman gushing over the glamour of cyber-threat analysis with Dune and Maude, Dune got down off his stool and excused himself. "Sorry, but I really have to go. I promised to meet my husband for dinner. It was nice meeting you, Suze. Hope to see you around. And if you ever get tired of doing accounting for whomever, come look us up." He handed her a business card and walked away.

DB shifted over onto Dune's vacated stool so he could join the conversation without talking to the woman's back. She was a little older than he was and a little taller, and he found himself warming to some strong presence she seemed to exude. She was so into the chat with Maude that he had ample time to study her face. It was a face that carried her years well, marked by creases that added character and projected a serious determination. He was already hoping she would follow up on Dune's invitation.

"I really have to go, too." Suze stepped down and away from the barstool with the taut grace of a circus cat. "It was fun talking with you, Maude. You really have a fascinating job. I wish I could say the same for mine." She half turned toward DB and held out her hand. "And it was nice meeting you, too. Maybe next time we'll get more of a chance to talk." There was sincerity in her tone and in the pressure of her hand.

As Suze slipped away into the crowd, Sam Parsons walked into the bar, looked around, and made a beeline for them. "Well, look who's here. Hi, DB." He faced Maude. "Hi, I'm Sam Parsons, NTSB. I'm ... doing some consulting with DB here."

"I'm Maude Girard, and I work for DB. Were you looking for him? I saw you looking around."

"No, actually, I confess I was supposed to meet somebody else. And there he is, heading our way."

DB looked genuinely surprised as Arkady Pohl approached. He waited as Sam and Arkady exchanged greetings and Maude introduced herself. He reached around to offer his hand to Arkady. "Agent Pohl, what brings you out our way? More international intrigue? Alleged intrigue, I should say. It's always alleged, isn't it."

Arkady stood his ground. "I thought your interests were more into data breaches and security software with spyware embedded in it."

DB was irritated at the thinly disguised dig but was at a loss for a response. "Actually, Parsons and I—and some others— are working on an independent research project." Sam gave him a look that said to drop it. Arkady's eyes darted back and forth between the two men, but he said nothing. Maude, growing uncomfortable at a situation she didn't quite understand, slipped down from her barstool and swayed next to it. DB took her arm to steady her. "I'll call you a cab, Maude. My thanks to you for all the overtime work."

"S'nothing." She grabbed at the barstool to keep from falling.

"But the cab's pro'ly a good idea."

When DB returned from seeing Maude into a taxi, Sam and Arkady abruptly stopped their conversation. He smiled. "Does this by any chance have anything to do with a difference of opinion, or maybe a difference of methods, regarding the last time you two worked together, or should I say didn't work together?"

The two of them looked at each other. Sam answered. "I think it has more to do with this time, right now, when we're still not working together. More of what you were talking about earlier, about putting our cards on the table, what we know but are not supposed to know. Agent Pohl hasn't anted up yet and is not playing by the same rules."

Pohl bristled. "You are speculating, Parsons, and working beyond your skillset, probably beyond your pay grade. The NTSB and the Bureau are not even playing on the same field, much less the same game. Stick to what you know. Pipelines, planes, whatever. We are not called the Federal Bureau of Investigation for nothing."

"Do you want me to make a scene here?"

"Do you want me to place you under arrest here?"

DB put himself between the two men. "Wouldn't you two like to take this conversation to somewhere less public? Let's go back to my office. I'll drive."

As they were heading toward the parking lot via the side door, Brian Mallory was entering by the front. He took a quick survey of the place, spotted Arkady at the tail end of the group as it exited, and immediately made a U-turn.

— — —

"Here, gentlemen, we can use Conference Room B." DB opened the door and smiled, then winked at Marwa and Ben. "Oh, wonderful, you're still here. Look who's back: our NTSB pal, Sam Parsons. Come on in, Sam. And the man standing in the hall displaying his displeasure is another old friend, our FBI pal, Agent Arkady Pohl. This little conference room looks like it's becoming the nerve center of a clandestine cartel or something.

"Pohl, I don't think you know these two. Meet Marwa and Ben. First names will do for now. Please, everybody. have a seat." He waited for Arkady to enter the room, then closed the door. "Ben, will you do the honors of bringing Agent Pohl up to speed on what we are working on?"

"Everything?"

"Sure, the good agent is here on his own, not on behalf of the Bureau, am I right?"

Arkady gritted his teeth.

"Right, so give him the précis, Ben."

Ben spelled out a cloud-level overview of what they had been doing and their tentative guesses about what was going on.

Arkady swept his index finger in an arc. "You realize, all of you, how many laws you've broken?"

"So, arrest us." DB held out his arms, wrists together.

"I'm not here to arrest you."

"Then what are you here for?"

"Originally to see what you have. Now, to warn you off."

Sam pointed sideways at Arkady. "As I told you all, this man knows something."

"I know a lot of things, many of them things that I could never share with you. I also know some things that my telling you would pin targets onto your backs."

"Then we'll just have to figure them out on our own."

"I hope not. There is some knowledge that it is dangerous to have, regardless of how it comes into your possession."

Ben fluttered his fingers in front of him. "Very scary, like an old Hollywood B-movie. Cue organ music." Arkady pressed his lips closed as Ben persisted. "You might as well tell us, because we're closing in on answers anyway."

"No, I won't be a party to your suicide, because that's what it would amount to." As Arkady started to stand, the phone in Sam's pocket beeped for an incoming text message.

Sam's face lit up with excitement as he read the message. "Yes!" He pumped his fist. "We got it. Listen to this. First, the delayed cargo was a pallet of electronics from a manufacturer in Singapore that is being looked into. And there's more. Singapore identified the no-show passenger but he had already left the country and returned to Malaysia. However, when he didn't show up to claim his luggage, the airport impounded it. In the mess following the diversion of PT20, the luggage was set aside and forgotten, along with the passenger, it seems. ISD is now studying the contents of the suitcase, which includes—get this—a laptop that was in hibernation because it had been left turned on in the case."

Ben was bouncing in his chair, and Arkady had paled.

"But, here's the best part. My contact is going to get an image of the contents of the hard drive and upload it to a dropbox for us to study."

Arkady looked like he was going to be sick. "Remember Pandora. Don't open this box."

"Then tell us why not."

"I'm a dead man if I do, Maybe I'm already dead. Probably all of you are dead as well."

"Very dramatic." Marwa clapped quietly. "Deserving of an Oscar for overacting. You make it sound like some monstrous malevolent conspiracy, some invisible empire with its tendrils into everything everywhere. That's the stuff of comic books and ..."

Ben finished her thought for her. "And conspiracy-theory wingnuts who blog for other nut cases. In the real world, stuff like that doesn't fly. It's impossible for one good reason: there are always leaks, always people in the know who let on. If there were anything like that, we'd know, or at least the CIA or Mossad would know. That's their business. They know things."

Arkady said nothing.

"If we are wrong, tell us."

"I really can't help you." He stood and leaned on the table as he looked sadly to each one in turn. "I'm serious, I'm telling you, be smart and drop this." He straightened up and left the conference room.

"What should we do?" DB waited for a response in the silent the room.

Ben looked at Marwa. "All in or nothing." She nodded and Sam followed suit.

"All right, then." DB reached for the phone in the middle of the conference table and punched four digits. "Hello. This is Botteneau. The man coming toward the front entrance, don't let him leave the building." He hung up, then pulled a cellphone from his pocket and hit redial. "It's me. We need you at Scenaria. Now."

Chapter 33

THE SCENARIA SECURITY GUARD posted at the reception desk was just a kid in his late twenties with a receding jaw and a pale face pocked by acne scars. He looked like he might lose his lunch at any moment. Brian Mallory winked at him. "I hear you have a situation."

"The man ... the man ... " He fought to control his stammer. "He says he's with the FBI. The boss says to hold 'im. What can I do? I don't want to lose my job, and I don't want to be facing federal charges."

"Don't sweat it, kid. I'll take care of it. Where is he?"

"Down the hall, in Conference Room A. I put the cuffs on him and took his piece. I really hope I'm not in trouble like he says."

Brian reassured the guard again. At the conference room, he opened the door slowly, took a look around, and then guffawed. "What in hell, Arkady? What manure heap did you land in this time? I thought we were supposed to meet for drinks at The Sting. I waited and waited. Finally got this call from an old buddy, had to push away the broad that was comin' on to me."

"Get these fuckin' cuffs off me, you half-breed idiot. Get 'em off so I can get to a phone and have everyone in this whole damn place arrested."

"Now that's no way to greet an old Bureau buddy, is it?"

"Don't old-Bureau-buddy me, Brian Mallory. Just unlock these cuffs, dammit. We can talk after I see the whole damn company brought up on federal charges."

"Now that there is most unfriendly, Arkady. You wouldn't want to cause no trouble for these nice people here. And you certainly wouldn't want to cause no trouble for me. By the way, whatever did happen to that young couple you were supposed to bring in for questioning on that pipeline caper? Lost 'em somewhere in upstate New York, if I got the story right. Did they really give you the slip? Or did you let them go? I always wondered."

"You can't blackmail me, Mallory."

"Who said anything about blackmail? Just wondering about setting the record straight. Course, that ain't all to the record that might need straightening, now is it? Little matter of Panama, right? And then there's your big brother?" He shook his head. "You know what they say, Arkady, about throwin' the first stone."

"Fuck you, Mallory."

"Well, okay, if that's how you want it. I'll just go and have me a chat with the good people here while you think about your options and your next move." He turned out the light and left Arkady fuming in the dark.

-- -- --

Brian returned to Conference Room A after talking with DB and meeting the rest of his ad hoc A-team. "You ready to play nice, Arkady? Or should I see if I can get your brother to come talk some sense into you?"

"Don't joke like that, Brian. Don't. This is a hell of a lot bigger and messier than you think."

"Yeah, I'm getting that idea. And knowin' your brother, big and messy might as well be tattooed on his forehead. You, you're neither as big nor nearly as messy. So let's just you and me go see how we can help out my friends here."

"That's what I was trying to do when they kidnapped me. I warned them, but they wouldn't listen."

"Well, maybe we should just talk through that warning of yours in a mite more detail." He unlocked the cuffs. They rattled as he tossed them on the table. "Then you know what? I think all of us, every jack one of us, should get some sleep. Let things kinda sort themselves out. Nothin' like a good night's sleep to make things in the morning look easier." He extended his hand to Arkady who shrugged it off and mumbled something that Brian took to be Slavic cursing. "Whatever you think, we are more likely to find a way through the brush if we help each other." He held the door as Arkady pushed through, still mumbling.

As he followed Arkady down the hall, Brian struggled against a wave of pain that spread like scalding water from a spot behind his stomach.

Chapter 34

THE PAIRED SPIRES OF Kuala Lumpur's iconic Petronas Towers, once the tallest buildings in the world, were blurred behind a scrim of ozone and hydrocarbon-heavy haze. Peter Ma hated Kuala Lumpur as much as he loved Singapore. Both were bustling, overcrowded East Asian cities, but in Singapore the streets were clean and safe, life was predictable, and the air was rarely this opaque. Technically, Ma should have passed his information on to the Malaysian authorities, but Peter had a low opinion of the KL police. He would have to bring them in on the case eventually, but he wanted to be the first to talk with the man.

For anyone who didn't mind the sun and smog, the address he sought was within a fifteen-minute walk of the Petronas Towers; otherwise, it was a twenty-minute ride in an air-conditioned taxi through turtle-paced traffic. The modest computer repair shop, not much more than a store front in a row of dingy street-level shops, seemed empty. Peter entered, tripping an infrared beam and setting off a synthesized bell tone, an arpeggiated minor chord that kept repeating until a man emerged from the back room and pressed a button under the counter. The man's head strained upward from a neck that was bent permanently down almost to the horizontal. His angular face looked much younger than the hunched and twisted body suggested. "*Selemat pagi,*" he greeted Peter in Malay. "Good morning. What can I do for you young man?"

"You repair computers, right?"

"Yes, that's what my sign says. You have a computer that needs repair?"

"I do, it looks like this." He showed the picture of the impounded laptop.

The man nervously licked his lips. "Many laptop computers look like that." He took the photo from Peter and studied it. "This is a cheap generic computer ... maybe from Taiwan, I think."

"It may be cheap, but this computer is special, however, because it was checked baggage on a flight from Singapore to Chicago. You were booked on that flight, Mr. Braud. You checked in but then you never boarded the plane. You left the airport and returned by train to Kuala Lumpur. So what do you think about this computer now?"

Braud took two steps back and stood, like a man-sized bobble-head doll, his head bouncing in slow, involuntary tremors. "Who are you? Are you from the police? Your accent is ..."

"I'm Peter Ma, with Singapore Internal Security." He brought out his badge case.

"I ... I did nothing. I ... I didn't know. I was afraid that it was a bomb or something. I got scared and left the airport. Then, when the plane was hijacked, I didn't dare say anything." The photo shook in his hand. "He asked me to make some changes and install some software and ... and deliver the computer in person to a man in Chicago. He paid for the ticket, round trip, and promised to give me 20,000 Ringgit for my trouble."

"He asked you. Who asked you?"

"I ... I really don't know. I've done some work for him a few times before. He telephones, tells me what he wants, I make the hardware changes or configure software, then he picks it up and pays in cash."

"This time, what did he want you to do?"

"He wanted me to replace the battery with a high capacity unit and to upgrade the radio with a better Wi-Fi module. He also wanted special software installed that he had found on the Internet. He gave me the web address for the download. I was told to launch the software before closing the laptop. He said to keep the computer with me as carry-on when I flew to Singapore but check it for the flight to America. When I was checking the bag at the counter in Singapore, I heard the disk drive engage as the computer woke up. That's when I worried that it was a bomb."

"What do you mean? How could the laptop be a bomb? It was a new computer that you yourself had worked on."

"But a bomb could be in more than one part. That laptop could be a controller for another part. I don't know; I'm a computer technician, not a bomb maker. I was just suddenly afraid to get on that plane, so I came back here. Then the next day, I heard on the news that the plane was missing. My guess was right."

"Why didn't you go to the police?"

"Do you know that a report last year ranked Malaysia as among the most anti-Semitic nations in the world?"

"You're Jewish, Mr. Braud?"

"My family originally came from Penang. The Jews all left there in the 40s. Some here stayed for a time. I was born here, but the rest of my family is long gone. I don't practice. There is no synagogue in KL. I could not find ten Jews in all of the city even if I wanted to form a minyan. No, I would never go to the police. I was a fool to come back here. There is no place to hide, no way to leave again without drawing attention."

Peter worked his jaw as he thought. "I'm placing you under arrest, Mr. Braud. You'll have to come with me."

"No!" The man backed away in horror. "You can't do that. You have no authority here."

"I can do that. I'm taking you into custody to be taken to Singapore for questioning." He lowered his head and tilted it slightly to look the man squarely in the eyes. "Do you understand what I'm saying to you. I'm taking you to Singapore for questioning."

The man's mouth hung open. "Can I take anything with me?"

"Like what?"

The man shuffled around behind a glass case that held an assortment of smartphones and tablet computers. He bent low and reached beneath a shelf. Peter tensed. The man's hand came up with a thick roll of American currency.

"No, you don't understand, Mr. Braud, I can't ..."

"Oh, I'm not trying to bribe you, not unless that becomes possible later. I'm only taking some traveling money with me. I don't expect to see the shop again."

Peter looked down at the roll of bills and noticed the number fifty on the corner of the outermost bill. "There must be—"

"There are large denominations underneath. This is $25,000."

"You keep that much cash in a drawer, with an elastic around it, ready to grab?"

"I'm a Jew. Jews must always be ready to leave and start over without notice—especially if you are the last Jew in Kuala Lumpur. I have an extra passport in my jacket, also. It's expired but it has been, shall we say, brought up to date."

Peter nodded. "I see. Then we should go. Perhaps you will need that passport."

Outside, Peter hailed a taxi for Sentral Railway Station. He did not want to draw attention by putting the man in handcuffs, but he wanted to keep a close eye on his charge. They rode in silence, and it was in silence they waited at Sentral before finally boarding the 14:35 express train for the seven-hour ride to Singapore. On the way, Peter read his newspaper and worked puzzles in his head, then paced the car to ward off sleep. He watched in envy as his charge slept through the last miles. By the time the train rolled into Singapore's sprawling Woodland Station, Peter was struggling to stay awake. He dragged himself from his seat and escorted his prisoner from the car to clear Customs and Immigration. The day that had started in the middle of the night had still not ended.

Chapter 35

THE EARLY SUN WAS just slicing through between the buildings of Phoenix Park in Singapore, and already Peter Ma was standing in his all-too-familiar stance: at respectful attention in front of Alon's desk. "It is not a problem, sir. There will be no diplomatic mess to sort out. The man traveled here on his own initiative. He will testify to that, I am sure. He entered Singapore legally, and then he voluntarily came in for questioning."

Alon did not look happy with the explanation. "In principle, perhaps, but it certainly won't help us the next time we seek a favor from the police in Malaysia. Does this man know anything? Was it worth the risk?"

"He thinks he could identify the man who offered to pay him to deliver the computer to America. We have him looking through photos."

"What about the destination?"

"It was supposed to be delivered to a Mr. Marlon Treet at Rothman-Wong Industries in Chicago. Izack Braud claims to have no knowledge of the man or the company, but he was given an address on Chicago's South Side. The FBI is checking it out for us."

He turned to leave, then turned back. "Oh, yes. We also have more information on the First Officer who went to Qatar. She had an interview with Qatar Airway. Seems she was being interviewed for a Captaincy. A human resources person from the airline said she was the top candidate, which is why they picked up the tab for her round-trip airfare. They hadn't made a formal offer, but had left her with the impression that they were serious. Looks like we can strike the last of the crew off our list."

== == ==

Arkady Pohl got the report through channels about the same time that Sam Parsons received an encrypted text message from Peter Ma. There was no company called Rothman-Wang Industries in Chicago or anywhere else in the United States, and no Marlon Treet could be located either. The address Braud had been given turned out to be the site of a recent demolition, with bricks and construction rubble all that remained of a two-story bakery that had been on the lot.

It was evident to everyone that the computer had never been intended to reach its destination. Arkady immediately requested that a batch of photos and fingerprint files from recent terrorist cases be forwarded to Singapore.

== == ==

In the headquarters of Singapore's ISD, Izack Braud's head hung bowed over a tablet computer on the table. He tapped his finger on the tablet, flipping through a display of mug shots. "No ... No ... No. Wait. This one I am not sure about. The face seems almost right, not quite. Perhaps it's the chin. The man who collected the computer last year had a beard, the kind that is called van something."

"You mean a Van Dyke? "

"Yes, a Van Dyke, like just here and around the mouth." He traced on his own face with a finger.

Peter picked up the tablet, fiddled with it, and laid it back on the table. "Like this?"

"Exactly. Yes, it does look like him."

Peter picked up the tablet again and swiped to turn to the

identification page for the photo. He glanced toward his partner, Mahmoud.

— — —

Sam Parsons ran down the hall toward Conference Room B. Out of breath, he pushed into the room. "I hurried back to tell you. We got a break." He scanned the room. "Where's everybody else? Where's Pohl?"

"DB's in his office. Pohl's gone. Brian took him for a walk after convincing him not to arrest us all." Ben put down the marker that he was using to update a to-do list on the whiteboard. "Ya know, that Mallory may look like he's all muscle and reflexes, but he's a damn clever talker. And that Pohl may look like a savvy investigator, but I was not impressed by his debating skills. Anyway, what have you got?"

"I just got another message from my contact in Singapore. The man who commissioned the special laptop has been identified by a computer technician from Kuala Lumpur who worked on the laptop. You'll never guess who he fingered."

Marwa shook her head and Ben shrugged. "I haven't a clue. Tell us."

"It's the shooter in Minnesota, the one who took out the two prisoners being held in connection with the bombing of that board meeting. That same guy arranges to send a computer by air from Singapore to Chicago, to a man who doesn't exist, then two days later kills two suspected terrorists in federal custody in Minneapolis. He, in turn, is killed in the attack, wiping the slate even cleaner."

Ben's face lit up. "Except for the guy in Singapore who ID'd the dead sniper. God, I hope they can protect him."

Chapter 36

THE PHONE ON THE conference table started ringing just as DB entered the room. He picked up the handset on the second ring. "Botteneau here. What's up?" There was a long silence as he listened and nodded. "Thanks, we'll be there." He smiled as he rose from the table. "That was Maude Girard in The Vault. They've customized a laptop to emulate the one in the abandoned luggage in Singapore and loaded the hard drive from the disk image supplied by Sam's contact there. They've been studying it and its software very closely. Now they want us to come down to The Vault so they can show us something."

== == ==

The walls of The Vault were a colorful collage of mismatched movie and high-tech conference posters. At a spot where an equipment cart had once rammed the wall and taken a chunk out of the plaster, the glint of bright copper could be seen, the exposed metal mesh that, like the perforated screen on the window of a microwave, shielded the room from radio waves. The Vault was Scenaria's sandbox, an electronically sealed environment where malicious software could be played with, tested, and studied without risk to the rest of the company's computers and without risk of signaling the outside world. Smartphones, tablets, and notebook computers were not permitted to be brought into The Vault, and other than the shielded electrical system, there was only one cable connecting The Vault to the outside world. That served the old-fashioned wall-mounted telephone and a single Internet-connected computer otherwise isolated from the rest of the company's network.

An assortment of desktop and laptop computers, no two alike, were arrayed around the room. At this hour, only three workstations were occupied. The young men in jeans and band-merch tee-shirts—Linkin Park, A Day to Remember, and Of Mice and Men—were all typing away with two fingers, all of them lost in the symbols and obscure text scrolling over their screens and in the sounds screaming through their white-corded earbuds.

Maude Girard rose from her workstation and motioned DB and the others over. She brushed aside bangs that flopped like a dark bridal veil over her eyes. "I won't interrupt my skeleton-crew over there to introduce the boys to you. We call them The Triplets. Left to right, that's Zack, Ari, and Bumpus—don't ask—and, no, they're not related, just geeks cast from the same mold, right down to their genius IQs and their tastes in music. If we can hear it from their earbuds all the way over here, you can imagine what it is doing to their hearing."

She sat down again. "This you gotta see, then you'll know why we made you come down here. This baby"—she patted an open laptop with a Windows 7 desktop on the display—"can't be trusted out of the room for reasons that will soon be clear."

Marwa craned her neck. "What's that thing at the end of the cable out the back?"

"Just a laptop battery. We lashed on a spare unit to match the hi-cap battery of the one in Singapore. We also installed an upgraded Wi-Fi/Bluetooth module that we had to really shop around for. It's much more powerful than the typical laptop unit and not exactly FCC approved."

"What does all that do?"

"Nothing much without the software, and that's the really interesting part."

Her smile broadened as she stepped around to face them before gesturing like a techie Vanna White. "Okay, this thing boots to Windows, as you can see, so it looks like an ordinary machine, but that's just window dressing, ha ha. There is actually a Linux kernel running underneath that is really calling the shots, beginning with loading some special programs that handle the Wi-Fi. When you close the cover"—she lowered it gently—"it goes to sleep immediately, but wakes itself up every eleven minutes to look around."

"Look around?"

"Yeah, it looks for Wi-Fi connections on all bands—802.11b, g, n, and a couple of little used frequencies that the special radio can handle—and tries to login." She flipped the display back open. "There, see all those lights suddenly start blinking over on our dummy access point? The comms software on the laptop has a database of passwords if it gets a request for credentials. The database seems to be loaded with an assortment of manufacturers' default passwords plus scads of oddball ones we never saw before.

"Once connected into a network, it looks for certain signatures—machine addresses, handshake sequences, node identifiers, manufacturer codes—that apparently tell it something about where it is. If it doesn't find what it's looking for, it disconnects, goes back to sleep, and waits another eleven minutes before trying again. We estimate it can keep up this sleep-wake-sleep cycle for at least a day on that big battery."

"What is it looking for?"

"The inside of an airplane. It verifies that it is connected to the public Wi-Fi of particular aircraft, and then the fun begins."

"And what fun is that?"

"Well, it took a lot of work to reverse engineer the code and then a lot of research to figure out what it was actually doing."

"But you figured it out, right?"

"Yes, most of it. The first section turns out to be an adaptation of techniques demo'd at the Black Hat conference in 2014 by a Spanish security researcher, Ruben Santamarta. He showed that it is possible to get into the supposedly secure network of the flight control computers through a plane's in-flight Wi-Fi. Once this thing is connected into the plane's Wi-Fi, it seeks out a bridge that shouldn't exist and is not supposed to be crossable. It negotiates access to a router, reprograms it, and then enters the flight control systems, the avionics. Ultimately, it finds its way to subsystems with particular chipsets, verifies their embedded serial numbers, executes an automated login sequence, and proceeds to upload new instructions and command structure to field-programmable gate arrays—that's specialized memory embedded in the chips. Voila! Pwned to own, as the hackers say. The plane is now under control of the malicious code."

DB fidgeted uncomfortably as Ben and Marwa nodded with excitement.

Sam asked the question that hung in the air. "What do these new instructions do?"

"We have no idea. It's apparently commands to the avionics. Give us a week or so with experts from Boeing and the chip manufacturer, and we could probably deconstruct it."

Marwa exchanged looks with Ben. "I think we could tell you what the code does in a lot less time than that."

— — —

Ben waited until they were in the elevator up from The Vault before confronting DB. "You know something about this reprogramming, don't you? You kept telling me to talk to my dad. The chipsets are not defective, they're doctored. Right?"

DB cleared his throat. "I really think you should be talking with Karl."

"I'll do that. I'll just do that." He waited for the elevator doors to reopen and dialed as he stepped into the hallway. To Ben's surprise, the phone was answered on the first ring. "Aba? Hi, it's Ben here. I have someone beside me who thinks we should talk about IsTac computer microchips."

"Perhaps we should. My flight just landed at JFK. I'm catching the next shuttle down from New York. We can do dinner together. I'll meet you at Meskerem at eight. Do you know it? In Adams Morgan. Great Ethiopian food."

"I'll find it. Are you going to tell me what suddenly brings you from Haifa to Washington, DC?"

"You. I'm here to talk with you, what else. See you at the restaurant."

Chapter 37

KARL LUSTIG'S CHINO-SMOOTH skin and flat stomach would allow him to be taken for vigorous middle-age, but his thinning white hair and snowy fringe of a beard were the tell that revealed a man in his seventies. In coveralls and seated in a horse-drawn buggy, he might pass for Pennsylvania Dutch in a television commercial. He rose from his seat against the wall when Ben entered the restaurant.

Ben hugged him. "Why did you have to fly all the way here? Do you have a new consulting contract? I thought you were retired for real this time."

"No, I don't have any new client. I have enough trouble still coming from old clients and work I finished years ago."

"Then why are you here?"

"What? Aren't you glad to see me?"

"Of course, I am, but ..."

"I already said, I'm here to talk with you. There are some talks that shouldn't happen over the phone." He sat down again and motioned Ben to follow suit. "Sometimes you need to meet in a noisy restaurant that neither you nor your son have ever been to before."

"This is one of those kinds of deals, huh? Please tell me you are not working with Anat and her people at Mossad again."

"How could I, Anat is retired. Even she doesn't mess in that world anymore. No, I told you why I am here. Let's order and talk over the meal."

== == ==

With a large *messob* platter filled with an array of exotic dishes between them, Karl finally opened the topic Ben was interested in. "Anat tells me you are curious about avionic chipsets."

"I thought you said Anat is retired."

"She is. So am I. It doesn't mean we hung up our brains when we cleaned out our desks."

Ben thought of Anat Dorfman and Lev Novikov, his aunt and uncle, whose years in Israel's elite intelligence service had been an added goad to his own vocational leanings. "I don't under—"

"No, you don't understand. Neither did I until people started disappearing or dropping like flies in a bug zapper. I want you to back off from this pursuit before it's too late. Maybe it is already, I don't know."

"You know, that's what others have been telling me, but it's my job. We're following up on the crash of a 787 in the Pacific."

"It's not your job anymore, not since you were laid off."

"You know about that?"

"I told, you, Anat and I have been talking, and she's been listening."

"Did Anat send you here?"

"Hell, no, she told me the same thing I am telling you. "Go back home,' she said. 'Forget about it. Get on with your life.' That's what she told me, that's what I'm telling you."

"But you need to tell me more than just Anat's advice to you." Ben tore off a piece of *injara*. He folded the spongy flatbread and used it to gather a scoop of spicy yellow lentils. "I don't know the names of any of these, but they're all so good."

Karl reached across the tray to scoop some lamb with his piece of *injara*. He paused with the bread almost to his mouth. "You know, I always find it odd that, after the mass immigrations of Operation Moses and Operation Solomon brought so many Ethiopian Jews to Israel, there are not more good Ethiopian restaurants back home."

"Back home. It is home for you, isn't it. You grew up in America and now Israel has become home. I grew up in Israel, and now I don't know where home is."

"You'll find where you belong."

"Perhaps some of us belong nowhere. Or everywhere. Your old apartment on Beacon Hill is as much home to me now as the one I grew up in back in Haifa. But, there you go. You keep cleverly changing topics to avoid talking about IsTac and avionics chipsets."

Karl leaned closer and spoke quietly and quickly. "The microchips in the 460 series have a built-in back door, kind of a hard-wired Trojan that makes it possible to hack into them and disable them or change the programming. Israel was not the first to pull this off. The Chinese had earlier been caught supplying doctored microchips for computers and consumer electronics complete with embedded spyware. With the IsTac chipset, it is even possible to get access using a modulated radar signal to cripple a fighter jet by remote control."

"And we use these chips in our own planes? That's insane. Why would we do that?"

"Piece it together, Bini. You're smart enough. If you were calling the shots, why might you do something like that?"

"Maybe to mislead other countries into thinking the chips were safe. If Israel uses them in its own planes, the chips can be trusted."

"Keep going."

"Well, maybe Israel thinks that the backdoor is securely locked, that nobody else could ever get access. Maybe we assume nobody else even knows about it."

"And what would happen if anyone else ever found out about the backdoor?"

Ben's mouth hung open. "Oh, shit. HaAvir is neutralized. Anyone who knew how could bring down Israel's air force without even firing a missile."

"Not only that, Bini. Even if they didn't know how to use the backdoor, if they just knew of its existence, that could essentially wipe out one of our biggest exports: military technology. Who would trust us again?"

Ben's head swung in a slow arc. "This is so screwed up."

"Maybe. But as long as no one else knows, we have the decisive advantage against any foe who uses the chips. Sweep their planes with the right radar beam and no more threat. See the appeal?"

"The Americans have these chips, too."

"Yes, but they don't know what we know."

"Unless they've figured that out by now."

"We, Israel, are the only ones who know how to actually use it."

"Wrong." Ben waved an accusatory finger. "Somebody else knows, somebody else who already brought down two passenger planes."

"The Israelis are the only ones who know."

"What are you saying? That the downing of those two planes was an Israeli operation?"

"I am not saying that or anything about that."

"Damn it, Aba, don't pull that patriotic speak-no-evil crap on me."

"I only know what I know and say what I know. But you understand now why this can't go further, why you must not pursue this anymore. It's only because you're my son that I've said as much as I have. And only then because I have hope that it will get you to give up."

"There's more that you are not saying, isn't there?"

"Like what?"

"Like who has actually been exploiting this embedded malware. The chips don't suddenly decide on their own to bring down a plane."

"Don't go there, Bini. Don't go there."

"If there is somebody out there who has the means to bring down commercial aircraft at will and with impunity, you think I'm going to just walk away and keep my mouth shut? Is that the kind of son you think you raised?"

Chapter 38

FOR ARKADY, THE LACK of coordination among law enforcement agencies in the US was a chronic pain in the side, but it was also sometimes useful. At the moment, the police in Bloomington, Minnesota, a suburb just south of the Twin Cities, did not yet realize that some confiscated property from a local motel had anything to do with a shooting at a hotel in downtown Minneapolis. Except for Arkady Pohl, who had a special interest in connecting these particular dots, the FBI knew nothing about the new evidence, either.

Upon landing at the Minneapolis-Saint Paul International Airport, Arkady hailed a taxi for the short ride down to Bloomington. At the police headquarters, he went directly to the Property and Evidence Division. The man working the window was one of those cops who never made lieutenant and had never tried. He'd been off the beat long enough to develop a barrel shape. The strained buttons on his uniform showed that he was still expanding.

"Yeah?"

Arkady read his name tag. "Hello, Officer Jensen. How're you doing?"

"Busy. What can I do you for?" His accent and expression were as pure Upper-Midwest as his blue-gray eyes and blond lashes.

"I'm with the FBI." Arkady flashed his badge. "The field office sent me down from Brooklyn Center to borrow some evidence for a few hours. Our forensic hotshots are on some kick or another. You know how those lab boys can be."

Jensen nodded. "So whaddaya need?"

"Don't know. All I got is a number. Here's the paperwork." He slipped a multipart form through the window.

Jensen grunted and headed down the rows of gray steel utility shelving that filled the evidence locker. He returned after a few minutes with a laptop computer inside a large clear plastic bag. "Ya gotta sign for it." He clipped a chain-of-custody form to a board, scribbled on it, and shoved it toward Arkady, who signed.

"When's it coming back?"

"Beats me. Sometime today, I was told. They wanna try running some new field tests or something."

"Okay." He turned away and returned to his chair.

Arkady slipped the laptop into the new briefcase he had purchased at Wilson's Leather before leaving Boston. It was real leather; the signature, the paperwork, and the badge were all fake. Ultimately, they could be traced back to him—it was a cover identity he had used before—but he would not be found immediately. Whenever the trail did finally lead to him, he would have the right story to justify his interest. Counterterrorism was convenient cover and an acceptable excuse for many activities in the borderlands beyond strictly proper procedure.

He strolled back to the main entrance where his cab was still waiting outside. Everything had clicked, and the cab dropped him off at a strip motel where he prepaid for a night in cash. In his room, he put on latex gloves and swapped out the hard drive. He looked at his watch. Plenty of time to grab a bite before another taxi would take him for a second quick stop at the police station.

The overweight property Officer took the laptop back without questioning the cock-and-bull story Arkady offered for the early return. Then it was back to the airport in time to make the return flight to DC—on the very plane that had brought him to Minneapolis. As the flight took off, Arkady was elated at how easily he had pulled off the whole operation to retrieve the drive from the laptop. He did not notice that one of the first-class passengers on the flight to Minneapolis was now sitting in the next-to-last coach row on the return flight.

▬▬ ▬▬ ▬▬

Ben slipped the coffee from the vending machine and took an airy sip. "I am telling you, Marwa, my dad covered it with bravado, but he was scared. He is not one to scare easily. What I get from the story he was not telling is that there is some sort of army of independents—rogue operatives, who knows—that is pulling strings behind the scenes and pulling the plug on anyone who might expose what they are doing."

"You're not serious." She held his eyes for long seconds. "You are. Does this mean we are, all of us, also in the crosshairs?"

"It might."

"What should we do?" She chewed at her lower lip. "We should tell somebody."

"And that's going to make it better? Who do we tell? Who do we trust? I mean, besides each other. Yes, my dad, but I don't think he's going to be much help at this point. Then there's DB."

"You know him that well? I thought you only worked together by remote access, back when you were a kid."

"Yes, but he put his life on the line for my dad. He's a straight shooter, in both senses of the term."

"What about Sam Parsons? And what about this FBI dude with the Slavic name?"

"I don't really know either of them. Both had some connection with my dad on a consult that he was briefly pulled in on then suddenly pulled off. Sam, as you know, has a somewhat messy past with some question marks in it. Arkady is a counter-terrorism spook with the FBI. Enough said. I assume that nothing he says or does can be taken at face value."

"So we have the six people, two we're not sure we can trust, one who might not be much help. That leaves"—she pointed successive fingers like a TV assistant director counting se-conds— "you, me, and DB."

"We left off this mysterious Mallory character, who rides in like the cavalry and gets Arkady off our backs."

"Right. DB says we can trust him, but Mallory and Arkady are supposedly old FBI buddies. He strikes me as muscle for hire."

Ben laughed. "I was just remembering 'The Princess Bride', when Inigo, Westley, and Fezzik are counting their assets before storming the castle. So what do we have among the three of us? No holocaust cloak, but we do have your ability with the psycho-social aspects of human networks, my skill with mathematical models and extracting signal from noise, and DB's command over a shitload of computing technology and an army of mal-ware wonks. What does that add up to?"

"We build a model of this nemesis network using clandestine computing skills—yours and the ones here—steered by my people-oriented perspective." She gave him an exaggerated grin.

"I see how you appointed yourself conspirator-in-chief. Still, nice abstract for an academic paper. I like that: nemesis net-work, a good working label. But how do we build a model of a network we can't see and know nothing about? We have to have at least a starting point, a single member or one node, a route in, don't we?"

"We do, we have a laptop—or at least a replica of the one used to bring down PT20. Let's go back to The Vault."

== == ==

Maude slouched beside her workstation. "So, what is it you want me to do?"

"Help us find a lead to the PT2o perpetrators," Marwa said. "According to Singapore, the technician in Malaysia claimed he had been directed to download and install software from the Web. Is there any chance we can find where he got the software?"

"Maybe, but it's relatively easy to hide your tracks, at least the obvious ones."

"But this guy was no espionage agent, just a technician doing a job, following instructions. And the laptop was never expected to be recovered; it was supposed to have gone down with the plane. We should give it a try, see what we can find."

Maude sat down, clicked a few times with her mouse, and pointed at the screen. "There it is, still in the browser history. There was no attempt to hide anything. I recognize it: a file sharing site often used by hackers. But chances are the file has already been taken down."

"Can you check?"

"Not from this machine; it's isolated." She spun her chair over to an adjacent workstation with a big nuclear-hazard warning sign above it. "We have this one machine, called The Hot Box, with direct connection to the Internet but isolated from everything else." She typed the long link address from memory. A pop-up message announced that the machine was infected with a virus. "Ignore that. It's a scam. They want us to click on OK, which actually does download a virus. But we just kill that message, and ... No, the file is gone."

"Is there any way we can find out who posted it?"

"Hmmm, if it is still there and the uploader used a handle that we recognized, maybe, but now—"

"You can still get it." It was one of the triplets, wearing a green-and-blue tee-shirt for the 2014 Global Warning Tour of Blue-Green Algae Invasion. He was pulling out his white earbuds as he walked over to them.

"I see you still have some hearing left, Bumpus."

He curled his upper lip at her and motioned for her to get out of her chair. "White noise. Helps me concentrate but doesn't completely screen loud voices. Like yours, my Lady Maude." He sat down and began to type. "We hacked this site long ago and installed a backdoor, direct route to the root directory, and ... click, click, clickety-click, here we have the upload logs. A lot of these dirty sites play dirty even with their own. Date and time?"

She told him an approximate range.

"There's the file name, user name, IP address, time stamp. Let me find out who owns the IP address for you."

"I can do a 'who-is' for myself."

"Just trying to help. There. It's Ooredoo, an ISP based in Qatar. And that address is in a block assigned to the Qatar Crescent Royal hotel chain."

"Any chance we can find out the name of the guest?"

"We can narrow it down. Give me five minutes."

"You can hack into hotel records in Qatar that fast?"

"It's all in 'the cloud.' People think what they store in the cloud is secure"—he typed and clicked as he talked— "but for people like us, it just narrows the possibilities." He scowled in concentration as he continued to work his way through links and layers of security. "There's the list of guests paying for Wi-Fi access on that day. Recognize any?"

"It's a long shot," Marwa said, "but can you pull off the same trick to get a list of guests at the Hotel Minneapolis on the day of the shooting there?"

"No prob." He typed and clicked away for several minutes, all the time bobbing his head to some unheard beat. "There we are. Now we run a compare for matches, and ... Woo hoo! We got one: Sergi Cardona."

"You are fast, Bumpus."

"Faster than you, old lady." He winked up at her before relinquishing the chair and holding it for her.

Marwa stepped toward the door. "Thanks, Maude. Thanks, Bumpus. I'm going to go back up to my network tools and see where that name leads."

== == ==

Brian Mallory slammed his thumbless right hand on the roof of the car. The thwack echoed in the concrete cave of the parking garage. He twirled his index finger in an outdated but still effective gesture. In response, Arkady lowered the car window, and Brian bent down to face him. "Well, well, Agent Pohl, back from a little quick trip to the Twin Cities, eh?"

"How ... ?"

"Oh, Arkady, I was always a better agent than you. You can be so obvious, even when you think you are being so ... so sneaky. You forget, I know your old cover names. I also know all about your surreptitious sibling. Where is Dima now? Last I heard he was in Boston. Wait a minute! Weren't you in Boston recently, maybe at the same time? You really shouldn't keep recycling your old cover IDs. Makes you too damn easy to track. That and driving this clunker." He slapped the roof of the car again and extended his hand through the window. "Now, give me the hard drive."

Arkady reached toward the briefcase on the passenger seat with his right hand, tugged up on the window control button with his left, and popped the clutch. The car lurched forward but the engine stalled. Brian jerked back his arm before it could be trapped by the closing window. With his left hand, he withdrew his Beretta and pointed it at Akady's head. "Don't be a dead jerk, Arkady. Just give me the damn disk drive."

"Listen to me. If you know my brother is involved in some way, you know this is nothing to fuck around with."

"Exactly, and that's why we're going straight to the best computer forensics people money can buy."

"That's official evidence in an FBI investigation. You can't—"

"If it was official, then why'd you cumshaw it from the Bloomington police with phony papers?" He pulled open the door and reached past Arkady to grab the briefcase from the passenger seat. He clipped Arkady's jaw as he whipped it out of the car.

"Shit!" Arkady put a hand to his jaw.

"It could be worse, Arkady. If you want the drive back or want to know what's on it, meet me at Scenaria. See you."

<hr/>

Mallory rounded the corner and stepped into the conference room. "You two still at it? How's it going?"

Ben was standing behind Marwa, intent on the screen of her laptop. "Meh," she said. "We got a name to attach to the man who had the laptop delivered to flight PT20: Sergi Cardona. We can track it to a number of countries through flight reservations, hotel bookings, car rentals, but the hits are disconnected. Looks like a phony ID that was used intermittently."

"Well, maybe this will help. Here, catch," He sent something spinning across the table. Ben snatched it before it could fly off the edge.

"A disk drive?" he said.

"Not just any disk drive. This one is a ruggedized one from a laptop that belonged to the sniper in Minneapolis."

"That would be Sergi Cardona. We now believe he's behind the 787 hijacking."

"Okay. Anyway, thought maybe you and the other whiz kids

here could make something of the disk."

"How did you manage this?"

"With a little help from the FBI. Course they don't know it's gone. Except for Agent Arkady Pohl, that is, but I don't think he's gonna be telling on us."

Marwa reached over for the disk drive. "We should get it down to The Vault. Call ahead, Ben, and tell them what we have. I'll run it down there."

▬▬ ▬▬ ▬▬

It was nearly midnight before they were invited back down to The Vault. Maude Girard greeted them with a grim face. "This new baby is going to be one tough nut to crack, if you can forgive my mixing metaphors. From the pattern written into free space on the disk, it looks like the system securely wipes temporary files every time it is shut down, so we don't know what it was last used for. It's got two separate operating systems, one of which has three-factor authentication, so you not only need the right user ID and password, but the system also reads a token from a Bluetooth device that must be in the vicinity, maybe a cellphone or a dedicated key server."

"How did you find all this out?"

"We mounted it as an external drive, bypassed a hardware interlock, and looked around. We are hindered by not being able to login to the second operating system. but we found a few things that might be useful. On the Windows side of the machine, it uses standard anti-virus software, not ours, but it's software sold by Portcullis, an Israeli company that licenses our update engine and subscribes to our updates."

Ben was smiling, but Marwa looked confused. "I don't get it. What does that buy us."

"I'm guessing that means that any system like this one has the same security hole that got us into the CAASS system. And, we can push an update to Portcullis subscribers that looks for something distinct to this system."

"Exactly. We can get any system like this that connects to the Internet to tell us who and where it is."

"That could allow us to build an inventory of similarly configured computers, if any, and possibly trace out the network. Can we get started on that?"

"Not until DB authorizes using our system this way. We're talking about a legal gray area here, and I mean like charcoal gray or darker. We called to update him, but there's no answer at either of the numbers we have for him. I'll keep trying."

Chapter 39

DB COULD HEAR HIS cellphone. The ringtone told him it was his office calling. He went to reach for his phone and discovered his arms were pinned beneath him. He was stung by pins-and-needles as he pulled his arms free. The phone was not in his pocket, but he could still hear it, as if it were on the other side of the bedroom door. He opened his eyes but it made no difference. The room was as black as the bottom of a mine. He rolled toward the side of the bed but ended up against a wall. He rolled the other way and collided with another wall. Wherever he was, he was certainly not in his bedroom.

He put out a hand to feel along the wall, only to be stopped by a sharp stab in his palm. He scratched and pulled at a splinter that broke off, leaving a point behind that jabbed him again whenever he moved his hand. Wherever he probed, he found rough wood. He was lying on what felt like a folded blanket and smelled like an outhouse.

The ringtone stopped. He listened carefully. In the distance he could hear machinery, some kind of construction equipment, the sound growing steadily louder. His wooden world flipped as something crashed against the side He was tumbling, slammed against one side then another, somersaulted like a rock in a polishing tumbler.

A pounding rain started as soon as the tumbling stopped, a heavy pelting that thundered like hail onto his box, then tapered off and stopped. Several sharp cracks that might have been an engine backfiring or a handgun discharging were followed by nothing: no engine, no hail, no cracks—just quiet.

DB twisted, doubled up, and kicked against the side of the box with all the force he could muster. Dirt tumbled down on him and a shaft of sodium-yellow light exposed the interior of the shipping crate.

"Ah, there you are." The voice sounded familiar but he couldn't place it.

DB kicked again and the side of the crate opened enough for him to see Brian Mallory picking his way down a slope of debris.

"You came darn close to becoming landfill, Mr. Botteneau."

"What the hell ... ?"

"Let's get you outa there." Mallory tucked his pistol into the front of his pants and bent over to give DB a hand climbing out of the half-open shipping crate. There was a flash of movement behind Mallory and the snip-snip of two rounds from a handgun with a silencer. Mallory fell forward across the opening in the crate. DB, operating on instinct and years of videogame reflexes, tugged the pistol from Mallory's belt as his body tumbled down. He thumbed the safety off and fired up at the silhouette haloed by the floodlight above. The man dropped to his knees, swaying with his gun hanging at his side. He looked at DB, open-mouthed, then slumped backward, firing wildly once more as he fell.

DB bent over to check Mallory.

"Get outa here, Botteneau."

"Let me help you."

"No, this is better, a lot quicker and probably less painful."

"What are you talking about?"

"The big C. This way I get to be on the job to the end. Leave me. You don't wanna be associated with this. And trust Suze

Kerchoff. She works for me. Did. Now she's in charge. Will be. When they read the ..." He choked and gagged. "Just get the fuck outa here." He grabbed DB's sleeve. "She'll fill ya in. Suze. Give me my gun back. You don't wanna be caught with ..."

DB slipped the pistol into Mallory's hand and closed the man's fingers around the handgrip.

"Go, Botteneau. Now!"

DB stood up and looked around. He was at the edge of a landfill, mountains of trash towering over him. He looked back at Brian Mallory one more time, then broke into a trot. Behind him, more shots split the night.

Chapter 40

SAM PARSONS ENTERED the office suite looking for Avery. The door to the adjacent washroom was open and DB was standing shirtless at the sink. "What in hell happened to you?"

"Let's just say I got dumped." DB used a wet paper towel to dab at his side.

"Shit, you're bleeding."

"Good call. Can you grab the first-aid kit from the guard station in reception and bring it back here?"

Sam returned with the metal box and handed it to DB. "That looks like a bullet wound."

"It does because it is. Not a biggy. Now, leave me alone. I'll meet you in Conference Room B. And not a word, not to anyone."

"Are you going to tell me what happened?"

"No. Just go ... No, wait. Send Ben back here. Okay?"

"Okay, if you say so."

DB was buttoning the top button of a fresh dress shirt from his emergency supply when Ben arrived.

"Where's Avery?"

"Running errands for me. Close the door and have a seat."

"You sound ominously serious."

"Good way to put it. Somebody tried to kill me. I would have been buried alive if it wasn't for Brian Mallory. He saved my life. He ... I ... I don't know what muck we stepped into this time, but it is now one bloody goddamn mess. You, Karl, and I go way back. We need to talk about how to proceed, whether to proceed. Is Karl still in town?"

"Yes, he's staying at the Meredith through the weekend."

"When did you last talk with him?"

"A couple hours ago. Why?"

"Just wanted to confirm he's okay. I'm going to have somebody from Saltmarsh pick him up and bring him here in a taxi."

"That sounds like a pretty big cab fare."

"I don't want to be using anyone's car that might have been hacked or might have a tracking device attached to it. The people we're up against are extremely sophisticated. I'm assuming you know what this is all about by now."

"You mean the chipsets? Yeah, Dad told me."

"Okay, by that I take it he didn't tell the rest of the story, so that means only I and maybe Arkady know ... hmmm."

"Are you going to clue me in or not?"

"In the conference room. I'll meet you there in ten."

•• •• ••

With his room keycard positioned to slip into the slot, Karl tensed, suddenly aware that the man who had exited the elevator with him had started to walk past but then stopped. Karl pretended to have changed his mind and turned back toward the elevators, almost running into the man. "Sorry, forgot my newspaper downstairs."

"Are you Karl Lustig? Saltmarsh sent me. I'm Freddie." The man, a Steven Segal type with a crew-cut, held out a hand that engulfed Karl's when they shook. "I work with Brian Mallory."

"Yes? And ..."

"The boss told me you were the cautious type. You can call Mallory if you want to verify. You probably also know his kid brother out in Utah. He's doing okay, by the way, now runs an IT consulting firm out there in Salt Lake."

Karl nodded. It was an insider reference that Mallory knew Karl would recognize. "Never met his brother, but I know the story well enough. So what can I do for you, Freddie?"

"What I can do for you is escort you out to Reston. Suze Kerchoff, Mallory's right-hand gal, wants everybody in one place with a defensible perimeter."

"Defensible perimeter? What's happened?"

"Suze will fill you in when we get there. She's in charge of this op. Let's go back downstairs and catch a cab on the street."

== == ==

Freddie directed the taxi driver to head north out toward Columbia, Maryland, then later pretended to change his mind to head to an address in Reston.

"I see," said Karl. "You like this sort of work, don't you."

"It's a job. Pays well." He leaned forward to read the name of the driver from the posted taxi license. "Hey, Gonzales, you like driving a cab?"

"It's a job."

"See, Lustig? We all just do what we gotta do. It's a job. Better than being out of work, right? What do you do?"

"I'm out of work: a retired journalist. No, I'm a just a journalist. I hate that word. 'Retired.' Sounds too much like golf carts and back problems and a slow shuffle off to the grave. Not for me."

"Hey, I'm with ya. Better to die with your boots on, right?" As they talked, Freddie kept finding excuses to check behind them. "Hey, Gonzales, try the right lane for a while, would ya?" He glanced back again. "Hmmm. I think we are going to take the next exit, Gonzales. Okay?"

Traffic was moving well on the Beltway despite a stretch of ongoing road repairs. They were approaching another construction zone just before the interchange, when the car behind suddenly accelerated and slammed into the left rear bumper of the taxi, sending it into a spinning skid.

"What the fuck!" Freddie grabbed the back of the seat as the driver struggled to regain control. The taxi slid sideways into the end of a line of Jersey barriers that cordoned off an idle bulldozer and several pickup trucks. The driver side of the car crumpled against the barrier, and the car tilted up, then slammed back down.

Brakes screeched and cars swerved as Karl struggled to open his door and climb out. A flicker of flames was licking at the edges of the hood. Karl struggled to drag Freddie from the rear seat, then managed to get the driver unbuckled and out of the cab. He pulled Freddie farther from the car and looked up in time to see the sedan that had hit them backing up toward him, racing in reverse at high speed alongside the Jersey barriers.

—— —— ——

Suze Kerchoff knocked and entered the office. "We got the perimeter secure, sir. My people are at the entrance and manning the reception desk. The office is doing background checks on employees."

DB raised his arm and looked down to check for any blood seeping through his shirt. "Looks all right." He managed a smile at Suze. "The checks won't be necessary. We're also in the security business. We do background checks on all new hires."

"Not like we do. If we're gonna be responsible for keeping you safe, you have to let us do our job—our way. We're also placing three of our tech-savvy people in newly created positions on your staff. They'll start tomorrow. You'll see, they'll be able to keep up with your people while giving us some inside eyes and ears."

"I told you, this is not an internal threat."

"So you say. Our job is to find out for ourselves. Oh, yeah, our inside people will be armed."

"You really are thorough."

"That's a tame term for how we see what we do." The faint buzz of a cellphone on vibrate could be heard. Suze pulled out her phone and checked the screen. "They picked up Karl Lustig at the Meredith and should be on their way here." She was just slipping the phone back in her pocket when it buzzed again. She looked at the screen, gritted her teeth, and closed her eyes.

"Bad news?"

"The hospital. Brian Mallory didn't make it."

"Oh God, I'm sorry."

"Me too." She cleared her throat and fought to maintain composure. "But it won't affect our services to you. If you could tell me anything more about what we are up against, who we are up against, it could help."

"I don't really know either who or what. We're working on finding out."

"Well, let me know as soon as you have anything."

"Hang around and you'll know as soon as we do."

Part Six: Topology
Chapter 41

MARWA FIDDLED WITH THE sleeve of her sweater, hooking and unhooking it from her thumb as she waited for confirmation that messages from Ben's patches were working with her software. She switched her laptop to display through the ceiling projector in the conference room. On the wall, a pattern of connected colored blobs—some brightening, some fading—was peppered over a spray of gray dots. "So, here's where we are. Since we got DB's approval, we've been pushing an update through to the Portcullis customer base of several million installations. We've reached a little over twenty percent of the base: those are the gray dots grouped by Portcullis sales region. We have confirmation of a dozen systems with Portcullis anti-virus software that also contain at least one of the signatures we're looking for, highlighted in red on the visualization. The size of the dots is proportional to the confidence level that a machine is part of the Nemesis Network. Remember, these machines only become visible to us as they are turned on, connected to the Internet, and have been loaded with our special version of the update engine, so we might be looking at only a tiny part of what could be a much larger network.

"That said, we've already made some interesting discoveries. Three of these machines connected briefly to the same IP address while online and those two in the Western Europe region actually exchanged data packets with each other directly." She highlighted the emerging structure of the displayed network. "And these two, which are actually connected live at the moment, have checked the same news stories in the last half hour. And look, there are two more machines that just showed up and ... Did you see that? They both accessed the same IP address right after power on, but it's different from the one used by the other machines."

"Can we get more precise locations or any other identifying information for any of these machines?" Sam asked.

"We're pulling in approximate locations based on IP addresses, and for systems that stay connected, we're doing some real-time scanning. Here, I'll switch to a map view of locations for the handful of machines we have data on. It's updating as new data comes in."

A new red dot appeared on the map and Ben gasped. "Can we zoom in on that last location, the one that just appeared in Israel?

Marwa manipulated the map and zoomed through successive expansions. "Looks like it's in Tel Aviv."

"Can we go all the way down to the street map?"

"Sure."

"Oh God, no." Ben slumped down in his chair. "Not possible."

"What is it? This looks to be a residential area in Tel Aviv."

"I know, and I think I know exactly where it is and who is at the computer."

"Can we get Israeli help on this, send somebody there? Notify Mossad or something?"

"This is Mossad. Or at least it might as well be."

DB entered the conference room, walking slowly and holding his side. "What's happening. You look like you just saw a zombie, Ben.

"A lot worse than that. I think I know somebody in the

217

Nemesis Network. I don't know what to do with the information. I think we should be talking with my dad."

"He's on his way. Should be here any minute. Let me check with Suze. Oh, here she is now."

Suze Kerchoff slipped her radio into the holster on her belt as she entered the room. "What are you going to check with me about?"

"About Ben's dad, Karl. Where is he now?"

"Should be turning into the parking lot about now. Let me ping my guy and get an update." She slipped a cellphone from her blazer and dialed. There was no answer. "That's funny. Let me try the radio. Saltmarsh Four, calling Saltmarsh Four. This is Kerchoff. Where are you and what's your ETA? Saltmarsh Four." She held the radio out and scowled at it. "Funny."

Ben pulled out his phone. "Let me try my dad." He dialed but there was no answer and he was redirected to voicemail.

Suze held up her radio again. "Saltmarsh Base. This is Kerchoff. I want you to track down Freddie. He was supposed to be in a DC cab escorting Karl Lustig out to Reston. I can't raise him and Lustig is not answering his phone."

The raspy voice came over the speaker on the radio handset. "Any chance that could be the same cab that was in a multi-car pileup on the Beltway?"

"Don't know. Hope not. Get the cab number from our logs—Freddie would have texted it in—and use our sources in Virginia and Maryland State Police. Call me right back." Suze laid the radio down on the conference table. "So, Ben, I think you better tell us what you suspect about this member of the—what do you call it?—Nemesis Network."

"One of the computers our probe has identified as possibly part of the network has been traced to a neighborhood in Tel Aviv that I know well. I—"

The radio spat a sharp hiss. "Kerchoff, this is Saltmarsh Base. We got the ID on the cab in the accident. It matched our logs. Freddie was pronounced dead at the scene. The client was taken by chopper to the trauma center at Inova Fairfax Hospital. Do you want me to get somebody over there?"

"Yes. I'm out in Reston. I'll get to the hospital myself as soon as I can."

"Roger."

"We have an on-call chopper on our corporate card," DB said. "You want me to see how soon it could pick us up and fly us there?"

Suze nodded. "Sounds good. Could save some time."

"I want to go, too," Ben said.

"Why not." DB picked up the phone and dialed. "Avery, can you call HeliTopper and find out how soon they can meet us here with a four-seater?"

"What about me?" Marwa asked.

"You and Sam stay here," Ben said. "Keep working on building the network model. I need to be with my dad."

―― ――― ――

As Ben, DB, and Suze approached, the man seated outside the hospital room stood. He was wearing a black windbreaker with 'FBI' in white block letters on it. "I'm sorry, you can't go in there," he said.

Already bracing for the worst, Ben started to go around the officer. "That's my dad in there."

The man sidestepped, blocking Ben's way. "I'm sorry. No one is allowed in."

"Why not? I'm his son."

"I'm sorry. The patient is in federal custody."

"Just let me check on him, just for a minute.

The man was determined. "Sorry, can't allow that."

Ben's eyes surveyed the hall as he weighed his options. The double doors at the end of the hallway swung open and Arkady Pohl pushed through. "Ben, you made it."

"Yes, I made it. And this guy won't let me in to see my dad."

"He's just doing his job. When I got word of the accident, I had Karl taken into custody for his own protection. It's okay, Agent Haverill, you can let these people in."

Monitors and medical paraphernalia were arrayed beside the bed, blocking Ben's view. He crossed over to look down at the battered face on the pillow. "It's not him. Who is this?"

"What do you mean? This is not Karl Lustig?"

"No, don't you think I'd know my own father. I don't know who this is."

"According to the ambulance driver who brought him in, this is the passenger taken from the scene of the accident"

"Well, it may be a passenger from the accident, but it is definitely not my dad."

Chapter 42

Marwa was so absorbed in tracing connections in the growing network model that she didn't hear the conference room door open. She jumped at the sound of the voice.

"I'm looking for Binyamin Markham."

"Who?" She looked up to face a white-haired man with traces of red mud dried on his face and dark spots of blood on his French-blue shirt.

"Bini Markham, my son."

"Oh, right. You mean Ben. And you must be Karl."

"I am. I thought I would find Bini here."

"He's out looking for you, at the hospital. What happened? We heard there was an accident, and you were taken to some trauma center."

"It was no accident. The taxi I was riding in was deliberately rear-ended and forced off the road. I dragged my escort and the driver out of the car before it caught fire. When I saw the car that hit us stop and head toward us, peddle-to-the metal in reverse, I slipped away. I hiked to a shopping mall, flagged a taxi, and came here hoping to find Bini and DB. They are both in danger."

"I think they're in good hands. That commando woman from the security service is with them."

"And they're at the hospital? We should get them back here. I'd call them, but I lost my phone."

"Maybe the guard at the desk can help. Suze had a radio with her. Say, how did you get in here anyway?"

"I came in through Talpa's old private entrance from the executive parking lot. From the looks of it, doesn't seem like anyone uses it anymore. I remembered it from when I worked with DB. I wasn't sure whether they had ever changed the security code. They hadn't."

"Talpa?"

"Uh, Richard Talpa, the guy who founded the company—long gone."

"Oh, right. Ben told me he was not one of the good guys."

"Not one of the bad guys either. There's a lot of that sort around, really smart people who rent out their smarts, play whatever side pays better or hires them first or spouts the most convincing rhetoric. Last I heard, Talpa was being paid well, working for the NSA, but he might have had a better offer by now. Frankly, some of the surveillance stuff Snowden uncovered looked like exactly the sort of sneaky business that was Talpa's signature style." Karl slumped down at the conference table. "Uff da, I'm definitely getting too old for this chase game. Could you give Bini a call? I lost my cellphone in the accident."

"You said that."

"Right. But can you call? Just don't say anything about me. Tell him you have something important to show him right away, something about whatever you're working on."

"Yeah, sure." She tapped on the smartphone beside her keyboard, put it to her ear, and waited. "Hi, Ben, it's me." Her smile blossomed. "Look, I found something in the network that you need to see. Can you all get back here right away? I know you are worried. But ... just trust me, this is something you'll want to see. Okay, bye."

She stared at the phone as she put it down. "He really loves you, you know. He wanted to be out there looking for you, but he's on his way. The chopper is bringing them all back."

— — —

As he turned the corner in the hallway, Ben caught sight of Karl and rushed to hug him. "Aba, what happened? Are you all right?"

Karl explained what had happened in a flood of words, and DB punctuated the account. "So, the bottom line is they've made attempts on both Karl and me. And they killed Mallory."

Suze looked from Karl to DB and back. "I get the feeling I'm the only one who doesn't yet know who 'they' are. Brian once said something about Pohl, the FBI guy, having a brother involved in some off-the-reservation ops. Is that connected?"

Karl stepped back from his son and spoke over his shoulder. "Did you figure it out, DB? I mean, after I told you to talk with that ex-CIA agent, the one who writes zombie fiction and knew about the chipset caper."

"More or less. I got the idea that the Americans were also in on the built-in backdoor for the avionics microchips, maybe that there was more than one compromise in the design. And I also got this sense that none of this was official, that it wasn't really the CIA or Mossad but some unspecified third party that was really behind it all."

Sam, who had been sitting quietly in the far corner studying a programming manual, offered an opinion. "Conspiracy-theory crap, I'd say. Unreal."

Marwa tapped the spacebar on her computer and a new diagram was projected on the wall. "Trust me, it's real. Look. This is the network as we have mapped it out so far. The red circles are computers with some or all of the software configuration that was used by that shooter in Minneapolis, the same guy who setup the hack into the onboard electronics of flight PT20. That's Sergi Cardona; he is what we call the index member of the network. The orange ones are missing computers that we assume should be there but we don't have confirmation on yet. The red lines are definite links among the nodes and the orange are presumed connections based on pattern matching. Interesting, huh?"

The displayed diagram consisted of a series of six-member clusters, like cells in a honeycomb. Within a cluster, each member connected with only some of the other members, so no one in any cluster would know all the other members. Within each cluster, at least one member was also connected to a member of another cluster, so no cluster in the network was completely isolated; all parts of the network could be reached.

Marwa stood up beside the displayed diagram. "What this means is we may actually know more about the total organization than anyone inside it. If you're inside the network, you'd see only a limited picture. So far, there doesn't seem to be any central group or command center. It's completely decentralized as far as we can tell, although there are some anomalies. One cluster seems to have seven members. Maybe that's the key.

"Our index member happens to be a connector who links to a member of another group. Some of those, in turn, are linked to more than one other group. All and all, it is a very clever configuration that allows for fast, simple communication without a central hub and without anyone having more than local knowledge of the network."

Sam looked up from his reading. "Other than this Sergi Cardona, do we know the identities of any of these alleged members of this alleged network?"

"We're pretty sure that Cardona is not Cardona, that it's a cover. Our intelligence placed him in Doha, Qatar, but no one by that name traveled from Doha to Minnesota. On the other hand, the day after the Pacificano disappearance, one Dexter Isaac

Nelson flew from Doha to Minneapolis via London. We have tentatively tagged a few other nodes with names based on retrieved content from the computers or names on service accounts. That includes one in Israel that has been traced to a subscriber with a billing address in Tel Aviv. The customer is named Anat Dorfman."

Ben and Karl stared at each other, both shaking their heads.

Chapter 43

"THERE HAS GOT to be some other explanation." Karl clenched his fists. "Anat saved your mother's life. Lev is my closest friend on the planet. He grew up with your father. These are not people who could be connected with all these killings."

"Oh, really? But they were both Mossad agents. And the way Ima told the story, she saved Anat's life."

"Yeah, well, but Anat was not a case officer. She was a desk jockey; she headed Technical Services after Lev retired."

"Technical Services. Like computers, networks, cyphers, spyware. And didn't you say she warned you off, told you not to investigate about the microchips?"

"It wasn't about the chipset. I already knew all about that. I was the one that uncovered the embedded hardware backdoor, remember. No, it was about some network that she knew about." He stopped, as if suddenly surprised at his own words.

DB put a hand on his shoulder. "This has gotta be really tough on you. I don't know about the clandestine stuff that you do, but, hell, don't they say that nothing is what it seems?"

"Sounds like a line from a movie."

"I think it is. But so what? Maybe you think you know them; maybe you don't know them at all."

"No, it doesn't make sense." Karl was not letting it go. "If she was really part of some super-secret, deadly black-ops network, why would she be on the Internet using an account in her own name? We already know that Sergi Cardona is a false identity. If these people are really as good as they seem to be, then none of the names you've tagged them with is going to match their birth certificates."

"Well, except those can be forged or faked, too." DB put up his hands. "Just saying."

"Look," Marwa said, "we need to think this through. If our analysis is right so far, we are dealing with a network that knows about the backdoor in the avionics chips and has access to very sophisticated technology as well as to, like, megabucks that it would take to finance such an operation. That sounds like they could have ties to some established espionage organization and it pretty much has to be either the US or Israel."

Karl coughed. "Not to throw a wrench into your works, but the Chinese may also know about the backdoor."

"Okay, but nothing so far points in that direction. If anything, it mostly points at Israel. It was rich American Jews, active Zionists, who were targeted by the Somali jihadi cell."

Suze had been waiting quietly by the door, like a bodyguard on executive detail. "I'm not big into puzzles. Not my strong suit. Mr. Botteneau hired us to keep you all safe. That requires knowing who to trust and who not to. If we can't trust this Dorfman in Israel, then we don't. We steer clear. Those are the people we have to fear." She gestured toward the diagram on the wall.

"And she is one of those dots," Marwa said.

"But maybe she isn't," Ben said. "You already said there's something funky there. She is connected in the only group with seven members. Plus, she appears to be one of a few with a traceable real identity. She—"

"So far," Marwa interjected.

"Right, okay, so far. But Suze said it. We need to know who we can trust. Let's find out if we can trust her."

"And how are we going to do that?" she asked.

"Without putting ourselves more at risk," DB added.

"And without putting her at risk if she is not really part of the network," Ben finished the thought.

Marwa was back at her computer, typing and clicking away. "I say we can trust her."

"Women's intuition?"

"No, social science and statistics. I've been doing an open-source scan for references to any of the handles we've retrieved so far, evidence of normal social activity, Web presence, commercial transactions. Look." She changed the projected display. "The size of the circles is now proportional to the amount of traceable activity. The big ball in the lower right is our Anat Dorfman. The rest are all tiny by comparison."

"Yeah, but you said traceable activity. There could be plenty that we can't trace."

"Exactly. Can't trace. Think about what not being able to trace activity means. This says Anat Dorfman is not like the others in the network. Everything we have on her is ordinary, except she happens to have this computer configured like the others in the network. It's almost as if she isn't really part of the network, just a bystander."

Ben looked over at Karl thumbing his smartphone. "What are you doing, Aba?"

"Ordering flowers."

— — —

Lev Novakov brought the package into the bedroom. It was a cool night after an unseasonably warm day in Tel Aviv, and a salt-scented breeze drifted in the open window. "It's for you."

"What is it? Isn't it rather late for a delivery?"

"Looks like flowers. The delivery boy was from a florist at one of the big hotels."

Anat undid the ribbon and opened the oblong box. "Roses. No card. Just two roses." She studied the roses: one a deep crimson, the other a peach-and-yellow peace rose. "I ..." She took in a sharp, shaky breath. "Karl's in trouble."

"What the hell are you talking about? Karl sent you roses?"

"Yes, and he is in real danger. Hand me my phone." She dialed quickly. "Shira? Hi, this is Anat. ... Yes, good. Is Karl there? ... So do you know where he is? ... Ah, so what took him to New York? ... No, nothing much, just something I wanted to ask him about. It can wait. ... Right, we should get together soon, maybe when Karl gets back from his consulting trip."

Lev sat down on the edge of the bed. "So Karl's come out of retirement, has he?"

"No, I'll wager that this consulting business is just a backstory. But he is stateside."

"What makes you think he's in danger?"

"These." She lifted the roses from the box and handed them to Lev. "Mind the thorns."

"I don't get it." He sniffed. "I like the perfume of this one; the red one smells like ... like cardboard. So what has this got to do with Karl?"

"He sent them, I'm sure. He's mixed up with HaVared. That's why he sent these to me. The blood-red one is their symbol. I once gave him a peace rose when I steered him away from digging too deep into the organization."

"What organization? The Rose? By any other name—"

"Would smell so sour."

"Enough riddles. Tell me what's going on."

"It could be treason to say anything."

"How long have we been married, darling? I still have my clearance, you know. If this is on a need-to-know basis, I need to know."

She took several slow breaths. "Shortly before I retired, my unit stumbled on a terrorist network using advanced encryption technology to coordinate assets dispersed around the world. We traced the network using our own advanced technology until one of the links pointed back to Mossad. When I took it to the Assistant Director, he told me to back off, that another team was handling it. I didn't believe him, so I had a friend from Shin Bet haul in for questioning an Israeli we had evidence was linked into the network. Shin Bet got nothing from him and released him after a few stressful hours, but while he was being questioned, I cloned the drive from his notebook computer. I plugged it into an open slot on our home-office computer, but was never able to get much from it beyond the barebones my team had already figured out.

"A few days after we picked up the guy, he disappeared. His body turned up later in a warehouse on the other side of the wall. No marks on the body, but an autopsy found traces of a poison, a ricin derivative developed at our own research labs at Nes Tziona. I stopped all work on the case and decided it was best to forget about it.

"These people, who call themselves HaVared, The Rose, do not want to be found out and will do whatever it takes to wipe out traces that might lead back to them."

"What exactly do they do? Which side are they on?"

"What they do is kill people. As to what side they're on, I think they believe they are on the side of the angels, or at least Israel. I don't know if they really are."

"And you say they have somebody inside Mossad?"

"Yes, we once tracked a computer to the campus."

"So, we can't turn to our friends there ... who, I now see, might not be our friends."

"No, but I do have a guess who the insider is."

"And ...?"

"I am pretty sure he was in the Director's office, the inner circle."

"Which means we absolutely cannot turn to anyone there; it might get back to him. And we need to get in touch with Karl without HaVared finding out. I don't think we should use the office computer until after I pop that hard drive. The phone is probably not a good idea either."

"I'll just have to send flowers. I can do that."

"But we don't know where he is."

"I'll figure something out."

Chapter 44

SAM WAS ABOUT TO head back to Georgetown when the sound of an alarm bell and the flash of a strobe from the hallway interrupted the discussion in Conference Room B.

DB stood up abruptly. "Fire alarm. We better evacuate."

Suze stepped in front of the door. "It's a trick, a false alarm, I'm certain. They're trying to get us outside, in the open."

"If it's a false alarm, why do I smell smoke?" Marwa said.

"Regardless, if we leave the building with chaos outside, it would just be too easy for us to disappear. I couldn't protect you out there."

"But we can't just stay here."

DB ground his teeth in concentration. "How about The Vault. It's two stories underground, with its own separate filtered ventilation system from outside. We should be okay there. There's a service stairway beside the elevator. Follow me and stay low."

Acrid smoke hung in the hall outside the room. DB crouched and half ran, half duck-walked down the hall. He held open the door while the others entered the stairwell. Halfway down, they met Maude Girard coming up.

DB blocked her way. "I wouldn't keep going that way, Maude. You're better off in The Vault. It's like a fallout shelter down there. We can wait until they get the fire out."

"Okay, if you say so. Hell, Kurt Vonnegut survived the firebombing of Dresden sheltered in a subway."

"Didn't know that, Maude."

She turned around and started down. "Yeah, for real," she said over her shoulder. "Permeated his writing,"

"You don't happen to have a TV down in The Vault, do you?" Karl asked.

"No, but we can get streaming webcasts on the Hot Box. If it's on the Internet, we can get it."

"Great, because we are going to need to know what's happening topside and when the all clear is sounded."

"And I assume we can Skype from the Hot Box." DB said as he slipped in behind Maude. "I need to call Arkady Pohl."

"No problem."

== == ==

Two fire trucks and the fire chief's red-and-white Ford Excursion swung into the Scenaria parking lot and lined up along the marked fire lane. As gear was being deployed, three firefighters in turnout coats and breathers entered to sweep the building and make sure everyone was out. Within ten minutes, they had located the source of the smoke: a smoldering fire burning in a supply closet on the first floor. The adjacent automatic sprinkler had been wrapped in a wet towel to keep it from being triggered. The fire was marked down as suspicious origin, and a call was put in to the Fire Marshall's office to initiate an investigation. As the fire crews were finishing stowing their gear and prepared to leave, they were surprised by six civilians emerging from the building. Before DB's people could cross the parking lot to the fire chief's vehicle, they were intercepted by three armed officers in black jackets who shuttled them aside toward a pair of unmarked cars.

The fire chief trotted over, heading them off. "What's going on?"

The man holding Sam's arm signaled his men to stop. "FBI.

We're taking these people into custody. What does it look like, Chief?"

Sam tried to step away from the man. "Look, my name is T. Samuel Parsons. I'm with the NTSB, and these people are with me. We haven't done anything."

With flashing blue lights and the whoop-whoop of sirens, two more cars entered the parking lot and braked in front of the knot of people. Arkady Pohl stepped out of the first car wearing riot gear, holding his badge high, and shouting, "FBI, you are under arrest. Keep your hands where we can see them." Three more men in body armor emerged from the cars with their guns drawn.

The fire chief, looking like he wasn't certain whether to raise his hands, stepped away from the group. "What is going on here. These are suspected arsonists, and they are already in custody."

As Arkady advanced, the man holding Sam started to push him backwards, toward the rear door of the car waiting behind them. "I told you, these people are already in our custody," he said. "We're taking them in."

"You'll stand down, agent. They're now our prisoners. Please get back in your vehicles and leave. We'll take it from here."

"On what authority?"

Arkady crossed the distance to the man in two steps and shoved his badge in the man's face. "On this authority," he said in a lowered voice, "and on the authority of the firepower pointing at you. An incident here would be very messy, wouldn't you say? And if you survived, it would be damned hard to explain, since our authority is real and yours is fake. You don't even have the letters F-B-I in the right place on your jackets, you cheap phonies. I don't suppose you know who hired you to pull this stunt."

Thrown off guard, the man answered bluntly. "Of course, we

know. He gave us a credit card for the deposit and it cleared."

"Really? Just wait until you try to put through for the rest of the charges. And if you don't get outta here, you might have to eat the cost of medical bills and maybe vehicle repairs, too. By the way, do you know what the penalty for imitating a federal law enforcement officer is? Look it up. Now, apologize to the fire chief over there and leave."

Chastened, the men mumbled an apology and climbed back into their cars. As the cars negotiated their way through the maze of vehicles crowding the parking lot, DB patted Arkady on the back. "Thanks for that. But you let them go. We had them. They're part of this Nemesis Network."

Arkady laughed. "Those idiots? They were just delivery boys. The people you are interested in are too smart to make a move themselves, not out in the open like this with so many witnesses." He laughed again. "Nemesis Network, now that's funny. Which one of you thinks he's Ian Fleming?"

DB was irritated but kept silent. Karl spoke up. "What might you call them, Agent Pohl? HaVared? It's Hebrew, you know, means The Rose. Very thorny issue."

Arkady blinked, then stiffened. "You don't know anything."

"Oh, I know a lot. We have the whole network mapped out. And we're working on attaching names to the members. We know there are eighteen cells. Did you know that eighteen is a special number to Jews? In Hebrew letters, eighteen is chai; it means life."

"You stupid idiot. Shut up."

Suze Kerchoff approached. "Is there something wrong? We should be getting out of here."

Arkady turned his back to her and addressed his ad hoc SWAT team. "Guys, you can go. Thanks for turning out and helping me teach those jokesters a lesson." The rest of his team returned to their cars. He waved them off. "Go ahead. I'll get back on my own."

Suze stood beside DB, watching. "So, what are we going to do?" she asked him.

"We're going to go back into our somewhat smoky head-quarters. You're going to double your detail and make sure no one else gets past you."

"No one got past us."

"Well, except for the arsonist, right?. But whatever. Just put enough men around so nothing like this happens again."

"Listen, cowboy, I know how many is enough. I'll do my job; you just pay the bills when you get them."

DB chuckled. "We all need to chill out. Why don't you come in, have a cup of chamomile tea with me, and let's figure out how we are going to stay alive. You, too, Arkady. Hey, everyone, back to Conference Room B. I'll crank up the ventilation fans and the air conditioning to help clear the air. Let's hope the fire department didn't decide to hose down our computers."

== == ==

The group, sans Sam, who had excused himself, slowly reassembled in the conference room. As Ben entered, he noticed that the display was still projected but had changed. "Why does that one blob now have a stroke through it, Marwa?"

"That means there has been a change in hardware or software detected by the Portcullis updater. Hey, that's the node belonging to your friend in Israel."

Karl slapped his thigh. "I'll be damned. She got the message and has acknowledged it. She knew what I meant by the roses I sent, and she has done something to her computer to signal us back."

Arkady narrowed his eyes. "Are you saying you know someone in HaVared? I mean, in the network."

"Not exactly."

"Then what, exactly?"

"We know someone who was linked into the network and was probably investigating it, at least at one time. And thanks for confirming the code name for the group. We now have it from multiple sources. So next step, I need a way to talk with her without risking drawing more attention. We need to know what she knows."

Ben's smartphone started playing *"Jerushalayim shel Zahav."* He slipped it from his cargo pants and thumbed it on. "Oh, hi, Ima."

"How are you? Where are you?" Her voice came through tinny on the speakerphone.

He looked around the room nervously. "Er, I'm visiting friends."

"Well, say hello to your Aba when you see him. I haven't heard from Karl." Before Ben could say that Karl was right there, she continued in a rush. "Oh, guess what? I was going through some of your old things and found your old laptop tucked under your bed and just had to try it. Amazing, it still works. Booted into Windows XP. Talk about nostalgia, all those ancient programs of yours. I'm having fun playing with it and just had to call you."

"Sure, wow, I ..." Ben stopped with a perplexed expression on his face. "I'll pass the message on to Aba."

"Wonderful. I better go. I'm having guests from Tel Aviv staying over. I love you."

"Love you, too, Ima." He thumbed off his phone and faced Karl. "Ima is acting weird. You heard. She says hello to you, then tells me she's been playing with software on my old XP laptop, then cuts the conversation short because she has, quote-unquote, guests from Tel Aviv staying over."

Karl grinned and put his hand on his son's shoulder. "You

don't get it, Bini? Who do we know in Tel Aviv who would stay over? And what software did you have on that laptop, the one you used for all your hacking back in the day?"

"Well, there is some homegrown stuff for controlling our botnet and for secure communication, but it's prehistoric. Plus, I'm not sure Ima would know what to launch."

"But didn't you have a way for your friends over here to wake up your system when they needed to reach you?"

"Right, but again, it's a really old system. We're talking XP Service Pack 1, I mean. I don't even have the software with me. And it was cobbled together by me and my friends. We were just kids. I don't know how secure it actually is."

"The very fact that it was homegrown might be a plus. I thought you were using some pretty sophisticated open source encryption."

"Well, duh. We used a souped-up version of Schneier's 448-bit Blowfish algorithm. That's still in use today."

"Whatever. Can you find a way to get a copy of your old program or jury rig something?"

"Hell, I can suck it off my old machine if it's running and online—and if I can remember how to access my backdoor. It's been years. Let me work on it." He sat down next to Marwa and waited as his laptop booted up. "I was just thinking, you know, about Ima. She is really smart."

"And you are just now learning that about your mother?"

— — —

Ben punched the air triumphantly. "I got it. I have our software off my old machine. Man that system was so, so slow. Don't know how we ever put up with that. I'll have to run the program in a compatibility box, but let's see. Here goes." The screen went black, then blue, and a title-bar appeared at the top: SECTEXT 1.0 INITIALIZING. PLEASE WAIT. "Woohoo! Now let's see whether we can text."

> LOCAL: Testing. Hello.
> REMOTE: Bini?
> LOCAL: Yup, it's me. Ima?
> REMOTE: No, Anat. Put Karl on.

Karl and Ben swapped places at the table. "Sorry, Aba. The latency is pretty bad because that old machine sucks, especially running Blowfish, which wasn't intended for this kind of job."

"It's okay." He started typing.

> LOCAL: Hi, Anat. This is Karl.
> REMOTE: You out in the rose garden?
> LOCAL: Yeah, tangled in the bushes.
> REMOTE: You know this goes all the way to the top.
> LOCAL: I do now. Here or there?
> REMOTE: Here, yes. There, maybe. I don't know.
> LOCAL: Any ideas of how to chop down wild roses?
> REMOTE: No. Find a way to live with them.
> LOCAL: Who are they?
> REMOTE: Names?
> Local: Real names.

There was a long pause before the next message appeared.

> REMOTE: Ricardo Baruch Mendonça, late of Brazil, known
> aliases: Monchu Po, Pedro Cabral. He tried to kill me. I
> walked away and grabbed his laptop.
> LOCAL: More?
> REMOTE: Shlomo Paz, last seen in Jerusalem, aliases unknown.
> His laptop proved it was a whole network. I cloned his hard
> drive.
> LOCAL: That's all?

Almost a minute passed with no response.

LOCAL: ???
REMOTE: And one of the top guns at the Office.
LOCAL: Current or former.
REMOTE: Former.

Karl whistled, closed his eyes, and bowed his head. When he looked up again, everyone in the room was watching him. He bent to the keyboard and typed another line.

LOCAL: We talking gardens?
REMOTE: You always were good at guessing games.
LOCAL: Watch your back.
REMOTE: You too.

A message appeared: REMOTE TERMINAL DISCONNECTED.

Karl looked up. "Well, we now have a total of four names, including Eben Ganim—gardens in Hebrew—a recently retired Assistant Director of Mossad—the Office, as insiders refer to it—plus several aliases. We need to fill in the blanks, Bini. We need to know who's in and who's not, or we could find ourselves talking with the wrong people."

Arkady sneered. "Talking? Do you think there is any talk in the world that can deal with this?"

"We have to do something," DB said. "They already tried to kill us all with that fire."

"I don't think that was their intent," Suze said. "They wanted to flush us out. They don't know what they are dealing with, any more than we do. They would need to question us, find out how much we know, who we told, how exposed they are."

"Well, they are pretty exposed." Marwa pointed toward the image of the network that now displayed flags with names next to a growing number of the nodes. "I've got bots out trawling the

Internet for anything that might connect those names or IP addresses with anything in our network or with each other. Dexter Isaac Nelson and Ricardo Baruch Mendonça were globetrotters. Needless to say, your dear former Assistant Director of Mossad did not travel as much, at least not under his own name, but we can tie him to cities and timeframes. Even as we speak, new data are filling in the blanks. We just added another name, a Philip Pressman who was recently in Boston."

Suze, who had been studying Arkady, noticed him stiffen. She placed a hand on his back. "Someone you know, Arkady?"

"Don't think so. Maybe the name or something similar came over my desk recently. I can look into it, though, if you want."

"Sure, you do that."

"I will. I need to get back to the office anyway. I can do a little research. I'll pass it on if I find anything."

Suze watched him leave, then checked to be sure the hallway was clear before getting on her radio. "The Bureau boy who's just leaving, I placed a tag-along on his coat. Keep track of him for me, will you?"

Chapter 45

DB WAITED FOR SUZE to finish her radio conversation. "What the hell was that about? Arkady will be really pissed when he finds out you bugged him. After all, he is a federal agent."

"He's a compromised federal agent with a history of skulking down the side streets. And whatever kind of agent he is, he's a lousy actor. He really perked up when that suspect in Boston was mentioned. When Brian was giving me the background on this case, he said that Arkady had a brother who worked in the shadows. I assumed he meant in drugs or something, but now I am beginning to wonder, particularly as Brian later mentioned that Arkady had made a recent trip up to Boston where he apparently met with his brother. If Arkady does have a brother in the game, it means that regardless of what he may have done for us, we just can't trust him."

The radio on her belt crackled. "This is Saltmarsh Two, front desk. Security cams show we have a visitor entering through a special door off the exec parking lot. Want me to get somebody back there?"

"No, I'll handle it." She looked at DB. "Do you know where he is talking about?"

"Ah, sure. Must be the old wheel-chair accessible entrance put in for Talpa. Follow me." He led her down the hall toward the back of the building. Before they reached the private entrance, they were met by someone speeding toward them.

Richard Talpa still had the wide shoulders and hammy arms of an NFL lineman, but his face had gone soft, and above the stumps of his legs, a pillow of fat padded his torso. He rolled down the hall toward them strapped into his high-tech wheelchair. As he approached DB, his wheelchair shifted onto two wheels and raised him up so his head was at eyelevel with DB. "Douglass Damn Botteneau. Aren't you looking good. What are you up to these days?"

"Running a company. Investigating security breaches. How about you? I see you still have your iBot chair. What have you been up to?"

"Same-old same-old, only now for my new bosses over at Fort Meade. Right now, though, I'm busy betraying my country and hoping I don't get caught at it. I heard about the fire on the news and made some guesses when the TV coverage showed you all reentering the building after the fire." He expertly swiveled the chair to face Suze and adjusted the height of his iBot to be looking her in the eye. "And you must be Suze Kerchoff, Brian Mallory's heir apparent."

"How did you ... ? Yes, of course, you and yours know pretty much about all of us."

"It's our job. Same-old same-old. And where is everybody?"

"In Conference Room B."

"Well, what are we waiting for? Let's go."

Talpa sped down the hallway, took the zee-turn to the main corridor, and waited just outside the door for DB and Suze to catch up. From the doorway, he studied Marwa's network diagram. "Holy shit. How long did it take you to put all that together?"

"A few days. Why?"

"Because at No Such Agency, we've been gathering intelligence over the last six years, and we don't have much more than that. You do this yourself?"

"Well, Ben and me, with a lot of help from DB and his people."

"DB was always good at that, that teamwork shit. I'm guessing you're Marwa Fredericksen, the resident Palestinian. I'm Richard Talpa. I built all this." He waved his arms before pivoting toward Ben. "And who are you?"

"You don't recognize me? I'm Bini, Karl's son."

"My, my, of course. You were just a cocky kid back then, but you were already wicked good at Internet hacking. I remember thinking that I hoped you didn't decide to go into business and start a rival company. Scenaria would have been doomed." He spun the chair smartly. "And Karl, welcome back. How are things in Israel?"

"Fucked as ever. But then, working where you do, you would know more about that than most."

"Not me. I just siphon the data. I leave making sense of it to others."

"But you seem to be taking a personal interest in this rosy little network."

"Ha ha. Well, sort of, but that's old business. At the moment I have more personal interest in you all. I would hate to see so many old friends hurt. And it occurred to me, you just might have the wherewithal to take care of a thorn in my side."

"If you've known about HaVered for six years, why didn't you deal with the thorn yourself. Why would the NSA just watch and wait?"

"Because that's our job, keeping watch. Taking action is up to other agencies. Besides, HaVered has been useful to us—and those other agencies. They did things we couldn't or didn't want to do—like rubbing out terrorists and would-be terrorists. That physical stuff draws too much unwanted attention and unsought scrutiny, and the wet work tends to backfire on our country. Better let the Jews do it."

Marwa cocked an eyebrow. "I take it you're not Jewish."

"Hell no. It's bad enough being a legless smartass. Why would I want to stack the deck even worse? No, I was raised atheist and never lost the faith. The more I know about the sorry state of our species and our poor planet, the more I know for certain there ain't nobody up there looking out for us. And I'm not too sure whether we are capable of looking out for ourselves, either, given our recent multi-ethnic performances in slaughtering each other. And don't get me started on the fat-cat white boys who think turning the whole world into an overheated wasteland is a good way to run a business."

Marwa was grinning. "I see you do not lack for opinions—nor lack confidence in them."

"Oh, my opinions are no better than yours, Marwa Khalidi. But I was not expressing opinions, just telling it like it is."

Marwa nodded toward the wall screen. "You said 'almost as much' about our network map. What are we missing?"

"Looks like you got most of the members, not all of the names. It's the topology that you are weakest on. You only have access to current activity, not the historical context we have, so you're missing a lot of the connections and don't seem to be able to differentiate the important ones from the minor ones. What software are you using?"

"GeMap 3.1, Garlock's open source visualization suite, Net-Base, a lot of statistics stuff we wrote ourselves in R. Why?"

Talpa spun his chair and deftly rounded the end of the table to roll in beside Marwa. "Do you mind?" He reached toward her laptop.

"No, be my guest." She shoved it toward him.

He lowered his chair a few inches and steered it under the lip of the table. "I'll add some of the missing connections, color them blue so you can keep them straight." The group watched as he spent the next fifteen minutes in a frenzy of clicking and tapping.

"There. Your biggest problem is not the actual topology of the network, but the way you are displaying it, which is not making it easy for you to see what is really going on." He started dragging nodes around, moving them into different groupings with the same connections. "There, now what do you see?"

Marwa squinted as she studied the display. "One of the clusters you pulled together is actually a kind of hub or an inner ring. Everyone in that group is connected to three other groups. Wait, one of those guys is only connected to two others, so, right, eighteen groups in all. The structure is much easier to understand the way you arranged it. Fewer crossing lines, and your blue lines complete the pattern."

"Right, and if you follow up on some of those missing associations, you will probably be able to fill in some of the missing names. How did you build the network in the first place, and how did you get this far?"

DB answered. "Actually, you showed us the way. We used pieces of your old corporate spyware. It was still baked into the update package in Scenaria's antivirus software, so we just used that to push some new patches that would look for the right software signatures. Then we planted our own loggers and scanners to monitor activity and dig into the Windows side of the systems. Isn't that how you do it at the NSA?"

Talpa let out a deep laugh that shook his ample belly. "Hell no. Data mining. You know how it works. Our approach is basically to put taps on every Internet pipeline we can get our hands on, sluice everything into storage, then look for things: keywords, associations, repeated patterns. We have teraflops of computing power analyzing terabytes of data. It's the sort of thing that happens when a group gets too much funding and too little oversight. Anyway, we eventually identified everyone in the network. Of course, every so often they lose somebody, so they will be down one for a while, but they always seem to recruit someone new fairly quickly." He squinted at the display in front of him. "But you seem to have added an extra member. You have one of the eighteen groups with seven instead of six. This one seems to be an outlier." He squinted at the flag on the node. "I recognize that name from somewhere: Anat Dorfman."

DB reached across the table and shoved the computer back in front of Marwa. "What do you want, Talpa. Why are you here? Who sent you?"

"Nobody sent me. In my position, I pretty much go where I please. Always did, of course. We can assume people watch where I go, but they watch pretty much everyone—at least everyone like those of us in this room. I came because I wanted to check out the fate of my old home in person. I could also see from CIA tracking data that you all were onsite. Well, all but our lady bodyguard here." He winked at Suze. "You're not yet on the radar, but you will be after this."

"That still doesn't answer my question."

"Questions. You always were good with questions, DB. Anyway, the problem is that this wonderful, well-organized network that has been so active and useful over the years, seems to have gotten out of hand of late. Overextending themselves, one might say. As I said before, my people don't take action, and the people who do either lack the will or the capability to deal with this particular problem. Before we knew the full extent of Thorn Bush—that's the code name by which we know it—the CIA made an attempt to deal with one small piece of it. They lost five good men and got the message that nothing was going to touch those people.

"Anyway, you have some idea, Karl, how segmented and dysfunctional the security community can be—working at cross purposes, keeping cards up the sleeve, hedging bets. Hell, even within the NSA, the various subgroups rarely share the cyber exploits they've worked out on their own. Nothing is going to get done by any of our agencies, and Mossad has made clear that they do not see Thorn Bush as a problem."

"Let me get this straight. The NSA is expecting us to do its dirty work and rein in this rogue network."

"Not the NSA, Richard Talpa. I'm the one who is looking to you for help with a problem that has gotten out of hand."

DB put on his best gape-mouthed what-the face. "Richard Talpa has suddenly acquired a conscience? Or is this still some overblown version of self-interest."

"I always had a conscience, DB. I just have a different sense of morality than you. Unlike some of those we have to live with, though, I don't go out and kill people who happen to be inconvenient. I don't bring down planeloads of innocents. And I don't approve of the officials who look the other way because it's convenient to let Thorn Bush continue to do our dirty work for us. For the most part, they take out terrorists, people we would rather see dead anyway. You know, it's so damned hard to capture and prosecute terrorists. Even on the rare occasion when we do take executive action, it's costly. Do you have any idea what it cost to deal with bin Laden? Thorn Bush, on the other hand, costs us nothing."

"There were plenty of Americans aboard both those planes."

"A price worth paying, my superiors would say."

"And you? What would you say?"

"I'm here, am I not. I can't give you any material support, but I hope I have planted some ideas worth following up on. Use what you know. Remember, it's a network, just a directed graph, subject to graph theory like any other digraph." He nodded toward the projected image of the network. "And now, in order not to spoil my cover story against the possibility of being asked to explain my visit, I had better be leaving. I'll check in on your progress in a couple of days." He maneuvered his chair back from the table but stopped at the door. "One more thing. If you look closely you will find that a couple of the nodes you are tracking are now located in the DC area. Worth noting."

— — —

Karl listened as the faint whine of Talpa's iBot wheelchair faded. "Well, who would have expected a visit from the Ghost of Christmas Past? How does that make you feel, DB, realizing he's been dogging your footsteps all these years?"

"Not terribly surprised. As we now know, the NSA has been dogging just about everybody's footsteps, although how you escaped scrutiny, Suze, escapes me."

"I don't believe Talpa for a minute. With all the hijinks we pull at Saltmarsh, I assume we are all closely tracked. And speaking of tracked, we better pay close attention to those two dots up there that Talpa said were tracked to the DC area."

Chapter 46

As he was turning into L'Enfant Plaza toward his office at NTSB headquarters, Sam realized there were benefits to heading a moribund work group with no current assignments. No one cared much if you showed up for work on time or at all. He arrived near the end of the day and spent much of his time making a token circuit of his floor of the building, being sure to chat with or nod to as many people as possible. Once in his office, he took his time drafting a response to an information request from another agency before ducking out to drive to the apartment.

Lottie, punctual as ever, had arrived home first. As Sam sorted through the packet of mail neatly stacked for him on the counter, he noticed Lottie's trench coat tossed carelessly on the floor in front of the bathroom door. He picked it up and slung it over his arm before tapping on the door. "I'm home, darling." The sound of rapidly dripping water was the only response. "You okay? I thought we could send out for pizza tonight. What do you think?" Nothing.

He twisted the handle and opened the door a crack. Steam-soaked air pushed out. "Hey, save some hot water for me." He opened the door the rest of the way and dropped the coat. The bathtub was nearly running over with bright pink water.

-- -- --

Marwa and Ben listened, shaking their heads in sympathy and

disbelief. Sam had poured out the account of finding Lottie's body as if he were vomiting the words, clearing his system of some poison.

"The police said there will be an autopsy and investigation as required, but ... it certainly looked like suicide. That's not possible. I know. That just isn't who Lottie was. She wasn't depressed. Hell, I don't think she was capable of depression; she wasn't really much of an emotional type. She was cool and analytic to a fault, except with me. She ..." He stared at the table, his face contorted in pain and disbelief.

Marwa put her hand atop his. "You've been mostly away from her for a few days. Maybe something hap—"

"Nothing fucking happened!" He stopped himself, lowered his voice. "Except she's dead. I told you, she didn't kill herself."

"Okay, okay," Ben tried to calm him. "This has gotta be hard, really hard. I can't imagine ..."

Sam's head shook in rhythm with his words. "There was no note, no warning signs, no nothing. It just doesn't make sense. And, of course, now I'm under suspicion, too, until the investigation is complete."

"If you want to just go, that's okay," Marwa said. "We understand. We can keep going here."

"No, I need to work, more than ever." He straightened up. "I have to figure out why she was killed. It makes no sense. She was a finance officer, a damn glorified accountant. She tracked expenditures."

Ben perked up. "What did you say?"

"She was in finance, budgeting, tracking expenditures."

"Like, what kind of expenditures?"

Sam's eyes widened. "She did say she was going to do some digging, try to find out something that might explain why my program was killed and your group was told to stand down."

Marwa leaned forward. "What if she found something, something that could embarrass the Board or the administration."

Sam lifted his head and faced them with tear-reddened eyes. "That makes sense in a nonsensical sort of way. She told me she had something to show me, but wouldn't say anything more over the phone. If it was connected with our work on the network, on HaVered. I ... Shit, I need to find out why she was killed and who did it."

"Is that realistic?" she said.

"Fuck realistic! What the fuck do we think we are doing? A random bunch of techno-nerds trying to outwit an organization of pros while they pick us off one by one. The bodies keep piling up. Maybe the real mystery is that any of us are still alive. We're sitting ducks. Everybody knows we're here. The old man, Talpa, even drops by to check up on us. The FBI knows. We can bet this HaVered network knows us all. They must be just waiting for the moment when it can look like an accident or when they can be sure to cover their tracks. It's just a matter of time."

"We could go to the press," Marwa said.

"Ah, Canadian-American faith in the power of a free press. Go to the press. Right. With what? A bunch of colorful diagrams that any middle school kid could create with PowerPoint?"

"We have names."

"Phony names."

"A few are real."

"We think. And most of those are already dead."

Ben, who had sat listening but seemed lost in thought, suddenly leaned forward. "Did your girlfriend have a laptop? Did she ever work from home?"

"Lottie had a laptop, but I don't remember her ever telecommuting. She did take it back and forth from the office now and then."

"Can you get it, bring it here? Maybe the team in The Vault can get something off of it."

"I suppose. It might be in the apartment, but that's cordoned off with police tape while they finish the investigation."

Suze snorted a laugh from the doorway. "Don't mean to barge in, but a little yellow ribbon never stopped Saltmarsh. Look, I'll swing into Georgetown and retrieve it if it's there. I'd like to do my own little investigation, anyway. You stay here, help the kids with their networking. I'll be back."

DB pushed past her into the room just as she exited. "You be careful, okay? Watch your back."

She glanced over her shoulder with a look of mild surprise. "Always do, always do. I'll put an extra man on duty here. With our three undercovers, that will make five. Should be enough."

"Should be. Hurry back, though." He continued to stare out the door as he listened to the fading sound of her boots on the tiled corridor.

Suze had the lock picked open and had ducked under the police tape before the doors of the elevator she had just exited were closed. She tried to slip the door shut silently, but the warped door refused to latch. She leaned on the handle and tried to twist it into place to no avail. Giving up, she surveyed the room. The apartment was a paragon of organized simplicity. A wide plate rail near the ceiling was lined with colorful glazed bowls and other objects of mixed utility and aesthetic appeal. Nothing seemed out of place. It was the territory of a couple who shared moderate obsessive-compulsive tendencies.

After a quick check of the closet and kitchen cabinets, Suze opened the bedroom door and entered another world. The canopy bed was draped with sheers, the walls were hung with tapestries, and the carpeted floor was nearly covered with colorful pillows in silk brocade. It was a playroom out of a Victorian edition of The Arabian Nights.

Suze stepped around pillows as she explored. "Where would an OCD accountant with a suppressed sense of play keep her laptop? If it's still here? Not in the bedroom. No. So I must have missed it." As she turned to leave, she tilted her head back and closed her eyes in concentration. When she opened her eyes again, she noticed the shelf above the door. A floppy fedora with an aquamarine feather rested beside a slim briefcase, it's handle just visible. She slid the briefcase off the shelf, set it on the nightstand beside the bed, and thumbed the latches. When it didn't open, she briefly considered puzzling out the combination before deciding to jimmy the simple locks. The snaps popped on her second try with her penknife, revealing a two-day-old copy of The Washington Times, a stack of stapled photocopies, and a MacBook Air.

Suze set the papers and the laptop aside to tuck into her backpack, used the tabs on the back of the locks to reset the combinations to three zeroes, and closed the briefcase. She carefully slid it back on the shelf. She had just zipped her backpack closed and was about to shoulder it when the groaning squeak of the warped door stopped her.

Cautious footsteps of someone in soft-soled shoes could be heard from the living room. Suze considered her options as she unholstered her pistol. The ground was two flights down by the fire escape. There were likely to be police watching the building. She hadn't thought about a story because she hadn't expected to be caught. Mallory would have chided her. "Always have a story," he would say. "Always have a backup plan." As quietly as possible, she attached the long suppressor to her compact Glock 29.

Part Seven: Theology
Chapter 47

"You SHOULD HAVE SEEN Arkady's face as he looked into the muzzle," she told the team in Conference Room B. "When I first got a peek around the corner and saw it was him, I was sure he had followed me. But no, he was just on a fishing expedition. He had noted that the door was not fully closed but figured it had been left that way for some reason by the crime-scene team.

"Anyway, I really can't be sure, but I am beginning to suspect he's not a threat to us, except maybe through bungling. Then again, I also got the impression he cultivates the image of Eastern European ineptitude to make himself seem less dangerous than he is. When he asked whether I had found anything, I told him no, zip. He seemed to believe me, but who knows" She put her backpack on the table and unzipped it. "Of course, I was lying. I found this, Sam. Is that her MacBook?"

"Looks like it. Where'd you find it?"

"On the shelf over the bedroom door. It would have been really easy to miss."

Sam was noticeably uncomfortable at the mention of the bedroom. "Yeah, that was ... where she kept her briefcase, on the shelf. She liked, you know, to stash things above eye level. It seemed to go with her being so tall."

Suze handed the laptop to DB. "Okay, let's see what you can get from it."

DB shook his head. "The gang down in The Vault doesn't

really do Macs."

"Why not? Some Apple antipathy or something? I know how some Mac fanboys can be about Windows, but I didn't know it worked the other way around, too."

"No, nothing like that. We just don't offer security solutions for Macs. Despite the urban myths, Apple computers are just as vulnerable to malware, but it's a much smaller market than Wintel machines, especially in the industrial world that's our main customer base. But I'll see what the crew can do." He took the computer and left.

== == ==

DB picked up the phone. "Botteneau here."

"This is Baumgarten from The Vault. Maude's not here. The Mac you gave us was password protected, but we still were able to get some stuff off the hard drive."

"Baumgarten?"

"Rufus Baumgarten. Uh, people down here call me Bumpus. Like I said, we pulled the disk and sucked some files off it. Had to fetch another Mac to get the software to be able read them, but the newest files were just long lists of recent expenses that seemed to have been pulled from various accounts identified by number and a code. I recognized the format."

"You recognized the format?"

"Yeah, my embarrassing past includes a stint in business school. Don't tell the others down here. My father always wanted me to take over the family chain of drug stores. What a disappointing son I was. Ha, ha. Well, anyway, some of the expense entries in the lists had been starred, but there's no footnote or explanation."

"If you could put that stuff in a Word doc or an Excel spreadsheet and send it up here, that would be great."

"Sure thing. I'll drop it off when I come up for lunch."

DB set down the phone and turned to the circle of expectant faces. "Looks like Sam's girlfriend had found some suspicious expenses. We don't know where they were leading, but maybe somebody didn't like the direction she was going. Either that or it was a megaphone message to poor Sam."

■■ ■■ ■■

The low purr of an electric motor was the only announcement that Richard Talpa was back. He shifted his chair up onto two wheels, expertly zigzagged between chairs, and stopped in front of the wall projection. "I see you have filled in some more of the blanks and have begun to weight the connections and classify them by direction and type. So what's your plan?"

DB gritted his teeth. "I don't think we have a plan. But what makes you think you can just come and go like you owned the place?"

"Technically, I do. Still. The majority of shares is in the hands of several of my shell companies. As CEO, you should have kept track of that sort of thing. So what's your plan?"

Ben looked around at the others. "We were hoping more information would give us some ideas, but this is not exactly our area of expertise. We thought about knocking out all the computers they're using, but it looks like some of these people know each other from other contexts and presumably could get back in touch by some means. We have to assume a certain amount of redundancy in the connections throughout the network. Plus, hardware can be replaced and software reinstalled. And it's not like we can go out and wipe them out one-by-one."

"What the hell do they teach at MIT these days, anyway? What do you mean this isn't in your area of goddamn expertise? How did you ever get through MIT without learning graph theory?"

"I studied at the Technion, not MIT. But yes, I understand graph theory."

"Then why the fuck haven't you used it?"

Both Marwa and Ben scowled. "Don't look at me," DB said. "I'm just an old database analyst. Database normalization is as sophisticated as my skills go. You want me to convert a table to third normal form, I'm your guy."

Talpa spun back from the projection. "Think, people. You can't destroy the network, so you want to cripple it. It's a problem in graph theory, finding a cut set that—"

"Partitions the graph into disjoint subsets." Ben nodded enthusiastically. "That's it. We are looking for a set of connections that, if we were to sever them, would leave the network fragmented into isolated pieces." He looked across at Marwa. "We were caught up in the content again, thinking about actual people and specific locations and about who knew what about whom—at least according to our guesses. We needed to step back and see it as an abstraction."

Marwa shrugged. "Whatever. But if I remember right, finding minimum and maximum cut sets is, like, computationally hard. Can take forever."

"Theoretically, yes, but we have a finite network of moderate size, and we can rely on shortcuts to simplify the problem. We don't have to find an optimal solution, just a workable one." Ben reached across the table and grabbed his laptop. "Let me setup some routines and crunch some numbers."

— — —

Ben took his time defining the problem, writing some fresh code, and importing data. Once the problem was set up properly, DB fed the program to the company's server network, which started searching for acceptable solutions. "Understand," DB said, "these are not like the big supercomputers over at your place in Fort Meade, Talpa. It could take some time to get results, but I do think we've done a fair job of exploiting what we have here with some parallel processing to speed up the search. Look, let's do lunch and see what results pop up by the time we're back."

—— —— ——

Eager to check the output, the group rushed lunch. After they returned, the first solution didn't arrive for another twenty minutes of heavy-duty number crunching. The computers had partitioned the network into two disconnected subsets at the cost of breaking thirty-three connections. "This is not an auspicious beginning," Ben commented.

Talpa snorted in derision. "Too soon to give up. Besides, we don't want to chop it in two. We shouldn't be wasting time looking for solutions with few subsets. Put a threshold on the number of partitions, and skew the criterion function to focus on the stronger, closer connections."

"But that could leave some of the subsets still weakly interconnected."

"Which could be okay," Marwa said. "This is not one of your mathematical optimization problems, Ben. We just need a bunch of semi-good solutions that we can examine and maybe tweak. You should change your program so it shows us lots of partial solutions instead of sitting there thinking for hours before showing us one mathematically pure one."

Ben heaved a sigh of annoyance but started rewriting his code.

—— —— ——

It took an afternoon of rewriting programs and playing with partial solutions to come up with a partitioning that looked like it might work. Ben summarized the progress to DB, who had left the group to catch up on some of his own work. "So, as often happens, making the problem a little more complicated made it easier to solve. We added nodes representing the fact that many

259

of the connections were by way of dropboxes we had identified. If we treat those as nodes that can be disconnected by hand, we are left with a solution that breaks the network into a dozen subsets that are essentially isolated from each other and, except in one or two cases, relatively weakly connected inside each group. This partitioning would require we disable or destroy nine dropboxes and block all communication to and from thirteen critical nodes: a little over ten percent of the network."

DB studied the diagram of the solution. "Now that you've found what you claim is a workable cut set, how do we break the connections? How can we prevent two agents who have been connected from ever again communicating?"

"We neutralize those thirteen nodes."

DB looked unhappy. "By neutralizing nodes, I take it you mean killing people. Am I right, Ben? You're talking about playing God. Or maybe I should say playing terrorist."

"Well, not necessarily. Maybe we can expose them and get them arrested and jailed or something."

Talpa was laughing and shaking his head. "Naïve. Hopelessly naïve. Keep in mind who you are dealing with. No, any solution will have to be essentially permanent."

Marwa was clearly distressed by the discussion. "We're not, like, field agents or hired assassins. I wouldn't even know where to start looking for that sort. Plus, the very act of trying to, like, put out contracts would almost certainly expose the agenda." She looked directly at Talpa. "I would think that even though the NSA doesn't do its own dirty work, you surely must know some people, the kind who could do this ... this stuff."

"Remember, I'm not the NSA, just Richard Talpa, and I definitely don't have any such contacts. But Suze might."

"Oh, no, not on this scale or at this level. In fact the very people I might reach out to could very likely overlap with the circles these guys travel in. It would take another network like HaVered, at their level, to take out these guys."

"That's it!" Marwa announced.

"That's what?"

"It's jujitsu, Ben. To fight people at this elite level, you would need people at this level. So, you turn HaVered against itself."

"I don't get it."

Marwa was bouncing with excitement. "In a sense, it's another social network problem. For each of those thirteen targets, we pick another agent who is only distantly connected and wouldn't know the target. We use our hacked connections into their computers to issue false orders to take out the target. They don't know the target is one of their own because they don't know who is in and who is not. They will just be doing their jobs. We don't have to, you know, take anybody out ourselves. They do the dirty work."

Ben reached across the table and grabbed Marwa's hands. "Brilliant! You are genius."

Suze was watching Talpa closely. "Looks like our spook from Fort Meade does not look entirely enthusiastic."

"I don't know," he said. "It might work, but it's very high risk. If everything doesn't happen just right, it will be found out, and once the threat is exposed, all the missiles will have your names scribbled on them. One of them might even end up headed my way."

"Always looking out for number one, eh Talpa."

"As you should, Suze, as you all should. Shit, I'm a survivor. I've dodged more than a few bullets in my time: landmines, assassination attempts, corporate blackmail. I've accumulated plenty of good reasons to protect my chair-bound backside and lots of practice doing so."

Karl, who had been quiet, pushed himself erect. "My list is

just as long as yours, Talpa, but I don't just think of myself."

"Lustig, don't go all self-righteous on me. I'm here, remember. I may be no boy scout, but I do draw lines. And all I was saying was that this would be a goddamn tricky operation to pull off. It's risky as all hell, but I didn't say it couldn't be done. And I didn't say I wouldn't stay in the game."

Suze walked over to the whiteboard. "Okay, boys and girls, listen up. We need to identify possible agents for each target. We need to figure out exactly how we get false orders to the agents. And we need to work out the timing. The agents will need time to plan their ops and get into place, but the more time we give them, the greater the chance of some part of the whole caper unraveling.

"My suggestion is we each focus on our strong suits. Ben, Marwa, DB: you're responsible for devising a foolproof way to direct the agents and track them. Talpa, Arkady, and I will concentrate on tradecraft, tactics, and personnel."

"Arkady? He's in on this?"

"Yeah. We have to have him on the inside."

"But he might have a family connection into HaVered."

"Exactly, which is why we have to have him with us where we can keep an eye on him. Besides, he might be able to give us some useful insights because of his connection. Anyway, I already invited him here. He should be along any minute now."

Karl was shaking his head. "Who put you in charge?"

"I did. Every SWAT team needs someone to take charge: a trained leader with on-the-ground experience. If Brian were still with us, he'd do it, but he's not, so you get me."

DB grinned. "All right! Go girl." She grinned back at him.

— — —

Arkady arrived within the hour. After some initial tension and sparring, the group settled into the job at hand, steadily working their way down the list of targets using what they knew, guessing at the rest, and arguing over everything.

Finally, Suze tapped on the whiteboard with a finger turned blue-and-red from the markers. "That takes care of Krumwalt, Malkusic, the two in LA, Brownfield and Zarco, Nussbaum in London, the German in Argentina, Roszhenki in Chicago, Breslow in Amsterdam, Mizrachi in Paris, the German army officer, the guy in Texas.

"We are down to our last two targets, and we need candidate agents to take them out. Let's start with the one flagged as Philip Pressman. Tracking data from his laptop and cellphone makes him still local, in Alexandria at the moment, but apparently staying in downtown DC. There was another operative in the DC area, but he's not a candidate because it appears he was working with Pressman, so knows him. The closest weakly connected operative was last tracked to Miami, but we already have the Florida assignment settled. Ideas?"

"Yes." Everyone looked at Arkady. "I'll take care of Pressman."

"That's not how this works," Suze said. "Each target is to be taken out by someone in the network. It's gotta be an inside job."

"I know that, but I also know Pressman. I can take care of him. It will mean one less insider who might go squirrelly or sound an alarm. I'll do it." He defiantly locked eyes with Suze.

"It's your brother, isn't it?" she said.

"Yes. Dima is part of HaVered. Pressman is one of his aliases."

There was a long silence before Suze spoke again. "We can't ask you to do this. Not with your own brother."

"You're not asking me; I'm telling you. It's something I have to do. Myself."

Talpa looked incredulous. "What kind of messed up family is this. And why would we trust you to really take care of this."

"Because I feel the same way as you, Talpa. Hell, he's probably the one who did Sam's girlfriend—either him or the other one who's been hanging around DC—or maybe they did it together. It's time this whole thing stopped. In some ways, it's really better that I do it than some asshole stranger. At least I'll make sure it's quick and painless."

Suze nodded gravely, then wrote his initials on the whiteboard after Philip Pressman's name. She crossed out the name and wrote 'Dima Pohl' under it.

"That's Dmitry," Arkady said, his voice emphatic, "not Dima. I'm the only one who calls him Dima."

She corrected the first name. "And that leaves us with maybe the toughest one of all: our Mossad mole, who our sources in Israel suggest might be former Assistant Director, Eben Ganim, who is still active there."

Karl raised his hand. "I'll take care of that one."

"What are you talking about, Aba?" Ben was out of his seat. "How can you … ?"

"It's another case of an inside connection. I can use my connections to have it dealt with internally. That will be swift and final. I know these people. If I can find the right channel in and the right way to tip them off, they will end it."

"How can we be sure?"

"How can we be sure about Arkady?" He swept his hand at the whiteboard. "Hell, how can we be sure about any of these … assignments? What if we're wrong, and we paired up somebody who knows his target or is known by the target?"

Suze tapped a marker against the whiteboard as she thought. "Actually, that could work to our advantage, if the agent thinks the target has gone sour. Likewise, if the target knows the agent it could mean being trusting, credulous. Anyway, I say we let Karl take the last one. I assume you will be using the dangling node, that Anat Dorfmann."

"Yeah, I just don't know exactly how. I'll have two days to work out the details, right? That's the lead time we're giving the agents we've picked out, right?"

"Right. Ben, how are you all doing with the technical details?"

"We got it just about worked out. It's a little bit different for each of those thirteen agents. Well, eleven, really, because Karl and Arkady just have to be told when the countdown starts. Anyway, it seems some nodes rely on drop boxes, others expect to be contacted by secure texting, and so forth. We have a baker's dozen customized orders counting the two just made in person."

"We're counting on you two," Suze said. "It all needs to be completed with surgical precision so there is no chance of an advance warning. And we have to be sure that they all look like accidents or natural causes."

"Marwa is still refining the wording of each of the messages, but the criteria will be made clear in each case. Talpa, Arkady, and you should check the wording to make sure the jargon and stuff is acceptable. We don't want to be tripped up by some amateur-sounding message."

"Yeah, don't tell any of them that you want somebody whacked." Suze winked at them. "They only say that on TV." She turned back to the whiteboard. "Okay, people, let's finalize all this and put a schedule on it. We'll need to double check airline schedules and travel times to be sure all the assignments are doable within the timeframe."

Ben noticed that Marwa had stopped her typing, "You okay?"

"I guess. I just never ... killed anyone before."

"You're not killing anyone now. They're doing it to themselves."

"And we're issuing their orders. At Nuremberg, that would have made us even more culpable. Did you ever kill anyone, Ben?

Like in the army?"

"You know, that's the one question you should never ask any soldier. But, no, I never saw combat. I served in military intelligence, and it was between wars. But I could still be called up at any time. I think I could do what I had to do."

"I don't know if I could. Except to defend someone in my family, I suppose."

"Yeah, me too, I suppose. Better finish your drafts so we can launch this operation. I don't like being poised on the edge, just waiting."

Chapter 48

BEN AND MARWA DROVE in silence back to the hotel. In the hotel garage, Marwa parked and turned off the ignition but sat staring at the gray concrete wall ahead. Ben pivoted in his seat to face her. "What are you thinking?"

"Lots of stuff."

"About the operation?"

"That and ... I got another phone call. Seth wants a divorce."

"Oh, I am sorry."

"Don't be. I suppose it's been a long time coming. It was never, like, easy. I think Seth was looking for an acolyte who would follow him anywhere, and I was this rebellious younger woman looking to have it both ways, to follow history and wipe it out at the same time. I didn't think of it this way at the time, of course, but by marrying Seth I could, with one stroke, be honoring my father's fantasy that I would marry a man of faith and also be thumbing my nose at him and his patriarchal pushing. Maybe I was also getting even with him for not being much of a part of my life growing up. Yeah, and I end up marrying a man equally distant. Surprise, surprise. Does that sound too much like self-serving psychoanalysis?"

"Well, it is sort of what you do. Anyway, you're digging for answers, trying to make sense of something that must be hard, especially now. Maybe things can work out."

"No, they can't. He's found someone. She works at the agency, she's Lutheran, and she's there. That's three strikes and I'm out. One, I probably don't even have a job anymore. Two, I'm not Lutheran. And three, I'm not there but some five hundred miles due south. Actually, I'm caught up in some ... some other world. It's a world I'm also struggling to make sense of, like in some movie about spies and assassins, where people kill and get killed." She closed her eyes as she talked. "It's happening, for real. Up to now, it's been, like, this exercise, a classroom project. You know what I'm saying?"

Ben nodded several times. "Yeah, like it was just problem solving."

"And now, it's like we launched the missiles, and there's no calling them back, and people are going to die—maybe us, too—but it's all, like, on autopilot." She started crying. "My god, it's just like that plane, preprogrammed to crash, programmed to end so many lives. Maybe we're no different than HaVered." She slapped her hand over her mouth. "Oh, my god! Don't you see? We don't know how each of those assignments might be carried out. What if one of the agents decides the best way to take out some target is a bomb in a shopping center ... or another airline crash?"

"It's not going to happen that way. These are pros; they have time to do it right. You're just borrowing trouble, building worse case scenarios."

"But we don't know, and the blood will be on our hands. And, hell, maybe we just killed ourselves and everyone we know in the process. Because, if they figure out what's happening, they will figure out who did it, and they will come after us. Think of what that Israeli team did to go after the terrorists who planned the Munich operation." She was shaking. "I'm scared."

Ben reached over and pulled her toward him, cradling her head. "Me too. Me too."

They sat for several minutes just holding each other.

"Ben?"

"Yes?"

"I don't want to be alone tonight."

Ben looked around as if the right response might be found somewhere in the car or written on the concrete walls. He took a deep breath and let it out slowly. "Okay."

Chapter 49

BEN ROLLED OVER AND looked into Marwa's sleeping face, half obscured by a cascade of thick brown hair. Her eyes flitted behind her lids. "You are so beautiful," he whispered, his voice so soft that the words barely escaped his lips. "I don't know how, but I am falling in love with you, Marwa Khalidi."

Her eyes fluttered open and she smiled over at him. "I was dreaming this wonderful dream. We were on a beach somewhere. Maybe Israel. We were watching children playing in the waves. We ..." She freed an arm from under the sheets and brushed his cheek with her hand. "I love you, Ben. I know that's impossible, but I do."

"Then we are doomed. We both know it could never work."

"I don't know that."

"That's because you're a romantic. You don't look at life with logic. Let's face it. Some things are impossible. I'm a Jew and you're a Muslim. Even worse, you're a vegetarian and I'm a confirmed carnivore."

"Be serious, Ben."

"I am." He started slapping out a beat on the headboard as he hummed the opening bars of a metal-core musical pulse. "Parallel lines, parallel lines of opposing signs ..." he chanted.

"But the voices of the many still murmur a dream," she finished.

"And it's still a dream."

"But it doesn't have to be. And you don't fool me, Binyamin Markham. You hide your passion and vulnerability under a screen of statistics, but behind that flimsy curtain of formulas, you're a mushy romantic."

"Am not." He tickled her under the sheets.

"Are too." She giggled and poked him back.

"Am not." He jerked the sheets off and looked down at her, naked, curled in defense against his next tickling onslaught. "You are so ... so beautiful." He bent to kiss her hip. She turned onto her back and his kiss landed on her belly. She took his head in both hands as he planted a row of kisses, inching steadily downward.

The room phone rang. "Go away," he shouted. "Whoever you are, we don't want any." He continued his kisses. The phone kept ringing.

"Oh, shit." He reached for the phone and answered it with evident annoyance. "What do you want?"

"Well, good morning to you, too, son."

"Oh, I'm sorry, Aba. I was ... er, just waking up."

"Right, I'm sure. But I need to use your laptop, Bini."

"Sure, I suppose. But why? Don't you have your laptop?"

"I need that encrypted chat tool of yours, the old software. I need it to connect with Anat."

"Okay, but do you need it right now? I ..."

"Yes, I need it right away; we're on the clock. I'm just down the hall. I'll be right there." He hung up.

Marwa had her arms out ready to pull Ben back on top of her.

"Not now, my dad's coming to borrow my laptop. Quick, duck into the shower."

"No way. I'll just stay here and pretend I'm sleeping."

"You are a troublemaker. Don't be silly. At least put some clothes on."

"Don't you think your father knows what's going on?" She sat up and pulled the sheets up to her neck.

Three taps on the door threw Ben into a panic. "Please, Marwa." He pulled his pants on, padded over to the door, and checked through the viewport to be sure it was Karl. Before twisting the door handle, he turned back to plead once more with Marwa, but she was gone.

He opened the door. "Uh, Aba, boker tov."

"Yes, good morning, Bini." Karl scanned the room. "Where's Marwa? I thought she was with you."

A shout came from the bathroom. "See, I told you, Ben."

"She's, uh, taking a shower, uh ..."

"Just give me the laptop, and I'll leave you two alone. Is there anything special I need to know to use the software?"

"Not really. Just launch the shortcut called 'CHATBOX' on the desktop. But it won't do anything unless my old XP machine is running and connected. And Anat may not be there."

"I'm going to lay odds that Anat has your machine with her and has kept it on since she borrowed it. I know Anat."

"Okay, give it a try." He handed the laptop to Karl. "It will be even more sluggish going through the hotel Wi-Fi, but it should be secure."

"What do I do to start a chat?"

"Just click 'connect home' and wait for the confirmation and the prompt."

Karl tucked the laptop under his arm. "How is she doing?" He spoke softly as he tilted his head toward the bathroom. The hiss of the shower on full could be heard through the door.

Ben shrugged.

Karl raised his eyebrows. "And you?"

"Same."

"Look, son, this is real. Real isn't always easy ... or clean."

"I know 'real', Aba. I'm not some teenager."

"And I know that. Neither am I, by a lot wider margin of years. But that doesn't make life-and-death stuff any easier. There are things we have to do."

Ben studied the mottled blue-and-brown pattern in the carpet. "But so many people have died. And now more are going to die. We ..."

"I can't grant you absolution, Bini. Only you—or God—can do that. I can tell you that you are a good man and hope that's enough. The same for Marwa. If I could offer a bracha that would put your souls at ease, I would."

"I thought you didn't believe in God."

"I don't, but that doesn't mean I don't believe in blessings ... or the power of prayer. Both of you have mine." Karl stepped out of the room, then stood smiling back through the doorway. "You know, she reminds me of your mother: smart, quick-tempered, and trouble in a small, sweet package." He turned and walked down the hall.

Ben closed the door, then jumped at the sound of the bathroom door opening. Marwa stepped into the room, naked, droplets of water still beaded on her milk-and-tea skin. She twisted her head to one side and down, twirling the towel she carried into a turban.

"That was a quick shower. And you look absolutely ..." He ran his tongue along his upper lip as he approached.

"Can we just talk?"

"Not with your dressed like that, we can't. I'll never be able to keep my mind on the topic of conversation no matter what it is. Let me at least get you a robe." He ducked into the bathroom and snatched one of the heavy chenille hotel bathrobes from the hook on the back of the door. "Are you sure you want to just talk?"

She swatted at him with the end of the belt as she finished tying it around her waist. "Yes, I'm sure. I want to know what this means, what happens next?"

"If by 'this' you mean us, I have no idea what happens next. All I know is that I want to find out, to find out with you. I assume once we wrap up things at Scenaria, we finally head back to Cambridge and your job."

"If I have a job. Woolyard is not happy with me—his emails make that clear—and Sam seems to think CAASS is not long for this world, anyway. As if that were not enough, pretty soon, I may not even have a place to stay. Seth is pushing for a quick and clean divorce—clean being easy, at least for him. The place in Danvers is in his name, I make more than he does, and he is now saying we should talk about how much alimony I ought to pay him. I asked why I should pay him anything, and he is all, like, you know, how he supported me through my second doctorate, how he's had to survive up there all on his own because of my work, how—"

"Move in with me."

"Whoa. You push even faster than my ex—or soon-to-be ex."

"Just being reasonable, logical. The place on Beacon Hill is mine for as long as I want it, job or no job."

"You really think it could work, I mean, us? We're so different, and we're from different worlds and—"

He kissed her. "And I ... yes, damn it, I'll say it. I'll shout it. I love you. Hell, Marwa, we're people of The Book, Semitic cousins. We should be able to make it work. I mean, just because our people have fought each other for thousands of years shouldn't stop us from trying." He slipped his hand inside her robe.

"Ben, stop it. This is serious. There's so much you don't know about me."

"Then enlighten me. What don't I know about you?"

She sucked in a breath through clenched teeth. "Lots."

"Like?"

"Like I'm a spy."

"Aren't we all these days?"

"No, spying for real."

"You? A spy? No way. Recent experience notwithstanding, you're not cut out for it."

"You can say that again. I was supposed to keep reporting back to Woolyard, but ..."

"Woolyard?"

"Yes, I was told to keep an eye on you. Well, I guess I did that part, but I was a complete fail when it came to passing anything on. He kept asking me what was going on, and I kept telling him I'd let him know if anything came up. Hah!"

Ben couldn't stop laughing. "If that's the worst secret you've kept from me—that you didn't snitch for Woolyard—I'd say we're on pretty good ground here."

"What about you? What haven't you told me?"

"That I had the hots for you from day one." He opened her robe and slipped his arms around her bare waist. "And I really have the hots for you right now."

She let the robe fall to the floor in a heap.

▬▬ ▬▬ ▬▬

After carefully rehearsing his part of every possible dialogue, Karl double-clicked the program shortcut and got a blank home screen with the SECTEXT title bar. For several minutes, Karl stared at a blinking cursor. He was about to give up and reboot when a line of text appeared.

REMOTE: ???
LOCAL: Karl here. Anat?
REMOTE: Anat here. What's up.

LOCAL: You need to figure out who you can trust at the Office.
REMOTE: I'm on it.
LOCAL: Good. Tell them they have a dangerous mole.
REMOTE: The one we talked about?
LOCAL: Right. But just to be sure, don't give a name. Give them this IP address and tell them they have thirty-six hours to figure out who it's connected with.

Karl slipped a folded Post-it note from his pocket and typed the thirty-two-digit IP address.

LOCAL: At the end of the thirty-six hours, they must take care of the mole. Not before. Tell them that whatever they do with him, he has to disappear completely, permanently. Understand?
REMOTE: Yes. Do I tell them this is about HaVered?
LOCAL: If they don't already know, let them figure it out.
REMOTE: Okay. Thanks.
LOCAL: Be careful.
REMOTE: You too. Shalom.

Karl shut down the laptop. He knew he was passing the buck, but he also knew it was the right thing to do. It would be in the hands of Mossad to solve the problem and do the dirty work. Anat would not be directly involved and neither would he. It was another judo move, but he felt no sense of triumph.

He put his head in his hands. "For better or worse, Karl Lustig, you just helped kill the guardians. Well, okay, the self-styled, self-appointed guardians." He fought back tears. "So many. And who will clean the blood from your knife, Karl? Who will forgive you?"

The tears came and wouldn't stop.

Chapter 50

THE FRESH RUBBERIZED COATING atop the half-completed office building tugged at Arkady's shoes, making clicking sounds with each step. Stacks of two-by-sixes and empty buckets from the roofing material were on one side, a refuse slide and a precipitous drop into dark nothing on the other.

Dima was waiting. "Ah, little cub, here at last. What exactly is it that you wanted to discuss on a rooftop in the dark?"

"Conclusions."

"And what have you concluded?"

"It's time, Dima, time to end this, to put an end to HaVered. Enough is enough. It's not even that so many have been killed—many were soldiers, and I'm not even saying they didn't earn their fate—but so many innocents have died as well."

"It's always a calculated risk, weighing the cost and benefits."

"Then your scales need recalibrating. To stop five terrorists, you kill nearly six hundred people: children, the elderly, women, men, dozens of Jews among them."

"Six hundred? How do you get six hundred? There were less than three hundred on the Singapore flight."

"What's a few hundred more or less, right? Just add in the Malaysian flight, your damn proof-of-concept." He spat out the last words.

"That was an accident. We only intended to take temporary control of the plane, then release it back to normal flight. It was a test, brief, that's all. Something went wrong—maybe the pilot, maybe a fire in the cargo of lithium batteries—we don't know. Nobody knows. As to the Pacificano flight, it was a last-minute decision by one man improvising on his own. You might say it was not according to plan or policy."

"As if that mattered now."

"Look, our resources were already stretched intercepting the other teams. We couldn't let that flight reach Chicago and risk the terrorists disappearing into the city. We didn't know their targets. Our only hope was to stop the terrorists before they deployed. We had no *kidon* in Singapore, only a couple of *sayanim*. So you see, we had 'assistants', not 'assassins'. Surely you understand the difference. Taking out the plane would probably not have been my choice, but, in the end, it succeeded."

"You have a warped sense of success."

"You know why we do this, don't you?"

"What's your version?"

"My version? Simple truth, history. After Operation Wrath of God against the planners of the Munich massacre was wrapped up and the teams were disbanded, some of us thought it was a mistake, that there was still work to be done. It could no longer be done within Mossad or the military, so HaVered was formed —unsanctioned, unofficial—to take direct, lethal action wherever and whenever needed. We do what is necessary to protect the homeland. It's about prevention rather than vengeance."

"How noble sounding, but it's also about self-protection. Worse, each of your operations demands a response. You take out a bomb maker and Hamas retaliates. Each round ups the stakes. You respond in kind, but there is 'collateral damage.' And you must take out anyone who is a threat to the organization, who might expose you for what you are. Don't you see? You have become the very thing you hate. You, yourselves, are terrorists, above the law: judges, juries, and executioners all in the hands of one invisible network."

"We watch out for the interests of the Jewish homeland."

"Bullshit. The IDF watches out for the interests of the Jewish homeland. The government, Mossad, Shin Bet: they watch out for the interests of the State of Israel. You are outlaws, Dima, accountable to no one. However noble you thought your aims might have been at the outset, your methods have turned you into monsters. The end doesn't justify the means; the means become the end.

"And what ever happened to being held to a higher standard, Dima? What kind of a light unto the nations are we now? 'Do not to others what is hateful to you.' No, it's time to put an end to it."

"You think quoting Hillel is going to sway me? But, you know, little cub, you may be right. Perhaps it is time to retire. I admit I've been thinking about it for some years, even planning. This ... this business is taxing. It weighs on the soul as well as taking its toll on the body. I've thought that South America might be nice. I really like Argentina, parts of Brazil. My Spanish is good, and after Operation Chipset, my Portuguese is almost there. I've always been a quick study—quicker than you, at least."

"I'm not talking about just you, Dima, not about retirement. It's time to close down the entire operation."

Dima laughed loudly. "Impossible."

"Not impossible. HaVered will be dismembered, chopped into small pieces."

"And who will do that bit of butchery? Your little band of egg-head amateurs? That's too pathetic to even contemplate. We are the very best. Who can stop us? The CIA? Mossad? No! We—"

"Exactly. You, your own best and brightest will do the job. We hacked HaVered. It will be a new Masada. You will kill yourselves."

Dima's smile melted. "You are serious. You really mean it."

"We really mean it. My egg-head amateurs, as you call them, may not know thirty ways to kill an enemy with their bare hands, they may not be stronger and may not have the advantages of size or experience, but they are a lot smarter. And they've outsmarted you, the whole organization. They've turned it against itself."

"Why are you telling me this?"

"Because I was hoping you could be persuaded to quit. So I wouldn't have to kill you." He pulled a pistol from his jacket; the bright metal glinted in the light from the security lamps at the corners of the roof.

"Kill me? With that?" Dima laughed again. "A cheap pistol that probably doesn't even shoot straight. Wait, now I get it. It's from off the street. And you are thinking you can just get rid of it after you're done."

"I don't want to have to get rid of it after I'm done. I want you to be done. Never again."

"We Jews seem to have an affinity for that phrase, never again—so easily said, so hard to enforce, so seldom sustained. Never always comes far sooner than anyone expects. You know, little brother, that you would have to be absolutely sure that it ends here. You can't take a chance on me outing your little operation. And you have to know to a certainty that, were your operation to succeed, I or someone else will not simply begin recruiting to regrow the network."

"Give me your word, and we can both walk away."

"And you would trust my word? I lie for a living. How could you trust a professional liar? I tell you that I am finished, and then what?"

"Dima, please. Don't make me do it."

Dima chewed on his lip for several seconds. "You do know

that I would kill you without a moment's hesitation if I thought it was needed ... or if I was given the order."

"Just promise me, Dima, and walk away."

Dima took a step closer. "Now I see why you chose this building, a construction site. The chute over there, an easy way to handle a body without having to haul it down yourself. You do realize that you'll have to do me at close range with that puny toy, and it will take more than one shot. Pity. Messy and unpleasant."

Arkady raised the pistol higher and tried to steady his hand.

Dima smirked. "You can't do it, can you? You can't kill me."

Arkady gritted his teeth in silence and struggled to slow his breathing.

"Here, I'll make it easier for you." Dima turned around. "There, now you don't have to look me in the eyes. Trust me, I know about these things. It's harder, at least at first, if you have to see their faces. It's easier in the back. Now, remember, the technique you want is called double tap, the second shot to the head." He started to walk away toward the temporary stairs to the roof.

"Stop!" It was a whispered shout, desperate and hoarse.

"Goodbye, my little brother. I'm tired of waiting."

Dima was almost to the opening in the roof when the shot caught him. He stumbled, pitched forward, and sprawled face down, his arm dangling over the edge of the open stairwell. Arkady walked over, lowered the pistol, and fired his second shot.

Chapter 51

THE CELLPHONE INSIDE HER purse rang with the sound of an old fashioned Bell telephone. When Heddy Krumwalt finally heard the muffled clanging, she put down her book and dragged herself into the cottage, leaving the warm Key West sea breeze behind. She grabbed her purse from the hall table and rummaged for the phone. It stopped ringing just as she found it at the bottom. She didn't recognize the caller's number, but it was in her 305 area code. She hesitated for a moment but decided to return the call. She brushed back her frizzy blond hair and put the phone to her ear.

"You just called me?"

"This is Cutlass."

"What? I don't know anyone named—"

"Is this Flintlock?"

"What the fuck?"

"Flintlock? This is Cutlass."

"And this is an open wireless line. What the fuck are you thinking?"

"Emergency. The hedgerow's been hacked. I need you. The marina in twenty minutes." The caller disconnected.

Heddy stood by the table for a minute as she slowed her pounding heart and forced herself to become a professional on short notice. She glanced at her watch before dashing into the bedroom to change out of her bathing suit into traveling clothes.

The shoe box with her tools was on the closet shelf, pushed to the very back. She took out her Beretta, loaded it, and pocketed extra ammunition. The tactical knife she strapped to her ankle and pulled the cuff of her baggy jeans down over it.

The well-lit pier was not quite deserted. Heddy strolled with carefully styled nonchalance along the broad boards, noting the position of every boat and person along the way. She was just past the last of a series of matching for-hire deep-sea fishing rigs when a man onboard spoke quietly. "In here, Flintlock."

She stopped but didn't turn. "What do you want?"

"I'm Cutlass. We need to talk."

She turned slowly, chagrined that she had missed the man in the shadows when she had approached the boat. But, of course, he was Cutlass. He was good.

He did not offer her a hand as she climbed aboard. They ducked into the semi-enclosed cabin without a word and sat on opposite benches.

"Talk," she said.

"The hedgerow has been breached."

"So you said." She noted his hands were in his lap, and she was calculating how quickly he could retrieve the piece she knew he must be carrying. He was older by a few years, perhaps slower, certainly more practiced. Was she fast enough? And what was her escape route?

"I got pinged with a message to pick up an assignment from my dropbox," he said. "But the ping was not in the usual form and the orders in the dropbox were missing the handshaking code I needed to authenticate."

"Faked?"

"Apparently."

"And the orders?"

"Neutralize you."

Heddy kept her face expressionless. She knew this man only by his codename, which had popped into a few exchanges in the past. She couldn't know for sure, but she suspected that, despite his reputation for efficiency, he was nowhere near as central or well-connected in the network as she was.

He smiled at her self-control. "It's cool, don't worry. But we're going to have to work together to figure out how extensive the breach is and who is behind it. Are you in?"

"Yeah, sure."

"Good. Obviously, we're on our own here, not a word through any channels because we don't know how wide this malignancy has spread and who can still be trusted."

"What about my link-pin? Shouldn't we at least ..."

"How do you know that's not who fingered you? Maybe he's the traitor."

"What next?"

"An evening boat ride up to a safe house I have that's not in the database." He stood and climbed up to take the helm. "You cast us off, and I'll start the engines. We can talk on the way."

Heddy hesitated, but then went back out to handle the lines.

Cutlass turned the key, and the deep rumble of the twin outboards covered his muttered words.

—— —— ——

Theodore Malkusic shivered in his peacoat as he waited for the outbound Red Line train on the platform at Boston's Park Street Station. He checked his watch; he would just make his meeting with a new contact in Harvard Square.

The rush hour commuters were only beginning to thin out. He was not happy. He hated the cold and the noise, and he hated and distrusted crowds. As the rumble of the approaching train grew, he reluctantly moved forward from the tiled back wall against which he had been leaning. At the edge, imagining himself alone in the station, he stared down the tunnel and watched the unsteady light of the approaching train.

— — —

Max "Dog Face" Brownfield was crawling along at eight miles-per-hour in northbound freeway traffic on Interstate 5 in Southern California. It had not been a good day. He had been unable to track down the information he was assigned to confirm, even after hours of painstaking and boring microfilm research. After only three days visiting his brother in Glendale, he had received new marching orders. There would be time only for hurried goodbyes and a hasty repacking of his bags before he would have to turn around and head for LAX.

He slammed on the brakes as an El Dorado wedged itself suddenly into the space ahead. He yelled at the motorist.

— — —

It was an eventful several hours. Aviva Nussbaum was electrocuted outside London when the clippers she was using to trim her garden hedge shorted out. Leo Zarco was accidentally shot and killed in a drive-by shooting outside a crack house in a neighborhood where he had no business walking. In Buenos Aires, a man known locally as El Alemán, the German, committed suicide with a handgun that he had hidden in his apartment. Arnold Roszhenki was stabbed to death in a carjacking that went awry. Tal Breslow disappeared without a trace from his suite in Amsterdam. Phillipe Mizrachi was shot and killed in a mob-style hit in the immigrant-packed Nineteenth Arrondissement of Paris. A shoot-out between state police in south Texas and a suspected drug runner left the suspect dead and two officers wounded. An unidentified German army officer was found dead at his home in Berlin, cause of death unknown. Max "Dog Face" Brownfield had a fatal heart attack on the way to his brother's house in Glendale, California. Theodore Malkusic slipped and fell from a platform on the Red Line at Boston's Park Street Station and was killed by the arriving subway train. A shark-scarred body that washed ashore near Key West, Florida, was identified as Heddwig Krumwalt.

Days would pass before the body of a man believed to have once been connected with Mossad would be found in Nablus, in the occupied West Bank. Mossad would not admit to any knowledge about the man or his death. The mutilated body would carry false papers and signs of beating and torture. No group would come forward claiming responsibility, but it will generally be assumed that the man was killed by Palestinian extremists.

A guest staying at The Hotel Meridith in Washington, DC, would be discovered to have skipped out without paying his bill. The hotel would have the police looking for a blond, middle-aged man who had been registered under the assumed name of Paul Demetrius. The credit card used on check-in to cover incidental charges will be rejected as no longer valid.

Chapter 52

BEN SLIPPED HIS ARM around Marwa's shoulder as they watched the display projected on the wall of the conference room. "There, that's the last of the agents checking in. Everyone has acknowledged mission complete. They really must be pros. We gave them a six-hour window in which to complete their assignments, and they made it with time to spare. Now we just have to wait to hear from Arkady before we can take down our system and erase our tracks."

Marwa nestled closer but started shivering as if suddenly cold. She twisted and looked up at Ben with teary eyes. "It just hit me again. It was so easy when we were using graph theory to partition a network, but each one of those Xs up there is a person: a person who was killed at our direction. "

"They were terrorists. That's what they really were."

"They were zealots, yes, extremists, but they were also real people, people who thought they were doing the right thing. And we killed them."

"You can't think of it that way. They killed themselves. It was collective suicide. They died by the very sword they lived by. Ultimately, we've saved lives."

"That's a rationalization, one I've heard too many times before. I'm looking for answers."

He shrugged. "Maybe there are no answers. Maybe it's just like the rest of life."

The quiet was broken by the sound of slow footsteps. Arkady ignored the two of them as he entered the conference room and slumped down in the nearest chair.

Marwa looked over Ben's shoulder. "You okay, Arkady?"

"Yeah, I guess."

"Did you ... ?"

"Yeah." He stared down at his right hand as he flexed his fingers. "It's taken care of."

"If you want to—"

"I said, it's taken care of. That's it."

"Okay." Ben made a patting gesture with both hands. "We already have confirmation from the others, so that's it. We can erase our tracks and slip away into the night. Marwa, do you want to do the honors and initiate —what did DB call it?—Operation Closed Account?"

"Sure." There was no enthusiasm in her voice. She sat down at her computer and typed a command. "Here goes." She tapped the return key like a pianist hitting the final note of a sonata with extra emphasis. After a few minutes, nodes on the display started flashing green, then fading to gray. The three of them watched without speaking, as more and more of the nodes winked out.

Arkady scowled. "Did we miss some? There's six or seven up there that are still showing red."

Ben reassured him. "It's not a problem. They'll get automatically purged when next they login to the network."

Marwa's face was spread with uncertainty as she looked up at Ben. "Is that the end of HaVered? Once those systems are clean, is it really dead?"

"As dead as it can be. It would be next to impossible for the isolated groups to reconnect. They not only don't know each other, but in many cases they don't even know of their existence.

And it will take time before most of the agents become aware that they might have been cut off. They'll just think nothing has been happening, that they haven't been needed. It will slowly, inexorably wither and die, like a potted vine chopped into pieces."

"But some of the clusters might continue to stay in touch or reestablish active exchanges. Possibly they could even take action on their own, right?"

"Sure, it's possible, but with the NSA surveillance that Talpa promised and both the CIA and Mossad alerted by all this new activity, any re-animated agents are also apt to be caught in the act. No, it's over." He checked his watch. "We should do something tonight."

Marwa gave him a look of disapproval. "A celebration? Not exactly something to celebrate."

"Sure it is. We're done. We're through with this business. We can get back to ... to normal."

Arkady pushed himself slowly up from his chair as if he had suddenly aged thirty years. "I'll leave you two to your normal or whatever. I've got paperwork to catch up on and one heap of explaining to do, both of which are my normal."

As he was leaving, Sam arrived at the doorway of the conference room. "I just touched base with my NTSB network. A team from Woods Hole recovered the black boxes."

Ben looked surprised. "Really? I hadn't heard. How?"

"They used a brand new underwater research robot, a semi-autonomous experimental model called DEEPDIP. It's good to over 25,000 feet. They knew exactly where to search, thanks to you guys, and they were lucky. Both recorders are being analyzed."

"Have they learned anything yet about what happened?"

"Nothing's been released to the press yet. They'll take their time doing a thoroughgoing analysis, but I got a copy of a preliminary assessment."

"And?"

"It looks similar to the conjectures about flight MH370. After the plane made its unplanned turn, it climbed to 47,000 feet, well above operating ceiling. The internal air pressure was allowed to drop slowly. Those aboard would have just gotten sleepy and slowly succumbed. After an hour, the plane dropped to thirteen thousand feet and maintained that altitude until it ditched in the Atacama Trench. By that time, everyone had been dead for many hours. They died in their sleep. Of course, the full truth as we know it is not the story that's going to hit the media."

"Another cover up, right?" Marwa said.

Sam sighed. "Deeper than the Atacama Trench. The truth would expose the doctored chipsets, and that's a story that can never come out."

"Your contacts in Singapore, do they know the whole story?" she said.

"No. In order to keep his job, my inside man at ISD will keep his mouth shut about the part he does know. I get the impression, though, he is ready to move on anyway. The Jewish technician from Kuala Lumpur never did know what exactly he was doing for the man he knew as Sergi Cardona. A Jewish charity is sponsoring the technician's immigration to Israel. He'll make a new life and consider himself blessed."

Ben nodded his approval. "What about those chipsets, Sam? There's still a herd of Trojan horses hiding inside a lot of planes. Taking out HaVered is not the end of that story."

"No, it's not, but Talpa is taking care of that."

"What can he do?" Ben said.

"He has connections in Defense," Sam explained. "Seems this secret backdoor was created without consulting them. They are ape-shit over it, but they also know they can't just bitch and blow the whistle, which would leave toxic egg on everyone's faces. No, they're already quietly upgrading the aircraft that had previously been upgraded with the IsTac avionics. At the same time, Boeing and other big players in aerospace are being alerted that some changes need to be made—and made without drawing too much attention. They don't call it the military-industrial complex for nothing. Karl says we can expect much the same thing from Israel. Eventually the other countries that were suckered into using the chipsets will get wind through their own clandestine services. No one will want to look stupid, and no one will want to be the last one with vulnerable systems."

"You think it will be over fairly fast," Ben said.

"Yup. That's the reason your group in Cambridge and mine here at NTSB were targeted to get the axe in the first place: to ensure the story of the chipsets didn't get out. The collaborators here and in Israel still wanted them as a weapon in reserve. Just because the chips are all now destined for the dump heap doesn't change the need to keep the story under wraps. My guess is it won't be long before this is history, lost history."

"Talpa can pull off all that?"

"Probably. It's leveraging dependencies, like a kid pulling out an apple from the bottom of the neat stack at a farm stand. The whole pile comes tumbling after under its own weight."

"What exactly is happening with Talpa?" Marwa asked. "Where is he?"

"Out there." Sam spread his arms. "He's like data in the cloud: somewhere, everywhere, nowhere. Remember, he's a survivor. He told us he was working for the NSA, but my contacts there claim they never heard of him. Who knows who he works for, but you can figure whoever it is, he's well compensated."

Sam turned at the sound of approaching footsteps. "And look who else is here: DB. And Suze Kerchoff. What's up?"

"Not much. I'm good. Suze is good. And it feels damn good to be able to say that and mean it for a change. I've got my people erasing tracks; Suze has been mending local law-enforcement fences. We were thinking of getting away from our little cave of conspiracy for a while. We've all spent way too much time in this room. If I never face another sociogram again, it won't be too soon. You all want to join us for dinner?"

"Thanks, but no," Sam said. "I think I just need to be alone for a while." He swallowed. "It's something I'll have to get used to again. I ..."

Ben looked at Marwa, then up at Sam. "It's gotta be tough."

"Yeah." He stood there, his mouth open, ready to say things for which the words would not come. "I guess the one consolation is that we put a stop to it. At least I hope we did. Anyway, thanks for the invite, DB, but I'll pass this time."

DB turned to Ben and Marwa. "How about you two? Want to join us for dinner? My treat."

"Thanks, but we have to get my dad to the airport. If he misses that flight my mom is going to have fits. Then, I think we'll just, you know ... hang out."

"Sure. I understand. So, everyone is going off their separate ways."

"It's a little scary, I admit." Marwa hooked Ben's arm and gave it a squeeze. "We don't know whether it really worked—or for how long."

DB took a slow breath and let it out. "True. But Suze promised to keep an eye on things. I hired her firm for the long haul. She's going to be watching our backs." He grinned at her. "Right?"

"Right. Especially yours." She gave him a slow wink.

■■ ■■ ■■

"That's it." Ben slipped his laptop into its sleeve. "We're the last ones out. I guess we turn out the lights."

Marwa hoisted her backpack onto one shoulder. "Or we can let the night crew take care of the lights, I suppose. I did erase the whiteboard, though."

He squinted at the whiteboard. "Just don't apply for a job with the cleaning crew here; I can still see some of the handwriting showing through. Funny, we were so careful online, but then we left things sitting around and posted on boards in rooms that were unlocked. I don't think we were destined for this espionage business. Maybe we're fated for something else, though." He let his smile grow steadily until his eyes crinkled at the corners.

"Don't tell me that Binyamin 'Always Rational' Markham believes in fate."

"Can't help it. I'm my mother's son. She's a believer. There's a Yiddish word for it."

"I think I know the word: *bashert.*"

"Right. Maybe it wasn't accidental that we ended up sharing an office. Maybe we are fated, *bashert.*"

"We'll see, my romantic rationalist, we'll see." She flipped off the light switch as they walked out hand-in-hand.

Epilogue: Oenology

AT AFONSO PENA International Airport in Curitiba, Brazil, a man with a cane awkwardly pushed his stacked luggage cart out onto the walkway. The morning fog that so often plagued the airport had cleared. Underneath the concrete canopy that stretched in shallow waves the length of the terminal building, a brisk breeze whistled and wove through the exposed tubular grid of the supporting structure. Leaning on the cane as he looked around for his driver, the man was beginning to wonder if he might have to hail a taxi for the ride to the estate.

"Mr. Pembroke?" The boy who came around from behind him was short and skinny. He looked to be at most sixteen or seventeen. "Are you Mr. Gaspar Pembroke?"

The reply came with some hesitation. "Yes, I am."

"I am so sorry I missed you inside. I am Paolo. Welcome to Brazil, welcome to Curitiba." The boy's smile was a white slash across a face the color of a coconut macaroon. "Mr. Cippolini, your manager, sent me to drive you. He is eager to meet you."

"As I am to meet him. Is it a long drive to the winery?"

"Oh, no. An hour, maybe less. But the vineyards are scattered and some are much farther from the city. But you know all this, since you are the one, the buyer who has been buying them and having them planted."

"Yes, of course. Shall we go then?"

"Please, this way, that is the Fiat over there. These bags I will take care of. I can fit them in. Everyone is so happy that at last our Mr. Pembroke is coming to visit."

"Oh, this is no visit. I'm here to stay, to live here."

"Ah, then that is even more reason to be happy."

Paolo pointed to the wolf-headed cane that Gaspar was using. "Did you hurt yourself?"

"It's"—he paused as if searching for the right translation—"just an old war wound."

"You were in a war? I was told that you are a capital adventurer."

"A venture capitalist. Yes."

"Did you have many capital adventures?"

The phrase set Gaspar chuckling to himself. "Yes, I guess you could say that. I have had many capital adventures."

―― ―― ――

Suburbs gave way to gently rolling highlands, and the paved roads gave out. Paolo kept up a running commentary and non-stop conversation.

"You must be a brave man," he said.

"Why do you say that?"

"Because you are planting grape vines where no one is growing grapes. Most of the wine is made farther to the south. Here it is a risk, a business only for a brave man."

"Perhaps, but I have researched this well over the years. It will be a challenge, yes, but I have always embraced challenges. And I think I can grow some wonderful grapes in these vineyards and make some wonderful wine."

"That will be most wonderful. And I can work for you making most wonderful wine."

Gaspar laughed. "How wonderful."

―― ―― ――

The grand tour of the estate and its newly completed wine-making facilities lasted much of the day, leaving Gaspar exhausted and his leg aching. Cippolini nevertheless insisted on a welcoming banquet. Finally, with the household staff clearing after the three-hour dinner, Gaspar limped out onto the veranda of the main house and closed the French doors behind him.

He breathed in the musky scent of warm soil and lush greenery as he looked out over the neat rows of young vines stretching out below him in the light of a nearly full moon just rising. He took a sip of wine, then held up the glass to view the moon turned into crimson ripples by the deep ruby liquid.

"Someday it will be my own wine that I'll be drinking." He lifted the glass yet higher. "L'chaim, to life." He faced north and lifted it again. "And to you as well, my distant brother. I drink to you, Arkady. In the end, you were right, wolf cub, it was time. And in the end, we did know each other, truly. I knew you couldn't do it, and you knew that I would walk away."

He set his glass down on the heavy wooden railing and rested with both hands on his cane. "Shalom, Arkady. What a wonderful word, that. Goodbye. Hello. Peace. So many meanings: endings and beginnings and resolution all in one word." He winced as a pain shot up his leg. "Ah, but I do wish you had chosen to make your penultimate point less dramatically, Arkady. A shot in the air might have delivered the message just as persuasively. Then again, perhaps not."

— — —

— — —

Appendix: Parallel Lines

BLUE-GREEN ALGAE INVASION, an Israeli-Palestinian rap-metal band, enjoyed a brief popularity in alternative and world-music circles in Israel and Europe during the early 2010s. Formed by Israelis Chaim Hassan and Nadal Gershon with Palestinians Abdullah Sirhan and Samih Sayed, the group was known for its eclectic and unpredictable style that often defied genre distinctions. The members first met and became friends through their work with the YTheater Project, the intercultural theater group started in Jerusalem by Bonna Devora Haberman and Kadar Herini. The band took its name from the green associated with Islam and the blue of the flag of Israel.

Most of their music is explicit political commentary centered on issues of justice, equality, and peace and reconciliation, although their second album, *Wall Songs*, included two cuts that, despite the hard-driving metal arrangement, have markedly romantic lyrics. One of these, "Even Handed," portrays an evidently homosexual love through alternating verses in Arabic and Hebrew with a chorus in English.

Their style has been hard to characterize, sometimes mixing spoken rap with eastern-influenced melodic lines styled after synagogue and mosque chanting. Their innovative arrangements generally featured lead vocalist Hassan on keyboards, Gershon on electric bass guitar, with Sirhan playing amplified Egyptian oud and lead guitar and Sayed on drums (later replaced by another Palestinian, Farikh al-Tikriti).

Asked about one of their unusual tracks, "Overripe Olives," classically trained leader Hassan described it as having a "classic trio sonata form, with a jazz-rock bridge sandwiched between metal-core fugal episodes—and a shitload of screaming in the coda." Some critics have argued that their eclecticism kept them from establishing a consistent fan base and enjoying greater popularity.

Outside the Middle East, their reputation rests largely on one of their few songs done entirely in English: "Parallel Lines" from their debut album, *Division by Zero*. Riding on the popularity of "Parallel Lines," the group toured the UK in the summer of 2011. Shortly after their return to Jerusalem, drummer Samih Sayed was struck by a motorcycle in a freak accident in the Old City's narrow streets. He later died at Shaare Zedek Medical Center as the result of his injuries. The band recruited Al-Quds University student Farikh al-Tikriti as a replacement. Al-Tikriti played with the group until they disbanded amicably two years later.

After the split, Hassan and Gershon formed a successful im-port-export business headquartered in Haifa. Sirhan went on to teach music at a secondary school in Nablus. The current where-abouts of al-Tikriti are not known.

In an interview with satellite-radio host Jassika Dervon of the MidlEast Channel, Hassan said that "Parallel Lines" was not the band's greatest work, but it was "the most fuckin' real. That's what is really going on, like, not just where I come from. Here, too. Most of us just want to get on with, like, living, you know. But we're out-shouted by extremists. They have the agenda, the ideology, the, you know, right answers. We just want to make music, grow olives, whatever."

Parallel Lines

words and music by Chaim Hassan and Samih Sayed
copyright, Planktonic Music Ltd (reprinted with permission)

Parallel lines:
    parallel lines of opposing signs,
    a shouting match of repeated attacks.
And in the middle, between,
Too subdued to be heard above the slogans and
    screams,
The voices of the many all murmur a dream.

A fanatical few invoking The Name:
    faithful fundamentalists and true reactionaries,
    orthodox extremists and revolutionaries,
True believers all distinctive
    but all sounding the same.
Controlling conversation,
Reciting revelation,
Shouting new invective,
Without nuance or perspective:
    Resolute truth and absolute right;
    black is still black and white is always white.
But the voices of the many all murmur a dream.
Too subdued to be heard above the slogans and
    screams,
The words and whimpers of those in midstream
Are lost in the chaos of the stubborn extremes.

Parallel lines,
    parallel lines of opposing signs,
    a shouting match of repeated attacks.

And in the middle, between,
Too subdued to be heard above the slogans and
   screams,
The voices of the many all murmur a dream.
The voices of the many still murmur a dream.
The voices of the many ...

Acknowledgements

No LITERARY PROJECT is truly the work of a single person. There are always collaborators and supporters whose contributions, acknowledged or not, are part of the story.

Although fiction, my novels are always grounded in reality. The scenarios in this book are based in the real capabilities and all-too-real vulnerabilities of contemporary technology. In today's fly-by-wire aircraft, the pilots do not fly the plane—computers do. Pilots use the cockpit controls to provide input to the computers, which then decide how best to fly the plane. Hacking into the avionics networks from the in-flight passenger Wi-Fi network has already been demonstrated, so a digital hijacking is actually possible—in theory but, we hope, not in practice.

I drew on my consulting experience for the cybersecurity details, but to make sure I got the aviation elements of the story spot on, I turned for help to a number of airline pilots and aviation specialists. To these professionals, who read various versions of the manuscript with care and a critical eye, I owe a great debt for giving me the benefit of their firsthand knowledge and long experience with flying. (One of them even read his advance review copy during off-duty hours on a long-haul 787-9 Dream-Liner flight.) The fact that some of these aviation professionals are fellow writers made their feedback doubly valuable. My thanks go out to Eric Auxier, Alan Hoffberg, Harrison Jones, Keith Lamb, and Jim Preston for their generous comments and suggestions. I also appreciate the comments from the readers, unnamed by preference, who reviewed the manuscript to guide me in better capturing some of the ethnic and cultural elements.

I am deeply indebted to my editors for their heavy lifting in shaping a manuscript into a finished book. Lucy Lockwood—my developmental editor, my best friend, and my wife of twenty years—took time out from her own work and graduate studies to offer a no-holds-barred, deep-dive review with extensive suggestions. I have learned, with good cause, to trust her uncensored but always constructive criticism. The final spit-and-polish that makes a book a book is professional copyediting. Once more, my copyeditor, Janet Lemnah, has worked her meticulous magic to move every misplaced comma, to clarify every unclear clause, and, in general, to transform my imperfect output into the much better book you are reading.

Finally, I want to thank the many readers of earlier works who, in personal messages or online postings and reviews, have shared their experiences reading my fiction. Most importantly, they have told me how much they valued my novels, and they have encouraged me to keep writing. Needless to say, I could never name them all, but I hope they all realize how grateful I am.

About the Author

LIOR SAMSON is the pen name of an emeritus university professor and award-winning consulting designer. His more than two dozen books include seven previous novels, a novella, and a collection of science fiction short stories. His focus is on writing intelligent, thought-provoking fiction addressing contemporary issues, and his intent is to keep readers both turning the pages and pondering what they have read. He is a part-time journalist, occasional composer of serious choral music, and full-time support for the three students in his family. He sings baritone whenever given the least bit of encouragement, makes archly bad puns with no encouragement at all, and regularly cooks inventive fusion cuisine with Indian, Italian. Mexican, and Portuguese influences.

He enjoys hearing from his readers and appreciates reviews posted anywhere. Reach him by email at Lior@LiorSamson.com